SCENT OF DARKNESS

This Large Print Book carries the
Seal of Approval of N.A.V.H.

SCENT OF DARKNESS

CHRISTINA DODD

THORNDIKE PRESS

An imprint of Thomson Gale, a part of The Thomson Corporation

THOMSON

GALE

Detroit • New York • San Francisco • New Haven, Conn. • Waterville, Maine • London

THOMSON

TM

GALE

Copyright © Christina Dodd, 2007.

Thorndike Press, an imprint of The Gale Group.

Thomson and Star Logo and Thorndike are trademarks and Gale is a registered trademark used herein under license.

Thorndike Press® Large Print Core.

The text of this Large Print edition is unabridged.

Other aspects of the book may vary from the original edition.

Set in 16 pt. Plantin.

LIBRARY OF CONGRESS CATALOGING-IN-PUBLICATION DATA

Dodd, Christina.
    Scent of darkness : darkness chosen / by Christina Dodd.
      p. cm. — (Thorndike Press large print core)
    ISBN-13: 978-0-7862-9920-1 (hardcover : alk. paper)
    ISBN-10: 0-7862-9920-7 (hardcover : alk. paper)
    1. Large type books. I. Title.
PS3554.O3175S285 2007
813'.54—dc22   2007030026

Published in 2007 by arrangement with NAL Signet,
a member of Penguin Group (USA) Inc.

Printed in the United States of America on permanent paper
10 9 8 7 6 5 4 3 2 1

For Lisa Kleypas,
my friend, my comrade-in-arms,
my sister-of-the-heart, and the person
who taught me to swear in Russian.
Za vas!

ACKNOWLEDGMENTS

Starting a new series requires guts, imagination, and planning, which is why I'm grateful to my editor, Kara Cesare, for being my cheerleader, sounding board, and steely-eyed Keeper of the Rules. Thanks to Lindsay Nouis for being Kara's right hand. A big thank-you to Kara Welsh and Claire Zion for their enthusiasm for *Darkness Chosen,* and to Anthony Ramondo and his team in the original publisher's art department for the inspiring and exhilarating covers.

Thank you to my friends, the ones who write and the ones who read.

Thank you to the Squawkers for their constant enthusiasm.

Thank you to Scott. For everything.

DARKNESS CHOSEN
FAMILY TREE

THE VARINSKIS

1000 AD—In the Ukraine
Konstantine Varinski
makes a deal with the devil.

A Thousand +
Years Later

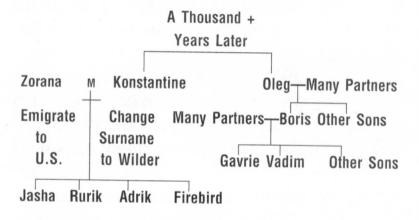

Zorana   M   Konstantine   Oleg—Many Partners

Emigrate   Change   Many Partners—Boris Other Sons
to   Surname
U.S.   to Wilder   Gavrie Vadim   Other Sons

Jasha   Rurik   Adrik   Firebird

THE BEGINNING

For centuries, the name of Cossack struck terror in the hearts of the peoples of central Asia, and the Family Varinski was the embodiment of merciless conquerors who murdered, maimed, and raped.

Even today, the Varinskis reside on the steppes of Russia. They are known for their scouting abilities, proving themselves again and again able to discover their enemies' weakness. They leave a trail of blood, fire, and death wherever they go. Terrible rumors swirl around them, rumors that say Konstantine Varinski, the founder of the Varinski tribe, made a deal with the devil — and, in fact, that is exactly right.

A thousand years ago, Konstantine Varinski, a magnificent warrior of great cruelty, a man driven by his craving for power, roamed the steppes. In return for the ability to hunt down his enemies and kill them, he promised his soul to the devil. To seal the pact, he promised the devil the family icon, a single painting divided into four images of the Madonna.

To obtain the holy piece, the heart of his home, he killed his own mother . . . and damned his soul.

Before she died, she pulled him close and spoke in his ear.

Konstantine paid no heed to her prophecy. She was, after all, only a woman. He didn't believe her dying words had the power to change the future — and more important, he would do nothing to jeopardize his pact with the Evil One.

But although Konstantine did not confess the prophecy his mother had made, the devil knew that Konstantine was a liar and a trickster. He suspected Konstantine's deception, and he comprehended the power of blood and kin and a mother's dying words. So to ensure he forever retained the Varinskis and their services, he secretly cut a small piece from the center of the icon, and gave it to a poor tribe of wanderers, promising it would bring them luck.

Then, while Konstantine drank to celebrate the deal, in a flash of fire the devil divided the Madonnas and hurled them to the four ends of the earth.

To Konstantine Varinski and to each

Varinski since, the devil bequeathed the ability to change at will into a hunting animal. They could not be killed in battle except by another demon, and each man was unusually long-lived, remaining hale and hearty well into old age. Because of their battle prowess, their endurance, and their decisiveness, they became rich, respected, and feared in Russia.

Through czars, Bolsheviks, and even presidents, they retained their warrior compound, went where they were paid to go, and, with flawless ferocity, crushed uprisings and demanded obedience.

They called themselves The Darkness.

They could breed only sons, a matter of much exultation to them. They took their women cruelly, and in their sprawling home they had a turnstile equipped with a bell. There the women who had been impregnated by the Varinskis' careless mating placed their newborn sons. Each woman rang the bell and fled, leaving the child to be taken by the Varinski men into their home. They hailed the birth of a new demon, and raised the child to be a ruthless warrior worthy of the name Varinski.

For no Varinski ever fell in love . . .

Until one did.

No Varinski ever married . . .

Until one did.

No Varinski ever fled the compound and that way of life . . .

Until one did.

For the first time, cracks appeared in the solid foundation of the deal with the devil.

Heaven took note.

So did hell.

CHAPTER 1

"Pass the vodka! I wish to make a toast." The Wilder children groaned, but Konstantine Wilder, descendant of a long line of demon warriors, would not be dissuaded by the bad manners of his own disreputable offspring. They might groan and his guests might grin, but everyone from the small mountain town of Blythe, Washington, expected him to give a speech during one of the Wilder family celebrations. His words were as much a part of their special occasions as the picnic tables loaded with Russian delicacies like *kasha* and *tabaka,* and American delicacies like hot dogs and corn on the cob, like the Russian music and dancing, like the poker games, like the good company.

He would not disappoint.

Striding over to the blazing bonfire, he took his place as the center of attention. His voice boomed out across the company. "My wife and I fled Mother Russia with the demons of hell on our heels. We come to this land of milk and honey." He threw out his big hands to embrace the long stretch of valley — his valley. "And here we have thrived. We grow grapes, the best grapes in Washington. We have our own garden. Our own goat. Our own chickens. More important, we grow our children."

The people of Blythe shifted in their seats to grin at his children, standing together like three lambs to the sacrifice.

"Jasha has grown strong and tall and handsome, like me." More like Konstantine than any of these people could imagine or understand. A wolf. "He owns — he is leader! — of his own wine-making company in Napa, California, and he uses his papa's grapes to make good wine." Konstantine lifted a bottle from the table and showed everyone the label. "He is smart. He is wealthy. He is my oldest, my firstborn son, yet still, at the age of thirty-four —"

"Here it comes," Jasha said out of the corner of his mouth.

"He shows no respect for his father, whose hearing is excellent."

"Sorry, Papa." Yet Jasha planted his feet shoulder-width to the ground and crossed his arms over his chest.

14

Konstantine was not impressed with the apology or the posturing. He saw the flash of red at the root of Jasha's golden eyes. "Yet still, at the age of thirty-four, he is single."

Rurik jabbed Jasha hard enough to make him sway sideways.

"He breaks my heart. Maybe one of you young ladies would consent to marry him. Next week, talk to me. We will make arrangements." Konstantine nodded, satisfied with crossing one item off his mental list. *Get my eldest son married off.*

He proceeded to his next victim. "Rurik is an adventurer."

"An *archaeologist,* Papa," Rurik said.

"Archaeologist, adventurer — I saw the Indiana Jones movies. They are the same." Konstantine dismissed Rurik's objection with a wave of his beefy hand. "Rurik is smart, so smart, with many fine degrees. He is also handsome, like his papa." Rurik's eyes, the color of brandy, his smooth brown hair, and his fine muscles made him a catch for the ladies. Even a father could tell that. "He is not so wealthy as his brother. Still, when I die, he will receive his share of my land here in the beautiful Cascade Mountains, so he would bring money to a marriage. I mention this because still, at the age of thirty-three —"

With a resounding *thwack,* Jasha punched Rurik in the shoulder.

"— he is single. He breaks my heart. Maybe one of you young ladies would consent to marry him. Next week, talk to me. We will make arrangements."

The men of Blythe were laughing, but the women, they were appraising his sons. True, Blythe was a small town, only 250 people including the outlying farms, so some women were very young and some past the age of childbearing, and quite a few had legs like tree trunks and skin like old tree bark. But the boys had been out in the wide world for more than ten years and neither had yet brought home a bride, and desperate situations called for desperate measures.

Konstantine wanted to cradle a grandchild before he died.

If all had turned out as he and Zorana had planned thirty-five years ago, when they came to this country, he would now talk about Adrik. . . .

His guests grew quiet as they waited, seeing his grief, respecting his anguish.

Adrik was lost to them. Lost to the wickedness of his own soul. Lost to the lure of the pact.

Konstantine took a long, quivering breath.

He squared his shoulders, and steadfastly pushed away the pain in his chest. With a broad smile, he gestured at Firebird. "And finally, we have my own baby daughter. Today we celebrate, not only Independence Day for the great United States, but also Firebird's twenty-first birthday." Even after all these years, he couldn't believe it. For a thousand years, no one in his family had fathered a daughter. Yet he had. His own girl child, his baby, his miracle.

Love and gratitude welled up in him so strongly, he could scarcely speak as he stood looking at her, so beautiful, with blond hair that she insisted on cutting into an unfeminine short length, and blue eyes so bright and determined. Always determined, his daughter. Determined as she toddled after her brothers, determined as she trained in her gymnastics, determined to walk again after the uneven bars broke, shattering her leg and ending her dreams.

Tonight her eyes were not so bright, though.

She had grown up during her senior year at college. She was a woman now, with a woman's silences and a woman's mysteries.

How had that happened?

"My Firebird, she is beautiful, and she is smarter than her brothers."

Both boys socked Firebird's shoulders, but gently. Her brothers were always gentle with Firebird.

"She won scholarships to four colleges." Konstantine held up four fingers for emphasis. "She went to Brown, a very prestigious school, and finished in only three years with a degree in software programming and one in Japanese." He thumped his chest in pride. "Now, you wonder — what good is so much education to a woman?"

His audience laughed again.

"I don't know. What man wants a wife who is smarter than he is?" he wondered.

"Yet that's what every man's got," Zorana said.

The crowd's roar of laughter caught Konstantine by surprise, and he pondered his reply until the tumult had died down. Then, shaking his head sadly, he said, "You see what I suffer. Two unmarried sons, a clever daughter, and an impertinent wife. I am truly the most put-upon of men."

"Poor guy." Sharon Szarvas, wife of River Szarvas, an immigrant from Eastern Europe, showed no sympathy for the dent in Konstantine's manly pride.

Ah, but she knew him too well. His manly pride didn't depend on praise or support. He knew who he was. "I think my daughter

18

should stay home now, but my wife, my Zorana, says no, that we must wish her well and release our little Firebird to flutter away. Someday she will return, her restlessness assuaged." He tried to smile at Firebird, to show her he meant every word, although his heart was breaking.

She smiled back and mouthed, "Thank you, Papa."

Her ambitions were his fault. His and his sons'. Always she had envied them, wishing for a wildness no one could tame. But they had gifts Firebird did not share, and although Konstantine had, from the day she was born, held her on his knee and called her his little miracle, she was discontented.

"So" — he pointed his finger around at his guests — "although Firebird is twenty-one and well past marriageable age, I do not offer her as a wife. So, you men, do not look on her."

They did, though. They looked on her, and lusted. The loggers, the farmers, the ranchers, the artists — they all wanted his Firebird.

She looked on none of them with favor, but stood with one hand pressed against her back and one resting on her belly, and watched her father with patient, sad eyes.

What was wrong with his girl?

But now was not the time to ask.

"For all my blessings, I have my Zorana to thank." He held out his hand, and with a smile, Zorana joined him.

She was tiny, his wife, only five feet one, with delicate bones, hair dark as a blackbird's wing, sparkling brown eyes, and a fiery spirit. She was younger than he was, but the first time he had seen her, she had entranced him. He had never recovered, and he loved her as no man in the history of the world had ever loved a woman.

Now she was fifty-one, and he worshipped her still. He wrapped his arm around her shoulders, looked down at her, and he saw himself reflected in her eyes. In her eyes, he was a good man. A great man. Her man.

He spoke more to her than to his audience. "This woman, she is worth dying for, but better than that — she is a woman worth living for." He kissed Zorana's smiling lips, then looked up at the people gathered around his tables, friends and strangers, his guests. His voice swelled. "Zorana and I and my children — all of my children — we thank the United States of America, who allowed us to immigrate from Russia to this place where we may be a normal American family and own this land and grow strong, and have wealth and health and safety, and have many good friends who come to celebrate the Independence Day with us."

The crowd was silent; then one person began to applaud. Then they all applauded, and stood and cheered.

From far away, Konstantine could almost hear the old enemies howling in fury and frustration, and he smiled. This life, the life he had built, was perfect.

He gestured, and everyone hurried to fill their glasses with vodka, wine, even water. Lifting his tumbler, he toasted his guests and his family. *"Za vas!"*

"Here's to you!" they answered, and everyone drank their shot, even Miss Mabel Joyce, the old maid schoolteacher, even Lisa, the crazy New Age herbalist with only one name, and especially the old doctor who had missed Firebird's birth because he'd been too drunk to walk.

Then Jasha and Rurik ignited fireworks that lit up the skies — and his foolish sons set the meadow on fire. So they led the neighbor boys as they ran through the grass, carrying washtubs of water and bellowing with laughter.

By the time the excitement was over and the fire was out, the neighbors were packing up to go home and reminiscing about the trouble the Wilder boys had created when they were younger.

The neighbors had no idea.

Miss Joyce hobbled over to Zorana, kissed her cheek, and said, "Well, folks, it's always an adventure when I visit, but it's time for this old woman to leave."

"Visit us again soon." Zorana had been only sixteen when she'd moved with Konstantine to the United States, and her accent was almost imperceptible. "We miss your visits."

Miss Joyce cackled. "I was up here every week while your kids were in school. Tonight really brought back the memories." She looked at the boys, still covered with soot and grinning, then at Firebird. "They almost made me quit teaching."

"Luckily for us, no one else would take the job." Jasha hugged his old teacher around the shoulders.

"Because of you kids. The Wilder Demons. The worst kids in the state." Miss Joyce's voice rang with pride. For thirty years in their tiny town of Blythe, she'd been the schoolteacher for grades seven through twelve. So when Konstantine's oldest had entered seventh grade, the elementary school teacher had breathed a sigh of relief, and Miss Joyce had girded her loins for battle.

Luckily, she'd had a lot of experience teaching — by then she'd taught for eleven years in a high school on the Houston ship channel, and after the incident with a student involving a knife that resulted in her six months' stay in the hospital, she'd come to Blythe and taught. No teacher wanted to instruct forty kids of different ages in a single classroom, so Miss Joyce had continued long past sixty-five. She said teaching kept her young, and maybe that was right. Only when Firebird graduated and Miss Joyce retired did she develop a dowager's hump and begin to use a cane.

But her eyes sparkled as brightly as ever.

"Do you need someone to drive you home?" Rurik asked. "I can take you."

"You're just trying to get out of cleaning up," Firebird said. "*I'll* take her."

The children began to squabble, but Miss Joyce held up a hand and an almost magical silence fell. "The Szarvas family brought me. I'll return with them."

"I've got to learn how to do that hand thing," Konstantine muttered.

"It's too late for you, *liubov maya*." Zorana patted his cheek. "Let us help River and Sharon Szarvas load up their guests. Some of them are much the worse for drink."

23

The Szarvases were artists of some note — Sharon painted amazing landscapes; River and their daughter, Meadow, fashioned beautiful, magnificent works in glass — and every night the floors of their rambling old house and their barn studio were full of sleeping bags and cots as other artists, young and old, came to learn and to serve as apprentices at the feet of their masters. The master artists used all their money to pay for food, blankets, heat, and teachers for their students.

They were good people.

Tonight they'd brought five students. Five students whose eyes had lit up at the sight of the loaded table. The three guys and two women who talked incessantly about their art. They'd eaten their own weight in *blini*. And they'd drunk — too much.

Now Konstantine threw one thin, pale, lank, unconscious young man over his shoulder and carried him to the rusty Volkswagen van.

Sharon and Zorana walked behind, their hands full of baskets and blankets, chatting about the day and the town and the weather.

River walked with Konstantine. "Sometimes the kids've got no talent, but they want it so badly they come and stay with us in the hopes it will rub off. And that's fine

24

— maybe they'll catch a whiff of the fever."

Konstantine nodded. This boy probably didn't weigh 130 pounds dripping wet, but he was heavy enough to make Konstantine gasp. *Must be getting old.*

"This young guy" — River nodded at the man over Konstantine's shoulder — "he's been with us for a week. Hasn't done a thing the whole time, just watched everyone create and learn. Sharon and I, we thought he was one of *those,* the ones with no talent. But you wouldn't believe what he did tonight. I can't wait to show you."

"Show me?" Konstantine didn't have the breath to say more.

"Right before he passed out, he told me it was a gift to Zorana." River shook his head. "It's amazing. Extraordinary."

A tingle shot through Konstantine's hands where he touched the young man. *Odd. Disturbing.*

"Fling him in there." River opened the door to the van. "This kid so has a crush on Firebird."

Konstantine placed the limp boy on the carpeted floor.

River gathered a towel-wrapped something out of the front seat. "Come on."

They headed back toward the fire and leftovers stacked on platters and the neighbors visiting before the drive home.

Sharon and Zorana followed, prodded by curiosity.

"Look!" River placed the thing on the table and pulled the towels away.

The still-damp lump of clay had been formed into a statue of Firebird. The boy artist had captured her as she stood with one hand on her hip, the other on her belly, watching the children play.

"My God." Zorana backed away. "My God. It is . . . Firebird."

"It's perfect." Konstantine threw the towel over the statue. "It's lovely!"

They didn't understand. None of the people here, the American people, understood. Zorana was a Gypsy. She was superstitious. Her people did not give life to lumps of clay, and this statue . . . this statue was amazing. Lifelike.

Eerie.

Zorana backed into Firebird's arms.

"Is that like me, Mama? I don't see it." Firebird hugged Zorana and whispered in her ear. "It's okay, Mama. It's okay."

Zorana slid an arm around her daughter's waist. She was so tiny beside Firebird, dark-skinned and dark-eyed where Firebird was fair and blond, and she allowed Firebird to comfort her. To River, she said, "When your

26

young man awakes, thank him for his art."

River nodded. He was an artist. He saw things most men did not. He understood things most men did not . . . but he didn't understand why the Wilder family hated that statue.

The neighbors from the surrounding farms, from the Chinese restaurant in town, from the only burger drive-in for fifty miles, lined up to say good-bye.

Konstantine shook hands with everyone, so happy that they came, that each bore witness to his home, his family, his life here in America.

The Catholic priest Father Ambrose reluctantly quit playing poker and joined the line. He was a traveling priest, wandering the roads of western Washington and celebrating Mass in small-town living rooms and backyards. He was a good man.

Konstantine respected him. Konstantine feared him. Putting his hands behind his back, he bowed low to the priest.

Father Ambrose laughed. "I wish all Catholic boys were as respectful as you are, Konstantine Wilder. Someday I'll get you to come to Mass."

"Not even." Reverend Geisler, the Congregationalist minister, shoved Father Ambrose aside. "When he comes to the light, he's mine."

Father Ambrose shoved back, laughing. "You're only interested in his tithes, you self-serving Protestant."

Reverend Doreen, the New Age minister, walked up behind them. "Everyone knows Konstantine Wilder is already in the light."

The two men rolled their eyes.

But all three were preachers of the Word, and Konstantine bowed to them all, but did not take their hands.

At last, the party was over. The last taillights had disappeared down the road. The dust settled. The family stood alone around the bonfire while the flames died down to a huge tumble of red embers.

A thin thread of smoke connected the earth to the heavens. The crimson glow bathed their faces, and Konstantine felt the first rumbling in his gut, that animal instinct that foretold trouble.

But they'd lived here for so long. So long. They were safe here.

"*We* are a normal American family? Papa, you have guts!"

Konstantine allowed Rurik's laughter to comfort him. "What?" He spread his hands wide. "We *are* a normal American family."

"Yeah, if normal American families grow grapes, speak Russian, and transform themselves into wild animals at will." Jasha was unsmiling, unamused.

"So." Konstantine shrugged. "Not so many Americans speak Russian."

Zorana slipped her arm around his waist and squeezed.

"I don't transform myself into a wild animal at will, and I'm part of this family." Firebird smiled her old, pert smile, the one that had been missing since she'd returned from college. "Do you, Mama?"

"No, I don't transform myself, either."

"Once a month you both turn into bears," Jasha muttered.

"We do not talk about that. Those are women's matters." Konstantine frowned at his unruly sons.

"Like laundry," Rurik said.

"Oh, man. You are in such trouble now." Jasha backed out of the way.

Konstantine thought so, too.

But Zorana didn't slap Rurik. Instead she looked up at Konstantine and said, "You didn't talk about Adrik."

Pain stabbed at Konstantine's heart, but he answered steadily, "Adrik is dead to us."

"No." Zorana shook her head.

"Dead to us," he repeated. His family watched him, all hurting for the loss of their brother. But Konstantine was the patriarch.

He had to remain strong.

Adrik had disobeyed him. He had reveled in his power to change, and the change had taken him deep into the heart of evil.

How well Konstantine knew that heart. Sometimes, at night, he felt as if he lived there still.

Every intimation of sun had disappeared. The moon hid her face, and the stars blazed like bits of broken glass in a black velvet sky.

The Wilders stood alone in the vastness of the primal forest. Alone . . . and yet their brothers and sisters stirred in the under-brush. The breeze ruffled the tree branches, and the cedars scented the cooling air.

Zorana broke Konstantine's hold on her. She turned her back to her family and stood with her hands clenched tightly. "I hate that thing."

"What thing?" Jasha hadn't seen it.

"Mama, leave it alone." Firebird sensed the wrongness, too.

"It's not right." Zorana tossed the towels away from the figure the artist boy had made. "It's not right." In sudden frenzy of action, she attacked the soft clay, smashing it with her fists.

"No, Mama. No!" Firebird caught her mother's arm.

And everybody froze.

No one knew why. They only knew something had happened.

Or something was about to happen.

Slowly Zorana turned and faced the embers, and she was . . . different. A stranger.

Her voice, when she spoke, was low, deep, smooth.

Not hers. Not his wife's. Not Zorana's.

"Each of my four sons must find one of the Varinski icons."

"Four . . . sons?" Konstantine looked at his children. At his two sons, at his daughter . . . and he thought about the only son left, his Adrik.

"Only their loves can bring the holy pieces home." Zorana's eyes were black — and wild. *"A child will perform the impossible. And the beloved of the family will be broken by treachery . . . and leap into the fire."*

Zorana was in a trance.

Before she married Konstantine, she had been the One, the female of her tribe who saw the future. But from the time he had seized her and taken her from her people, she had never had a vision.

Now it was as if all the repressed prophecies had overtaken her.

Zorana raised her hand and, one by one, pointed at her children.

"The blind can see, and the sons of Oleg Varinski have found us."

Jasha straightened and as if he could command the tides, he said, "Mother, stop this at once."

Foolish lad.

She didn't hear him. She was not now of this earth. *"You can never be safe, for they will do anything to destroy you and keep the pact intact."*

Her finger steadied and pointed at Konstantine. *"If the Wilders do not break the devil's pact before your death, you will go to hell and be forever separated from your beloved Zorana. . . ."*

"Mama, why are you saying this? Why are you talking about yourself as if you're not here?" Firebird's voice tottered on the edge of hysteria.

"And you, my love —" Zorana's eyes filled with tears, and for the first time, Konstantine realized that she was not gone, but here, and she knew exactly what she was saying. *"You are not long for this earth. You are dying."*

Answering tears sprang to his eyes. He couldn't breathe for the weight of his sorrow. Like a feral cat, the nagging pain in his chest dug its claws into his flesh and tore the flesh from the bones. Bright colored lights flashed in his brain.

And like a great felled oak, he crashed to the ground.

CHAPTER 2

All her life, Ann Smith had followed the rules. When she laughed, she covered her mouth with her hand to muffle the sound. When she cried, she cried in the privacy of her apartment. She didn't use the *f*-word except for that time when she dropped the casserole and spread lasagna all over the kitchen floor, and even then, she had been alone.

Of course. She was single, and always alone.

She dressed appropriately, first for a typist, then for a secretary, then for the executive assistant to the president of Wilder Wines.

So what was she doing driving from California to Washington, on her own initiative, adorned in her new, inappropriate clothes, to deliver important papers to her boss's vacation home on the coast?

What else? She was in love. In love with

Jasha Wilder.

Yeah. Who wasn't?

He was tall, six three and a half. Which was good, because she was six feet in her stocking feet. Or her stalking feet, as her friend Celia Kim said. He had the face of a fallen angel: dark hair, dark brows, long, dark, curly lashes that framed eyes a most peculiar shade of gold, and a tattoo that rippled down one arm from his shoulder to his wrist. The tattoo twisted like two snakes twining together, dark and mysterious against his tanned skin; silly, but it made her feel as if they had something extraordinary in common. Not that she ever wanted to explain to him what it was — or even could.

The eyes, the tattoo, and the height made him look dangerous, which he wasn't, at least as long as you didn't oppose him in business.

Then he got his way, every single time.

He had a jutting nose, and a smiling mouth with the most beautiful, gleaming white teeth Ann had ever seen.

Most important, at least for her, was his body. It was perfect. Broad shoulders tapered to a sculpted butt that made her fingers itch to squeeze it. Or them, depending on how one viewed the matter.

She saw his bare legs every day when he came into the office, sweating from his run, and she could testify that his calves and thighs deserved to be licked. Repeatedly. She would, too, if she had a lot of guts and another job to go to.

Not that she couldn't have; she was an excellent administrative assistant, and other wineries and restaurants throughout the Napa Valley had made offers.

She refused them all. Jasha Wilder operated only one company, and she was interested only in Jasha Wilder.

That was why she was here, driving along Highway 101 as it clung to the cliffs along the coast, the treacherous, narrow two lanes trapped between the raging ocean and the primal forest, and sometimes dipping down between the raging ocean and the rocky cliffs.

Since the tiny Washington town she'd passed twenty-five miles back, she hadn't seen a single house or car, nothing more than a few stray seagulls fighting the wind. She knew that was right; when Jasha bought this place, he'd bought the land for twenty miles in every direction. He said he liked to be alone, but the isolation had begun to prey on her. What if her car broke down?

But she had her cell phone, fully charged,

in her purse, and anyway, the car wouldn't break down. The Miata was brand-new and sporty, just the right car for her new image. Like the new clothes, the new hair, the new makeup, the laser eye correction, the new boobs — okay, Jasha paid her well, very well, but she hadn't been able to afford new boobs. Still, she had bought a Wonderbra that gave her wonder boobies. She was an all-new Ann!

She rolled down the window to let the wind blow through her shoulder-length hair, and pressed on the gas, determined to whip around the corners like the professional driver in the commercial.

Do not try this at home!

The wind blasted through the window, tossing one artfully highlighted strand in her mouth. She spit it out. Another strand whipped into her eyes. She blinked. When she pried one eye open in time to see a curve, coming fast, she swerved. Overcorrected. With a sickening thump, the tires dropped off the pavement and onto the narrow shoulder. In a panic, she took her foot off the gas. The car fishtailed. Branches slapped at the side mirror.

She managed to guide the car back onto the road and slowed almost to a crawl, shaking, and so, so glad no one had seen her make a fool of herself. Taking a long breath, she returned to her former reasonable and legal speed, and maintained it through the curves.

She checked the odometer. She still had another five miles to go before she reached the turn to Jasha's house. Then she would see him, and explain about the phone call and the documents, and it would be so close to evening he'd have to let her stay. She'd worn casual oatmeal linen pants with the tight-fitting pumpkin camisole that bared her arms — quite buff after workouts at the gym — and emphasized her narrow waist.

But it was a lot easier to be brave and consider seducing Jasha when she was in Napa, surrounded by grapevines and tourist buses and expensive hotels and civilization. Not here on this wild coast, fighting the wind that blew in gusts off the ocean, seeing the branches thrashing with ever-increasing vigor, watching the gray clouds whipping in ragged streams across the silver blue sky.

If she hadn't been watching the odometer, she would have missed the turn into Jasha's estate.

Tall rhododendrons hid the entrance and once she slammed on the brakes and made the corner, she was on a gravel road so narrow, if she met another car, one of them would have to give way. Her beautiful new car dropped into pothole after pothole, and indignantly she remembered the bill she'd received from the paving company.

And Jasha had signed the check to pay them.

Two hundred feet in, she passed between two stone pillars topped with snarling lions. Suddenly she was driving on asphalt. Here the forest pressed close, deep green, ancient, and lofty.

The road took a wide curve, turning west until she thought she would drive out over the ocean.

Then she did.

The trees broke away and far below, the Pacific was revealed in a wide sweep of view, glorious, wild, on a rampage. Ann pulled off and braked to a stop. Stepping out, she inhaled the salty air. When she'd left Napa, the Weather Channel had said nothing about a storm, but it was coming. She could sense it in her bones and in her heart, and she reveled in the whipping wind, the ferocity of the waves against the base of the cliff.

This was the way Jasha made her feel. Mad, bad, and dangerous to know. In her secret heart of hearts, she led a street gang, fought with the Navy SEALs, spied for the

CIA, and killed Bill time and again.

She laughed aloud. As if dull Miss Ann Smith could ever do — be — any of those things.

Her amusement faded, but determination lifted her chin. Maybe she wasn't glamorous, but once she had Jasha Wilder, she would keep him, which was more than Meghan Nakamura had been able to do. Ann wanted him to look at her, to see her, to say, "My darling, I couldn't live without you," rather than, "Ann, when you're done cataloging the pinots, send Jennifer Chavez roses and a note apologizing on my behalf about her cat."

"What's wrong with her cat?"

"It had an allergic reaction."

"To what?"

"To me."

"Don't you like cats?" Ann thought about Kresley, her old tomcat.

"Very tasty."

Ann laughed uncertainly.

But she wasn't sure he was joking.

As the house came into view, she slowed to a crawl, knowing what Jasha had said about his home — that it was a castle built by an early twentieth-century timber baron indulging in a grandiose gesture of courtship to the young woman of his dreams. She

40

hadn't been impressed, and he'd lived in splendid isolation to the end of his days.

Jasha bought it at auction, stripped the interior, and completely refinished everything, then relied on Ann to choose the furniture, fixtures, and appliances. She felt as if this were *their* house, and her heart pounded in anticipation. . . .

The drive widened. The trees parted. The castle came into view.

She slammed on her brakes.

This wasn't what she had expected. Not at all.

In her mind's eye, she'd pictured a palace, sort of like Cinderella's, although perhaps the roofs would not be such an obnoxious shade of blue.

Instead the place was tall and narrow, jutting up toward the racing clouds like a primitive penis symbol. It dwarfed the mighty trees around it, and it sat too close to the edge of the cliff. To her stunned gaze, it looked like a monster, the last of its species, hovering on the edge of lonely suicide. The wind had blasted away every hint of softness from the gray stones, leaving the rough surfaces bare and bleak. Sightless gargoyles stared out from the corners on each of the three levels, and the peak of the gray slate roof caught wisps of clouds as they billowed and faded.

The broad front porch was a vast expanse of shale set one step up from the earth, with rough granite columns that supported the Neanderthal brow of a roof.

Ann told herself that when the sun came out, the house would look better.

The sun came out.

The house didn't look better.

Golden rays shot from the west and glinted on the windowpanes, turning them from empty sockets to watching eyes, and the shadows grew more clearly defined.

Ann searched the area around the house, looking for any sign of Jasha, but no one moved in the grass or among the shrubs inside the circular drive before the house, and not even the sunlight could penetrate the shadows beneath the trees that surrounded the house. The garage was behind the house; perhaps he was there. Or perhaps he'd gone to town, or was off on a run. He could be anywhere — but she was here, and here she would stay.

Ann drove toward the porch. She braked, gripped the wheel, and took a long, deep breath.

This was what she wanted. This was what she'd prepared for, shopped for, dreamed of. If she turned back now, she would never forgive herself.

If she turned back now, she didn't deserve happiness.

She could do this thing.

She set the emergency brake — she always set the emergency brake, even on level ground, for it was the responsible thing to do. She lifted her leather briefcase — a gift from Jasha — and her purse out of the passenger seat. As she stepped out, the wind caught the car door, springing it back so decisively she feared for the hinges. She shoved the door shut with her hip, popped the trunk with the key control, and extracted her suitcase — her large, heavy, completely loaded suitcase. It took both hands and all her newly acquired gym-built muscles to heft it out of the trunk. She thanked God for luggage wheels as she dragged it onto the sidewalk and toward the entrance.

The wind shoved her sideways, tousled her hair, grabbed at her camisole. She heard the waves far below, angrier than ever. The air smelled like brine and seaweed, evergreens and wilderness.

And as she walked — one foot, then the other foot, then the other foot — the castle loomed above her. The shadows embraced her. When she stepped onto the stone floor of the porch, she stopped. She blinked, letting her eyes adjust to the dim light. Here she was protected from the brutal wind, yet she shivered in the cool, earthy atmosphere.

She dragged her suitcase up the single step, and the wheels rattled as she rolled it over the slabs of gray slate. The custom door loomed before her; she had ordered it herself from the eccentric artist, and knew it was black walnut trimmed with Brazilian mahogany. Yet she could see nothing of the grain of the wood or its luster, and the massive brass lion's-head knocker was only a glint in the darkness. Finding the small button on the trim, she pressed it.

The chimes rang inside.

No one answered.

She rang again, then cautiously tried the large iron handle. It was locked.

Jasha wasn't home.

She could turn back now. Tell herself she'd tried, plan for another day.

But there would never be another day, she knew that. It was now or never. So she shuffled through the keys on her key ring and found the one that opened the lock.

She was, after all, Jasha's administrative assistant. She had witnessed his will. She called his mother by her first name. She even held the extra key that opened his safe-deposit box. She had every right to use the

44

house key he'd given her.

Slipping it into the lock, she turned it. The door opened easily, silently. She looked into the foyer — and breathed a sigh of relief.

Better. This was better. Not brutal and overwhelming, but warm and civilized. The ceiling soared far above her head, and when she flicked on the light, a thousand prisms danced across the pale cream walls. One of the prisms touched the blinking light on the security system; she caught her breath. Dropped her purse and keys on the table by the door. And hurried toward the control panel.

She punched in the code.

"Jasha? Mr. Wilder?" she called.

No answer.

Well. She would wait for him inside.

She dragged the suitcase across the threshold. As she shut the substantial door behind her, she admired the windows set on either side. They were nineteenth-century leaded glass from one of the great houses on the East Coast. She'd found them, and she was glad to see they were as elegant as the price had indicated. Each pane had been cut in a diamond shape, then set in mahogany, and they caught and reflected and divided the light into glints of color.

Eager now to see the interior she'd decorated from afar, she walked forward.

The foyer opened into the great room. Ruby and gold Oriental rugs lay on the golden hardwood floorings. Warm shades and textures tinted the walls. A baby grand piano of shiny ebony stood in one corner. The paintings were bright, cheerful splashes of color, framed in the same shiny ebony. A simple, comfortable grouping of furniture formed a seating area before the huge fireplace that rose toward the second-story ceiling, and where the gas logs now merrily burned.

She'd designed the room, and it was a personal triumph for her.

The curved staircase rose smoothly toward the second-floor gallery. She walked to the foot and called, "Jasha?"

She went to the doorway of his study, then to the kitchen. "Mr. Wilder?"

Nothing but silence answered her. He just wasn't here. So he was outside. Running, probably, impervious to the weather, his strong legs covering the miles. He said running cleared his mind. He told her she should try it, and invited her along.

She told him her mind was clear enough.

She wasn't about to put on shorts and run with him. Half the time he took off his shirt and showed off a trail of black hair down his breastbone and over rippling muscles, and the exotic tattoo that rippled as he pumped his arms. Every time he came in from running, she wanted to lick the bead of sweat off his nipple, and run her hands over his thighs to see if they really were as solid as they looked.

Run with him? Yeah, right. She'd hyperventilate before they were out of the parking lot. It was bad enough that he kept a weight bench in his office and lifted weights when he'd been working long hours, and he said his neck was tight.

So she was alone in this house, waiting on pins and needles for her first lover to arrive home.

She rubbed her palms on her pants.

He didn't know he was her first lover, or even that he was her lover at all. It was her task to explain her plan. She'd thought about putting together a Power-Point presentation; after all, conferencing was a tool they both extensively used and understood.

But a brief contemplation of the scene recalled the humiliating lecture about reproduction, abstinence, and sin given by old Sister Theresa in eighth-grade health, and Ann had hastily returned to her scheme — an enlightening discussion conducted in seductive circumstances.

So it was a good thing he wasn't here, because this gave her time to freshen up from her long drive and implement said seductive circumstances.

She already knew which bedroom she planned to take — the master. Jasha's room.

She was bold. She was valiant.

So why was she tiptoeing over to her suitcase, picking it up as quietly as she could, and tiptoeing back to the stairs?

Because she'd spent her life waiting in the wings, desperately wanting love to find her, and now she was stepping onstage and demanding attention . . . and she would get that attention any way she could. With great clothes . . . or no clothes.

Abruptly, clouds covered the sun. The light disappeared. The wind hit the house with a blast that shook the windows, and rain splattered against the glass.

The storm was here.

CHAPTER 3

Stranger was back.

He'd come out of the big rock cave at the edge of the cliff. Only rarely did he run with the wolf pack, but when he did, he always came out of the big rock cave like some domesticated dog. But he didn't act like a domesticated dog — if he had, the pack could have killed him.

Instead, Stranger pranced along, big, handsome, his eyes golden and framed with black lashes. He had broad shoulders and a mark like two snakes that twisted and wrestled down one front leg. The dappled sunlight sparkled on Stranger's black and silver fur, and as he dodged through the forest, his muscles rippled with strength. He challenged the wind with his speed and grace.

Leader hated him, for the young female with the smooth brown fur watched Stranger, moist eyes gleaming. She would be in heat soon, and she made it clear that when she was, she'd run with Stranger.

But Stranger never looked back at the young female. He ran at the edge of the pack, keeping his gaze straight ahead, never challenging Leader's authority.

But if he wished, he could.

Leader knew that, so he loped along, his senses attuned to Stranger, to his motions, to the sounds of his panting breath and the thud of his paws on the ground.

For those senses told him there was something *not right* with the male. Something . . . bad.

That was the real reason Leader didn't challenge Stranger. Not because Stranger would win, but because the stench of something worse than death clung to his fur. Something unlucky. Something ruined, burned . . . hopeless.

A curse. Or perhaps a pact with the shadow that lurked right outside the range of Leader's vision . . .

Today, as Stranger ran, grim and bitter fury ran with him.

The storm was coming. The storm was here.

Leader feared it, for this time, the storm wasn't merely lashing wind and cold rain. Leader could feel a fire in the earth, as if a great shift was coming to their land, and everything he knew would soon be blasted and twisted.

Stranger carried the storm in his fur, in his heart. The mark on his leg moved and twisted, and his eyes . . . they glowed in the dim light of the forest.

That was why Leader failed to notice the scent of a human and take action.

Then it was too late. The human stepped out from behind his tree and took aim.

Leader saw him, turned to protect his female — and the killing blast rocked the forest. Pushed by an invisible hand, Leader flipped in the air. He came to his feet at once, prepared to fight. Prepared to run. *In pain.*

But Stranger raced toward the human.

The human pointed his stick.

Stranger leaped, and as he leaped he changed.

The fur shrank away from his skin. His body lengthened. His front legs became arms. His face grew horrible. *Human.*

A strong gust of wind bent the trees and hit them like a blast.

The first human screamed. He lifted the stick over his head and, in a panicked movement, lashed out.

Stranger hit him from the side. The humans rolled in the dirt. The stick flashed and roared. Overhead, branches exploded and chips and needles flew like snowflakes.

Stranger came to his feet, clutching the stick. He swung it in a circle. Smashed it against a boulder. Rock chips and moss flew. The stick broke in two.

The first human leaped up and ran.

Stranger stood still, looked at Leader, and spoke.

Leader didn't understand human-speak, but he understood this man. He recognized this man — he stood naked, with dark hair on his head, and dark brows, long, dark, curly lashes that framed familiar golden eyes, and a tattoo that rippled down one arm from his shoulder to his wrist that matched the marks on Stranger's fur.

"Are you all right?" Stranger asked.

Leader looked down. Blood dripped off his chest. His flesh burned like fire. His alpha female licked it, and Leader knew he would survive.

He inclined his head.

"He won't bother you again." The human changed again. More slowly this time, as if the effort cost him. But when he was done, he was a wolf. A wolf wrong. A wolf damned. But a wolf.

Then he sprinted after the human.

Leader took his pack deep into the forest, and hid. Hid from the humans, from Stranger, and from the scent he now recognized.

The scent of damnation.

The storm broke.

How appropriate.

Ann had broken into Jasha's home. Of course, now an unpredicted storm would trap her here. It was no more than she deserved.

She made it up the stairs and into the bedroom without tripping or dropping anything, and as she unpacked and hung her clothes in the closet, she gave herself brownie points for coordination, for good unpacking skills, for not burying her nose in Jasha's suit and breathing in his scent. . . . Nope, she had to take those points away. Sniffing his sleeve while she hung up her coat constituted cheating.

As she worked, she kept straining, listening, waiting for that whisper of awareness that said Jasha had returned to his home. Nothing. She even walked back to the top of the stairs, but he wasn't here.

Her active imagination created the scenario — he'd gone for a walk in the woods, tripped, and broke his leg. Or better yet, he'd been attacked by a cougar, had fought it off, and was even now calling for her.

And she . . . she sensed his distress and hunted through the night until she found him, cleaned and bandaged his wounds, built a stretcher out of saplings, dragged him back to the house, and nursed him. . . . Unfortunately, she couldn't convince even herself of that story.

Not that Jasha couldn't get hurt. He was a daredevil — he rappelled, he skydived, he participated in the Ironman Triathlon once, but the training took too much time from his surfing. He'd been in a cast for three weeks after that ski accident last winter.

She was the problem. Wounds made her faint, and anyway, why wouldn't she use her cell to call for help?

Immediately, in her imagination, she found herself garbed like Scarlett O'Hara — but there was still that yucky blood problem.

Nope. If Jasha knew what was good for him, he'd stay healthy.

One thing she knew for sure — if he *was* healthy, he'd be here for dinner — Jasha never missed a meal. And if she hurried, she could shower and be dressed in her wraparound black-and-white silk dress, the one that fastened with a single button at the

Empire waist.

Her friend Celia had called it the perfect dress for getting laid.

Ann tended to agree, for every time she took a step, the slit in the skirt opened all the way up her thigh, and when she thought about Jasha's tanned hand sliding up her leg, her skin prickled. But, as Celia was fond of pointing out, only the Carmelite nuns who lived near the beach kept Ann from being the oldest virgin in California, and something had to be done.

In a sudden and violent hurry, Ann grabbed the dress, a pair of panties so minuscule they were nothing but lace and elastic, and black stiletto Betsey Johnson sandals with a hard wooden sole that added an inch to her height, and sprinted into the bathroom.

The rich copper tile shower enclosure welcomed her. She set the land-speed record for bathing with Jasha's shampoo and Jasha's soap — made especially for him, and unscented, as he demanded. As soon as she was done, she ran to the locked door and listened, then cracked it and listened again.

Nothing. No sound. He wasn't here yet.

Her heart raced as she toweled herself dry.

It used to embarrass her, the way she

longed and lusted when he was nearby. She used to worry that he would notice the way she stammered when he got too close or the way she blushed every time he looked at her.

But he didn't. To Jasha, she was a highly efficient method of filing papers, producing correspondence, and making phone calls. When he was gone, he left Wilder Wines in her hands, and when his executives complained, he stared at them blankly and said, "But Ann does a better job than you."

Of course she did. She had something to prove.

She had *everything* to prove — but she'd been afraid to live, until six months ago when she'd been blindsided by a blow that woke her to the fact that Jasha didn't even know the two basic facts about her.

She was alive. And she was a woman.

Yet she knew everything about him, including that he liked good-looking confident women. So she set out to remake herself.

And she had.

She blew her hair into a shining, slippery mass of strands, and put on makeup — not too much, because she still wasn't particularly skillful, but enough blush to conceal her blanched skin and enough mascara to turn her lashes dark and her eyes bluer.

But if she was going to get naked with a man, she had one more matter to care for. . . .

She twisted so her back was to the mirror, and frowned at her distinctive birthmark. Over the years, it hadn't faded. She'd thought about having it removed, but the idea of showing it to a doctor who would ask questions, be incredulous, maybe see more than Ann wanted . . . she couldn't explain that mark. Because how did one explain the impossible?

Swiftly, she used her makeup sponge to dab a splash of foundation over it. Last of all, she donned the panties, the dress, and the shoes.

She stared at herself in the mirror.

How could she look so good, yet feel so much like the Cowardly Lion?

Okay. She was going to go to the great room, get a glass of wine, pose artfully in front of the fire, and wait for Jasha to show up. She could do it. All she had to do was walk downstairs. . . .

Above the battering of the storm, she heard a blast of sound from outside.

She knew that sound. She'd grown up in downtown LA.

A gunshot.

Running to the window, she crouched low

and off to the side. Warily she separated the curtains and peeked out.

The window faced the front of the house. Late-afternoon sunshine was diffused by billows of storm clouds. Wind blew the rain sideways. Lightning flickered across the branches of the cedars and pines, Douglas firs and rhododendrons, casting them in bleak shades of black-and-white.

She could see the shiny-wet roof of her car, but no one on the driveway or in the yard, no glint of a gun or sign of movement under the encroaching forest.

Yet this was the wilderness. Maybe someone was out there hunting.

She let the curtains fall — and heard a high, distant scream, then another shot. She leaped back from the window and knelt on the floor.

For long minutes, she heard nothing.

Finally, she looked out again, and stared hard at the ground beneath the thrashing trees.

Gunfire, and an inhuman scream. Weren't panthers supposed to scream? Had someone shot a panther?

Were there panthers in Washington?

Her impression about Jasha's bleak, ominous castle changed — she was nestled inside, safe from the elements, from the beasts, from a madman with a gun. Maybe that was why Jasha loved this place; once inside, he could let down the guard she sensed he kept around him.

Uneasily, she opened the bedroom door.

Someone was moving around downstairs. Someone — or something.

She heard a soft snuffling interrupted by repeated growls.

Had she reset the alarm?

No. She hadn't. And someone in the forest had a gun.

Had someone who was not Jasha — someone crazy, someone Ted Kaczynski — shot him and walked into his house?

She felt silly. Overly dramatic. She was plain Ann Smith, administrative assistant and nerd. Nothing harrowing ever happened to her. Yet she tasted fear. Taking off her stiletto heels, she held one in each hand as she walked quietly down the corridor. She paused on the balcony.

She heard snarling. Panting.

Did Jasha have a dog?

She peeked over the rail.

Yes — a dog stood facing the flickering fire. It was tall at the shoulders, long, and gaunt, yet it easily weighed 150 pounds, with a black and silver coat that gleamed with red and gold in the flames. It was growling, a distinct, constant, bass rumble of displeasure rising from deep in its chest.

Ann wasn't afraid of dogs, but she'd never heard such a menacing sound in her life.

Then the dog turned its head, and its pointed snout, its scarred cheek, and its white-fanged snarl sent her scurrying back against the wall.

A wolf. A wolf stood before the fire.

Her heart pounded so hard the sound thundered in her ears.

How had a wolf broken into the house? Was the back door open? Had it crashed through a window?

Where was Jasha? If he walked in on this thing, he could get hurt.

She sidled forward and slid along the rail, examining the room from every angle.

No sign of her boss, but although the wolf's rumblings had subsided, Ann knew it was dangerous. A killer. A predator.

As she retreated, the clear-minded planning that made her such a valuable administrative assistant kicked in. *Return to my room. Lock the door. Call Jasha on his cell and warn him. Then call 911 so they can get animal services out here. . . .*

She stopped backing up, and stared.

The wolf looked different somehow.

She squeezed her eyes shut. She opened

them again.

I'm allergic to something. The new-car smell . . . Jasha's soap . . . I have to be. Because I'm hallucinating.

But no, really.

He looked . . . longer. His muscular shoulders had lost hair, and his ears . . . his ears grew bare and rounded, and slid down the side of his head.

The wolf had begun to . . . had begun to resemble a man.

The man had begun to resemble Jasha.

CHAPTER 4

Oh, yes. Ann was definitely nuts. The stress of coming up here to confront Jasha had caused her hold on reality to snap.

Now shock ripped away her good sense. Without making a sound on the hardwood, and drawn by the same fascination that always plagued her in Jasha's presence, she walked toward the top of the stairs.

The wolf stood on its hind paws. Stood erect, like a man.

Her blood stirred. Her skin grew sensitive. The air in the house had grown thick and heated.

She recognized the signs. That *was* Jasha. That . . . that *thing* was really Jasha.

The pelt retreated to the top of his head and became Jasha's black, black hair with a premature streak of silver on each side. His skin absorbed the fur, and she saw his right arm, and its distinctive tattoo. . . . She broke into a light sweat.

He was naked. Nude. Absolutely without covering of any kind.

And apparently she was the weirdest perv ever to walk the earth, for even in the midst of her madness, she found the sight of his bare, toned butt riveting. She wanted to shut her eyes against the sight, to take a deep breath and give herself a stern warning about the dangers she faced.

But as she inched down each step, she couldn't risk shutting her eyes, and she certainly didn't dare take a deep breath.

Don't stumble, Ann.

Don't make a sound, Ann.

The transition was happening slowly, and once or twice, it — he — groaned as if the growth and change pained him. The paws became hands, large hands with Jasha's long fingers, and he used those fingers to push back his hair in a gesture she recognized as one of exasperation and worry.

With each step down the stairs, her frozen disbelief became certainty . . . and fear. The man she adored was a wolf. A beast. Something unholy, unnatural.

She brought the bad people. She always brought the bad people.

But Jasha wasn't bad. He couldn't be. She couldn't stand that.

Yet . . . yet here she was. She'd finally

worked up the nerve to chase her dreams only to find he had become her worst nightmare, and she was stuck in the house with him. It.

Jasha.

Think.

Her keys were on the end table by the door.

He hadn't noticed her yet.

If she could get from the stairs to her keys, she could open the door and race to her car ahead of him. She could drive off, and for once she wouldn't care about the speed limit.

He hadn't noticed her yet.

She would drive as if her life depended on escape — and it did.

Five steps from the bottom.

He hadn't noticed her yet.

She'd go back to her apartment, grab Kresley, and run as far away as possible. She would never look back. Never.

But first she had to get her keys. Open the door. Start her car . . .

And just like in her nightmares, the thing in the great room lifted its head and sniffed. Its head turned slowly in her direction. It looked at her.

Almost human. That thing was almost human. Except that deep in its golden eyes, a red glow burned. "Ann." Its deep voice sounded rough, as if it had a cold. It looked human again.

It looked like Jasha, the man she loved.

Her gaze fixed on the small, dark red smear at the corner of his mouth.

Blood.

He walked toward her. Naked. He was as glorious naked as she had always dreamed, and now she didn't dare take the time to check and see if the rumors were true.

Because he had blood on his face.

Blood.

"You little fool," he said, "what are you doing here?"

She screamed and with all her might, she flung first one heavy-soled shoe, then the other.

He dodged the first one. The second caught him squarely in the chest. The stiletto heel smacked his breastbone. She heard him grunt. Saw him stagger back, and blood spurt.

She ran. Ran so hard she skidded into the door. She grabbed the keys. Her sweaty palms slid on the doorknob.

Any second now and he'd have her.

The heavy door swung toward her. The wind swept through the door, taking her breath. She ran onto the porch.

Behind her, she heard a growl. In terror, she glanced back — and saw it.

The transformation was reversing.

Inexorably, Jasha was becoming the wolf once more.

Fangs . . . and claws . . . and an intelligent, vengeful, red-rimmed gaze fixed on *her.*

Using every ounce of courage she possessed, she ran back, grabbed the door, and slammed it shut.

Let Mr. Wolf Man claw his way through *that.*

As she sprinted toward the car, she sorted through the keys. The windblown rain slapped her in the face, clearing her brain. . . . What good did a clear brain do her?

Everything she believed in — everything she knew as true — was vanquished by the reality of that *thing* in the house.

Jasha.

The Miata's lights flashed as she unlocked the door with the remote. She slid into the seat and scraped her knee on the steering column. She knew it must hurt. She just couldn't feel it. Not now. Not yet. She didn't have time.

She slammed the door. Glanced at the house. Tried to get the key in the ignition. Tried again.

Her hand was shaking too hard to make the connection.

She glanced at the house again — and saw the wolf leap through the sidelight beside the front door. The glorious, expensive, leaded glass sprayed outward as his sleek body arched through, head outstretched, teeth bared.

Magically, her hand steadied and the key slid into the ignition. She started the car; she'd never heard a sound as wonderful as that of her engine turning over.

She put her foot to the floor. The car leaped forward and she whipped around the circle drive with the verve and expertise of a driver in the Grand Prix.

Rain sluiced down the windshield. She fumbled with the wipers, got them on . . . in the intermittent mode. As the wipers slid unhurriedly across the windshield, she cursed the new car, the unfamiliar controls, the desire that had brought her here.

She should have known better. She was an orphan, abandoned and alone, marked by evil, rejected by the Almighty. Sister Mary Magdalene had urged her to accept her fate and live her life alone, but Ann had rebelled.

Now she swore she'd thank God if she lived at all — especially since she hadn't even put on her seat belt.

Then she glanced into the rearview mirror.

The wolf raced across the grass after the car.

To hell with the seat belt.

He couldn't catch her. She knew it was impossible. Wolves couldn't move as fast as a car.

But men didn't turn into wolves, either. Maybe Jasha was a freaking Transformer. Maybe he was going to turn into a giant mechanized robot and stomp on her and her car.

She bent her attention to the road, driving faster than she had ever driven in her life.

The wind buffeted the tiny Miata. Lightning flashed and thunder cracked. Her hair dripped into her eyes. Her hands slipped on the steering wheel, from the rain, from fear-induced sweat. She squinted through the blurry windshield, taking the winding curves too fast, seeing the ocean cliffs flash past as she cleared the forest, then, as she turned inland again, the trees loom above her. Soon she would skirt the cliffs again. She needed to concentrate, to remember the route she'd driven only once. . . .

And without warning, the road rose, then dipped, then rose. The car was airborne.

She was airborne. With a jaw-snapping impact, the wheels hit the asphalt. The air bag exploded in her face, smothering her in white for one vital moment.

As it subsided, she desperately clawed it out of the way. Then she could see. The car was headed straight — but the road curved. Curved to the left, and ahead she saw nothing but rain and clouds and the edge of the cliff.

She slammed on the brakes. The car hydroplaned, the rear wheels sliding sideways.

At last the tread caught. She was in control.

But too late. Too late. The rear wheels dropped off the precipice. Half the car hung over the cliff, over the rocks and the ocean. The undercarriage screamed as it scraped the asphalt.

She was going to die.

The side panel smacked something. Something big. A boulder. A tree trunk. Something. The metal crunched. The car stopped. Stopped so suddenly she slid sideways into the passenger seat. She lost her grip on the wheel. Her legs tangled with the console.

She sat frozen, waiting for the car to tip, to plunge her into the ocean.

Nothing moved. The stench of hot metal

and burning rubber filled her nose. She was still alive — and if she wanted to stay that way, she had to get out. Get out before the car plunged off the cliff. Get out before it burst into flame.

She put on the emergency brake, then closed her eyes.

Taking care not to suddenly shift her weight, she grasped the handle and opened the door. All her care was wasted; the wind caught it and jerked it open. She held her breath, waiting for the inevitable shift and tumble.

Nothing.

Distantly she noted that her hand was now steady as a rock.

Somewhere on this wild ride, she had transcended terror.

She slid her legs out, inched her butt along the seat, then gradually stood.

The car hung there, suspended over the cliff, resting on the front tires and the frame.

She stepped away from it. Backed away, waiting for it to take the plunge.

The Miata remained still.

She stood alone on a one-lane private road. Her new car was smashed and unsalvageable, a testament to her bad driving — and a sign to Jasha that she was helpless and on foot. She was barefoot, rain lashed her, and — she faced back the way she came — nothing made sense, especially not the wolf who was Jasha.

She had to hide.

On one side of the road, the ocean ripped at the base of the cliff. On the other, the primeval forest loomed, dark and thick, branches lashing in the wind. She didn't want to go in there.

Then in the distance, a wolf howled.

He was coming for her.

Ann sprinted across the road and into the forest.

CHAPTER 5

The trees closed in around Ann, muting the already-dim light, protecting her from the lash of the wind and rain. Her bare feet sank into the damp loam. The scent of spicy pine drifted on the air currents, and for a second, she felt protected, absorbed by nature.

Then lightning struck and thunder boomed. The rain and wind struck with renewed force, and she heard one wolf howl, then another, then another. It sounded as if a whole pack was stalking her.

They probably were. Jasha's buddies.

The false sense of security was stripped away. She shoved her sopping hair out of her face, and her hands came away smeared with black. Her mascara was in ruins. Her dress was in ruins. Her dreams were in ruins. Her life . . .

As she jogged along, pine needles slipped beneath her soles, and she listened to the groan of the trees as they fought the wind.

Behind her, a single wolf howled again, and something in the sound, some note of fury and frustration, alerted her — that was Jasha.

What was he? Not some Wolf Man of legend; the full moon controlled those beasts. He was some other . . . thing.

Lightning flickered, turning the tall boulders into long faces that grinned and mocked. She ran along, looking for the best place to take cover, knowing that no place could be good enough. She was lost to civilization. She would probably die of exposure . . . or at Jasha's hands.

Paws. Whatever.

A stream crossed her path, and some long-buried Girl Scout memory surfaced. . . . Jasha couldn't track her if she walked through the water.

She stepped in. The cold water soothed her tender soles. She tried to hurry, but the large, smooth, mossy stones slipped beneath her feet. She strained, listening for the pad of a wolf's paws, but heard nothing. For a few minutes she imagined she'd saved herself.

Then she heard it. A splash downstream, and the slowly escalating sound of an animal loping through the water.

He'd found her. He was here.

She had nowhere to go.

She ran anyway, out of the stream and down a path between two great boulders. The way narrowed, and for a horrible moment, she thought she'd come to a dead end. But she squeezed through the crack, and beyond her, the forest opened. She was in a meadow, empty except for one immense hemlock. Its trunk was wide, and the crown touched the clouds.

She sprinted through the short grass. Rain splattered her face. The storm raged, gathering its strength until with one mighty strike and roar, lightning ripped through the hemlock. She felt the heat, covered her ears, smelled the brimstone . . . sank to her knees. Birds flew free, crying their anguish to the skies, and squirrels scattered as if bewildered.

As she watched in horror, the vindictive wind grabbed and shoved at the tree. Slowly, so slowly, the hemlock tilted toward the far end of the meadow. Its roots gripped the earth almost at her feet. But that was not enough; they ripped free in a great wide circle that took the green grass and clods of dirt and carried them high into the sky. The blackened branches flailed in protest, yet inevitably, gravity took command, and the tree slammed to earth so hard the ground shook beneath Ann's feet. Now, like the rest of the wild creatures, she rose to flee. Flee nature. Flee Jasha. Flee to survive . . . she scampered across the freshly exposed earth, imagining that somehow she could find a way to hide in the broken branches where Jasha couldn't find her.

Then the wolf howled, shattering her hopes. Startled, she slipped on a clod of earth, fell to the ground, glanced behind her — and saw, not the wolf coming through the gap in the rocks, but a glint of gold, and a woman looking at her.

A painting. A miniature. On a ceramic tile?

Ann blinked. She extended her hand. She curled her fingers around the small piece of polished clay.

The noise of the storm faded.

She lifted the image from the dirt, brushed it clean, looked closely.

This was old. So old. The painting was stilted, stylized, yet the paint had been fired onto the tile and the colors glowed as if they were new. The Virgin Mary held the infant Jesus, while Joseph stood at her right hand, and their halos glittered with gold leaf. Her robes were cherry red, the background was gold, and her eyes . . . her eyes were large and dark, filled with wisdom and compassion.

Ann's heart lifted. She wasn't going to give up. She wasn't going to die. She clutched the tile so hard the edges cut into her hand, and one ragged corner drew a single drop of blood. She stood, and ran again, heading right for the forest.

Overhead, the gray clouds swelled with renewed life. The thunder rumbled evilly. As she reached the circle of trees, she glanced back — and saw the wolf bounding across the meadow, his intelligent gaze fixed on her.

The rush of adrenaline hit her. Her heart leaped in her chest. She had thirty seconds to escape, and before her she saw only the wilderness filled with fallen branches, wide trunks, and swirls of moss. Fired by the intention to climb to safety, she raced toward a tumble of huge boulders, but as she took her first step up, something hit her from the side.

Jasha.

The wolf.

Whatever it was.

She toppled into a pile of leaves, rolling over and over, and when she came around the last time, she put all her strength behind her arm and hit it in the face with the painting.

With a yelp, it leaped back. It blocked her

arm as she wound up for another blow. The wet tile flew out of her grasp, and she found herself nose to nose with a snarling wolf.

He straddled her body, his body trembling with fury, his white fangs bared, his eyes yellow while, deep within his pupils, some *thing* glowed red.

As she fought for breath, her chest heaved, and the wolf's gaze wandered downward. Slowly, his head dipped, and he ran his tongue from the base of her throat to her chin. Again. And again.

She closed her eyes. Did wolves wash their prey before they killed it? For any minute she expected his teeth to close over her windpipe and crush it. Then he would rip out her throat, then drag her body away into the forest where it would never be found. . . .

But, my God, the long stroke of his tongue felt almost . . . erotic, and unwillingly her pounding heart changed its rhythm. He nuzzled under her ear, a gentle touch that prepared her for the nip on her ear. She felt his breath over the artery in her neck, and tensed again, expecting . . . but he kissed the side of her mouth.

She was confused. He felt human, but when she opened her eyes, she expected to see a wolf.

She saw Jasha. Jasha, with his intense gold

eyes, his generous mouth, and a new red mark on his cheek.

He knelt over the top of her, this man who smiled and asked, "Who sent you?"

"What?" What did he mean? She didn't know, she didn't understand.

"Who sent you?" Jasha's voice was smooth, warm, but with an edge that ripped through her like straight brandy. "Why did you follow me here?"

"I came . . . I came because the international deal will fall through unless you sign the papers. I brought them. They're in my briefcase. In the house." My God. His eyes were so gold, so intent. And his gaze wandered. . . . She looked down at herself.

She was splattered with mud, soaked to the skin. Her silk gown was ruined, and the stark white bodice showed everything — the shape of her breasts, the color of her nipples, that she was cold . . . and aroused. The black wraparound skirt was plastered to her thighs, and as she watched, Jasha placed his hand on her knee and slowly slid it up her thigh.

Her breath caught.

She was still afraid. Terrified. How could she not be? But mixed with that unfamiliar emotion was another, newer emotion — she was aroused. She was needy. She was ready.

How, when the lightning flashed overhead, and rain splattered on her face, could she want a man — a monster — like Jasha?

Yet she did.

Ann was a creature of instinct. Or perhaps of madness. She didn't know. She knew only that when he pressed his palm against her flat belly, she wanted his hand to move lower.

"Refresh my memory." Jasha sniffed her hair where it grew away from her forehead. "Where does the international deal originate?"

"The Ukraine."

"Of course." He laughed huskily. "The Ukraine. You're innocent. Of course you are. Like the devil. Like the illegal hunter. Like my own mother."

She didn't understand what he was talking about, whom he was talking about. "I didn't come to hurt you. How can you think I would hurt you when I . . . ?"

"Love me? Do you love me, little Ann?"

"No!"

"Yes, you do."

"You don't know that." He didn't. Did he?

"Of course I do. I know you better than you know yourself. I'm a beast, remember?

I have instincts that no mere man can match."

He was mocking her — wasn't he? He didn't really have instincts, did he? Not those kind. Not the kind that would help him see into her soul.

"Do you still love me now that you've seen what I am?"

"I don't love you." *Did* she still love him? She didn't know. She knew only that his touch changed her from a frightened girl to a ready woman, that regardless of her fear and her exhaustion, her unwilling body wanted him. Now. "Are you going to kill me?"

"Kill you?" His golden eyes narrowed. The pupils shifted, and for a second, his eyes flared with red. "Yes. I'm going to kill you — over and over and over again."

It was a threat her mind couldn't comprehend . . . but her body knew perfectly well what he meant.

She grabbed his wrists and twisted, trying to move him aside.

Dumb. He outweighed her by eighty well-muscled pounds. She couldn't budge him. But she couldn't bear to kick him, either. Even now, she couldn't hurt Jasha.

"What are you thinking, Ann? Are you thinking that I could tear your throat out?"

His hand slid inside the band of her minuscule panties. His finger slid between her folds, found her clitoris, and stroked with a leisurely, almost imperceptible touch.

But the only person who'd ever touched her there was . . . herself, and each motion bit at her nerves like the strike of a snake. She forgot who she had been — she had no past, no future — and became the person who lived now, and only now.

"Are you thinking of the cold earth against your back and the rain splattering your face?" He was crooning as if she were a wild bird he lured to its destruction.

Each one of her senses widened, embracing the scent of the earth, the cold rain, the wilderness around them . . . the wildness in him.

"Or is every fiber of your being concentrated between your legs? Are your nerves tightening as you wait for me to slide my finger inside you?"

He was reading her mind. He was taunting her.

"Maybe just an inch. Maybe all the way in —"

"Stop laughing at me!"

He bared his teeth. They were not at all fanglike, but they were very white. "I have never been farther from laughter than I am at this moment. Look at me."

She stared at his face, stark and fierce, with golden eyes that blazed in the dim light and, where she'd hit him, a scarlet patch of skin on his cheek.

"No. I mean — *look* at me."

With a shock, she realized what he wanted. She'd avoided running her gaze over the naked body crouched over her. And why? Fear of the wolf?

Or fear of the man and what he would demand?

She took a fortifying breath, then slid her gaze over his shoulders, so broad they blocked the rain, down his chest with its narrow band of dark, curling hair. The tattoo twisted down the length of his muscled arm, black and enigmatic.

He had a bruise on his left pec, and in the middle of his chest a small, bloody puncture wound. It looked like an arrow had struck him or — no, not an arrow. The narrow heel of her stiletto.

She chewed her lip. She should be pleased with herself. She'd got him good, and he'd deserved it.

But she'd cried when Bambi's mother died. She'd covered her eyes when she saw *Ghostbusters.* She was softhearted and a chicken, and she'd hurt Jasha, really hurt him. She touched the bloody mark with her fingertips, a quick, apologetic pat. "Sorry. You scared me and I, um . . . ."

"You've got a good arm." He impatiently brushed her apology away. "Now stop making excuses and *look at me.*"

She could feel the heat radiating from above her; it was the only thing that kept her from shivering as the wind howled through the rocks and lightning blistered the air. She looked down at his sculpted belly. . . . His erection was pale, deeply veined, and larger than . . . well, in the magazines, they just didn't look that big.

"Touch me."

"What?"

"Touch me."

He was furious — with life, with nature, with her — and a smart woman would do as he ordered.

But to touch his erection? When before she'd never had the nerve to do more than shake his hand?

He must have read her refusal in her face, for the hand in her panties pressed hard, and his finger stroked a circle around the entrance to her vagina.

The pleasure was so sudden, so intense, she found herself flattened, her arms stretched out to her sides, grasping handfuls of last year's fallen leaves as if gravity's law had been repealed and the earth threatened to throw her free.

"Touch me," he repeated.

She looked at her hands, dusted them clean, then reached up and grasped his shoulders. The muscles in them shifted, as fascinating a sensation as she could have imagined, and he took a breath as if to instruct her better. Then she dragged one hand down his chest.

The hand between her legs was still. Perhaps to tease her with anticipation. Perhaps because the way she stroked his nipple, circled it, pinched it, made him lose the power of movement. As both his nipples tightened, she heard his breath rasp in his throat.

So. She was not quite as helpless as she thought.

Except that she was — now that she'd started touching him, she couldn't stop. She loved the feeling of his warm skin, loved realizing that he might have chased her down, this not-quite-human man, but she held power over him as she *didn't* touch him. Didn't —

He freed his hand from her panties, grasped her fingers, and wrapped them around his penis. "There," he rasped.

"Touch me."

The heat he radiated originated here. She wanted to pull her hand away before he burned her with lust . . . but then he used her hand to stroke himself. His voice was gravelly as he said, "This is not a sign of laughter, Ann. That is a sign of arousal. You ran. I chased you down. You were frightened. Now . . . you're not afraid."

"Yes, I am," she said quickly. She'd be stupid not to be afraid, and she was not stupid. She *had* run. He *had* chased her down. He intended to . . . to screw her here and now, and she knew without a doubt that no matter what argument she made or how loud she screamed, he would have her.

Then he let go of her hand.

She found she couldn't — didn't want to? — take it away and be righteously indignant. Instead, she used her thumb to find a silky bead of semen at the tip and spread it in a small circle.

His breath hissed between his teeth, and for a second she feared she'd driven him to wolfish shape again.

But no. He was still human.

And his body was still fascinating.

He leaned his head close and spoke softly into her ear. "Do you know that a wolf can smell arousal in a female?"

Snatching her hand away, she turned to stare into his eyes. "No, you can't."

He sniffed her hair, behind her ear. He laughed, a deep, husky, wolfish laugh. "I know your scent as well as I know my own. I know your moods. I know your cycle. I even know your cat."

"No." He couldn't know that she wanted him all the time every day. That was too humiliating.

"Yes. And I know when I do this" — once again his hand slid into her panties — "the smell of fear retreats, and the scent of sweet arousal rises from you to fill my head and drive me half-mad."

"I've been aroused before, and you've always seemed sane enough to me," she said tartly.

"But never for me. It wasn't truly me who aroused you." He chuckled again, and his finger stirred the dusting of hair above her clit.

She closed her eyes, trapping the sensation inside her. Her brief burst of good sense faded, and her lips barely moved as she said, "Who else?"

"For a dream man that didn't exist. Because I'm not your dream man." As he had threatened, his finger slid all the way inside her. "I'm your worst nightmare."

CHAPTER 6

How did Jasha know Ann had thought exactly that? He was part wolf, part man — did he read minds, too?

Then he rubbed strongly with the heel of his hand. He stroked her inside and out, and as surely as he had transformed, she changed, too. She became a creature composed of passion and lit by an inner fire.

She dug her heels into the ground. Her back arched. She lifted herself, pressed herself against him, grinding her hips against his hand.

Abruptly, he took his finger away and stripped off her panties. Rising to his knees, he moved close between her legs. His eyes closed, his neck corded with strain, and his expression was exquisite agony. He held her thighs in his palms, and pressed the length of his erection to the softest part of her. As he rocked back and forth, he grew damp. Not from the rain, but rather from the torturous pleasure he forced on her.

Then — oh God — his penis probed, and he almost slipped inside. Except he *didn't* slip — her body resisted. Resisted and informed her, far too clearly, how painful their joining would be.

She whimpered. She couldn't help it. She was a born coward, and he . . . he was a wolf.

He shuddered. Opened his eyes and glared. "Virgin," he whispered.

"So?" She glowered back at him.

"So." He lowered her to the ground. "I'm a barbarian, the son of barbarians, a predator —"

"A killer." She flung the words as a challenge, hoping he would deny them.

Deep in his golden eyes, she saw a flare of murderous red. "Yes. A killer."

Lightning flashed and thunder blasted, reminding her — as if she could forget — where she was, and why. Vividly she recalled the yellow-eyed wolf, the terrifying chase . . . the blood on his mouth. He'd chased her down through a storm that roared around them, striking down great trees and shaking the earth. She'd left the trappings of civilization far behind, and her first time would be in the woods on the ground with a man who might at any moment turn on her and kill her — or who might give her the greatest pleasure a woman had ever known.

Her teeth chattered with sudden chill, and she tried to scoot out from underneath him.

But he captured her with his body.

"Are you afraid, Ann?" he crooned as he settled between her legs. "You should be. Because what I want from you isn't your death, but your surrender."

When he talked like that, his lips moving against her neck, he made her panicky. "What do you mean?"

"I mean I'm not going to take your virginity." Lifting his head, he smiled, and his teeth shone white and sharp. "You're going to give it to me."

"No!" For three years, she'd been his administrative assistant, and she'd never seen him fail any challenge.

"I swear you will."

"I . . . will . . . not!" She aimed the heel of her hand at his nose.

Barely in time, he jerked away.

She slammed his cheekbone. Her hand skidded up to smack his eye.

He caught her hand, and all semblance of the civilized man disappeared. "That's the third time today you've landed a blow on me. Since the day I became an adult, that's twice more than anyone else." Catching her other hand, he lifted them both above her head and pinned them in one of his.

For the first time, she felt the weight of a man: heavy, muscled, hard. He held her down, keeping her in place to do with as he wished.

"No more secrets." With his free hand, he loosened the button that kept her bodice together. As if he were unwrapping a present, he lifted the two halves away from her body.

The expression on his face made her swallow nervously.

He looked as hungry as the big bad wolf.

But when he cupped one breast and placed his mouth on the other, he was as gentle as a whisper. He was more of a breath than a touch, and every nerve in her body sighed in response.

The earth cradled her below. His body heated her above. The rain fell directly on her upturned face. Everything about this moment was primal, intense . . . primitive. She was a victim of nature's fury. She was a sacrifice to Jasha's need. Yet a willing sacrifice: Each time his tongue circled her nipple, she yielded more wholly.

The discomfort of unwilling arousal and the dampness between her legs grew, and she twisted beneath him, fighting to free herself before she gave him what he wanted.

Everything.

He pressed his cheek on her collarbone and chuckled. "Wrap your legs around my hips and you'll be more comfortable."

And open herself to him even more? She was already uncomfortable with this level of intimacy — and uncomfortable was an understatement. "How dumb do you think I am?"

He lifted his head from her chest. The rain blistered down. His hair dripped, and water beaded on his face. Behind him, lightning zigzagged so brightly, a negative photographic image of him seared her retinas. He smiled, but that smile told her all too clearly that this was another battle he intended to win. "I have *never* thought you were dumb. But I do think — know — that before this is over, you'll do as I command. Ann . . ."

Even the way he said her name had changed. In the office, he used it as a helpful piece of furniture, like "File cabinet" or "Copy machine." Now his warm tones lingered over the single vowel, the double consonant, transforming a name she'd always considered the ultimate in dull into something exotic and tempting.

He used his voice to possess her.

He kissed each one of her eyelids closed, then put his mouth to hers.

Her eyes sprang open.

Jasha and Ann were naked, as close as a man and woman could be, yet they'd never kissed. How often she dreamed of a single kiss, intense, deep, immediate. . . .

How wrong she'd been! For he savored her lips as gently as he'd savored her breast. He stroked his tongue along the seam of her lips, and when she refused to open, he stroked again in a rhythm that echoed the rumble of the thunder and the heartbeat of the earth . . . or was that her heartbeat she heard?

She found her eyelids drooping. She tried to focus on his unbearably large forehead — large from this angle, at least — but she couldn't focus her interest on his face. Not when his tongue slipped so neatly between her lips and caressed the inside of her mouth, or when his fingers caressed her ear-lobes — when had he released her hands? — or when he whispered, "Ann, come out and play."

Come out and play? What did that mean?

But he answered the question immediately when the tip of his tongue swirled around hers, and when she followed, he drew her into his mouth and let her . . . explore.

She clutched his wrists, her fingers barely circling the bones, sinews, and muscles. A sensible woman would realize that a man as large as this would dominate her in the act of love.

But he wasn't dominating; he was seducing, and he was good at it. When she opened her eyes again, his mouth had wandered back to her breasts.

And she'd wrapped her legs around his waist.

He'd won.

But she hadn't lost. With his every movement, she won, too.

She didn't intend to give him her blessing or her permission, yet irresistibly her hands crept up his shoulders, relishing the stretch of smooth skin over warm muscle. When her fingers tangled with the silky curl at his neckline, he froze, and for a moment all she could feel was his warm breath against her damp breast.

"Touch me some more." His voice wasn't loud, yet she heard it above the thunder. Pulling her nipple into his mouth, he suckled hard, assaulting her senses with his lips and tongue until she forgot to be timid and released the faintest moan.

A betraying moan.

Then he sank his teeth lightly into her

flesh, scraping across the fragile nerve endings.

Her fingers clutched at his hair, tugging hard. And when she grew used to his mouth on her breast, he somehow knew . . . and moved on, kissing his way down her rib cage, across her belly, taut with anticipation, and between her legs. He licked her, a wolf claiming his mate with pleasure. He thrust his tongue into her body, imitating intercourse. Tenderly he sucked on her clit, and when she battled against the rage of passion, he held her still and forced her to accept his attentions.

She wasn't unconscious; she knew what she was doing, but he conjured an orgasm beyond anything she'd ever imagined. One glorious spasm followed another. Her fragile control crumbled completely. All the moans she'd restrained could no longer be suppressed. She strained, struggled, panted, conscious of her body, the earth, the storm, the crash of thunder in her ears, and of Jasha.

"Jasha . . ."

"What?" He slid up her body, grasped her shoulders, massaged them in his large hands. "What? Ann, tell me what I should do."

He made it sound as if he would do what

94

she wanted, when in fact he had not only chased her down and held her captive to his body; he'd also forced her to relinquish her will.

"Jasha, please."

"What?" He used his thigh to keep the rush of her climax tumbling through her veins. He kissed her ear, and his voice was tender, gentle, encouraging. "Tell me, Ann. What do you want?"

She lifted her lids, the effort almost more than she could manage.

He sounded gentle.

He looked fierce, his yellow eyes narrowed, intent, unrelenting. He looked like a man, and he moved like an animal, all sleek, oiled muscles moving beneath glorious damp skin.

Rain slid down his cheek, and moved by some previously undiscovered instinct, she licked the droplet. It tasted salty.

He stilled. Slid into position, his legs between hers, his arms beneath her shoulders, his hand cupping her skull, holding her so he could look into her eyes.

The storm, the earth, the skies, stilled as he made his plea; his voice was hoarse, gravelly, desperate. "Ann, for shit's sake, ask me."

"Jasha, please, please" — she skimmed his

hair with her fingers — "make love to me."

The triumphant smile he flashed showed far too much of his white teeth, reminding her of the predator.

But it was too late for panic. He thrust into her, a hard, steady push.

And the storm raged again.

It was too much. He was too big. He hurt her. The world narrowed to the two of them, and as he possessed her with his body, he dominated her with his gaze. His body moved on hers, pulling back, coming in, farther and farther each time, touching new places inside her, his teeth and eyes gleaming with triumph. He was slow, savoring each motion, giving her time to adjust yet proceeding relentlessly.

And she resisted the pain, fighting him, cries breaking from her, and at the same time she struggled toward something — satisfaction, or joy, or maybe the joining of two bodies and two souls.

Finally he was all the way inside. His chest heaved with effort, and the way he watched her . . . as if she were now a part of him.

She shuddered. Never in her life had she been part of anything. Somehow she had thought that sex would be the same, that she would retain her identity, be the outsider looking in. Instead they were joined so closely she didn't know where she ended and he began. He moved, slowly at first, then faster, each movement long and deep, provoking sensations too raw for her to comprehend. She wanted to run again, to escape the onslaught of passion, but he held her close. His chest rubbed against hers. He seduced her with desire and dark, sexual words muttered in her ear. The rain fell on her face, and mixed with her tears of pleasure and exaltation, and it seemed the earth moved, not from the roar of thunder, but from the cataclysm of her joining with Jasha.

This was sex. This was possession. This was wild and feral, nothing like she'd imagined — and so much better.

The storm reached its height, a cacophony of lightning and thunder, of purple clouds fleeing across a sky black with turmoil.

At the same time, his body moved on hers, dragging her through anguish to climax.

He groaned, deep in his chest, as he thrust and thrust again, and shuddered as he came.

Lightning struck nearby; she heard the blast, smelled smoke and fire. As she came, the whole world changed.

She changed.

The lightning surrounded her. It was in her. It heated her, fused her . . . to Jasha.

Red flared in his eyes, and she saw his

face, transformed by passion.

He had changed, too.

They were one.

Then, little by little, her body calmed. Jasha's breathing slowed. They came to rest.

Slowly he pulled away from her; she couldn't believe how hollow she felt. But good . . .

Right now he looked totally human. If you didn't count being outside and doing it on the ground in the storm, they'd made love normally, without any weird doggy-style positions or any animal-eyed metamorphosis. If she wanted to, she could pretend she'd never seen him transform. Pretend everything was normal.

Then he did something she didn't believe; he placed his palm between her legs. He showed her his hand, red with her lost virginity. Carefully he placed it on the boulder beside them, leaving a smear of blood. "An offering to the earth," he said. And he was serious.

Normal?

Nothing would ever be normal again.

CHAPTER 7

Moving with a care for the ache between her legs, Ann sat up and without taking her gaze off Jasha, she scooted away from him.

He knelt where he was and watched her, his gaze knowing.

He saw too much, heard too much. . . . According to him, his sense of smell was acute.

How was she supposed to keep her secrets?

As with their passion, the violence of the storm had abated, leaving a steady drizzle that wet the sunset and made her wonder with melancholy if she'd imagined everything.

Jasha . . . a wolf? Her boss . . . a ruthless seducer?

Yet here she was, sitting in the trackless wilderness as the sun dipped toward the horizon, a virgin no longer.

And she *was* afraid of the man who'd

taken her.

Not because he'd hurt her, although he had, but because she *hadn't* hallucinated. He *had* been a wolf. In what universe did that make sense?

He looked as if he wanted to speak.

She avoided his gaze. Tried to wrap her dress around her. Realized it was ruined — the black silk skirt see-through and muddy, the white bodice torn.

"Stay here." He rose.

"What are you doing?"

"I'll be back," he said.

She noted that he didn't answer her question. Didn't even make a token attempt.

"Promise me you'll stay here," he insisted.

If he didn't have to respond to her, she didn't have to promise him. "What else am I going to do? Run away? You've already proved *that* doesn't work."

"Promise," he repeated. Without the words, he didn't trust her. Yes, he did know too much.

"What makes you think I will keep a promise?"

He chuckled and leaned down to look into her eyes. "You've worked for me as my assistant for how many years, Ann?"

"Three."

"Do you think I don't know you at all?"

All her defiance collapsed. "I promise."

"Don't sulk." He kissed her lightly, then vanished into the woods, and not even a branch wiggled to show where he'd gone.

No matter how much her legs trembled with the desire to rise and flee, she wouldn't do it. She didn't want to incite him again. Last time he'd just chased her down and screwed her. Next time, he might . . . kill her.

She couldn't believe that thought even crossed her mind, much less that she was giving it due consideration. But a girl had to be sensible, especially when she was sleeping with a wolf.

She had the marks to prove it. Her feet hurt; somewhere on the run through the woods, she'd stubbed every one of her toes. Her legs ached; vaguely she remembered scratching her thigh on an outstretched branch. Her hand . . . she stared down at the pale, whorled skin. The painted tile had sliced her fingers and her palm.

She'd hit Jasha with the tile. It had flown out of her hand.

All too clearly Ann remembered the Madonna's dark, serene eyes, the golden halo, the cherry red robes.

Where had the painting gone?

She studied the little cove, and hidden

101

between two boulders, deep within a crevice, she spotted a glint of white in a crispy-brown pile of last autumn's leaves. She cleared the debris away, freeing the lady from her hiding place. Carefully she lifted the tile, turned the picture toward the failing light, and studied it.

It was a historic rendering of the Virgin Mary. In the little vignette, the Madonna had surrounded herself with family, and that . . . that spoke to Ann's innermost desires. Turning it over, she saw faint burn marks along the edges of the unfinished clay.

Where had it come from? How old was it?

How had it come here, now, to her?

"Ann," Jasha called from the boulder across the way, a warning he'd returned.

Ann tucked the painting into the leaves beside her, and watched him leap into their little clearing.

He was respectably dressed in jeans, a T-shirt, and running shoes.

Indignation boiled up in her.

After what had happened between them, she wouldn't have thought she could be embarrassed about anything.

But she was, and she winced when she thought how bizarre she looked — mud in her hair, on her face, bruises and scabs everywhere. And this for her first experience at lovemaking! If what had happened between them could be called lovemaking. The term seemed trite for something so cosmic. God knew it had shaken her world.

"Where did you get those clothes?" she demanded.

"In case of emergency, I have stashes hidden around in the woods." He shook out a man's long-sleeved button-up shirt.

"Emergency? Like when you chase women through the woods to ravish them?" What a dumb thing to say. She needed to remember — he was a wolf.

The trouble was, he looked so very *Jasha*. "I've only ever chased one woman through the woods to ravish her." He wrapped the shirt around her shoulders. "It was wrong of me, but I —"

"You what?" He couldn't stop now.

Jasha stuffed her arms into the shirt, then held the two lapels apart and gazed at her. At her breasts, her belly, the junction of her thighs. "Someday, I'll tell you."

His expression made her tweak the shirt out of his hands and, in brisk movements, button it herself. That was better than responding to his hunger with a renewed hunger of her own, and reaching for him — wasn't it?

Of course it was. He'd admitted it himself.

He'd ravished her and any self-respecting modern maiden would get herself to a police station and file charges.

But she was glad to be rid of her virginity. Had come here for this exact purpose. She just wanted him to be what she had thought he was before — the perfect man. And a completely human man, too.

She stole a glance at him.

He squatted on his heels, his hands dangling on his knees, and watched her with amusement. "You should have let me button that for you."

"Why?"

"Because you buttoned it crooked."

In exasperation, she started again.

"You're feeling better."

"I'm a little less —" She hesitated.

"In pain?"

"Petrified."

But was that good? That she was accepting the impossible?

"It's all right. Next time we make love, I promise I won't hurt you." His golden eyes warmed to a sizzle. "In fact, I promise I will make you a very happy woman."

"That is *not* why I —" He knew that, she realized. He wanted to avoid that conversation.

She looked around at the dripping wet

woods. The branches rustled as animals moved through the brush. She remembered the howling of the pack and realized — he might have a point.

He folded her collar down. "I'm always naked when I turn, and if the FedEx man shows up and needs a signature, he's less likely to think I'm crazy if I'm wearing something."

Jasha talked about it so casually. *Turning.* As if he were a leaf. Or a door handle. And he looked directly at her, challenging her to accept him without question.

She shook back the long sleeves that drooped over her hands, took one of the cuffs, and folded it back. Anything was better than meeting his eyes.

"Of course, this is Washington. There are nudists all over the place, so the FedEx man probably would simply lecture me on the dangers of sunburn." Jasha took the task away from her, unrolling the slapdash job she'd done and neatly refolding the cuff.

"I can do it." Because she didn't know how to let him work while she did nothing.

But he brushed her hands aside. "I think you've never had anyone help you do anything."

"What do you mean?" She was feeling a little hostile.

"When you were a kid, was there ever a time when someone helped you dress yourself?"

"No. Why?" She didn't understand his point.

"You do everything with a frightening efficiency, and I always wonder — were you ever a child?"

She suffered an odd combination of hurt — for he seemed to be criticizing her — and surprise — for she never thought he noticed her. "*My* efficiency is the reason I'm *your* administrative assistant."

"One of the reasons. So" — he finished with the cuffs and adjusted her collar — "*were* you ever a child?"

"I thought you were asking a rhetorical question."

"And I'm fascinated that you don't want to answer it. Who taught you to be so self-sufficient, Ann Smith?"

Was he sorry for what he'd done? Was he trying to make conversation, to make amends before telling her the whole experience had been equal parts rage and foolishness? "The nuns."

"You went to a Catholic school?"

"Yes." That was true — as far as it went.

"Hm." His eyes were skeptical.

She shivered. She remembered how often

she'd seen him look at an employee or a business rival and *know* the person was withholding information. She'd always been pleased and impressed, thinking he showed an almost supernatural insight into human behavior.

Well . . . yeah.

"Let me see your feet." He lifted first one, then the other, and *tsk*ed. "We need to get you back and put some antiseptic on these cuts. Are they painful?"

"They're too cold to be painful."

He chafed her toes. "They're ice cubes."

"They always are."

"I'll have to carry you." He slipped his arms behind her back and under her knees. He pulled her against him and stood. "You can put them on my back in bed."

"Put what on your back?" She grabbed at his shoulders. He was warm. He was so warm.

"Your ice-cold toes." As if the prospect delighted him, he smiled down at her.

He intended to sleep with her.

"So you're not going to eat me?" she blurted.

He started to walk. "Now and again."

She wanted to hide her head. She wasn't used to this kind of flesh-to-flesh contact, or to sexual teasing . . . or to the relief in

107

knowing that Jasha always kept his word, and she had something more to look forward to.

Being eaten by a wolf who was really good with his tongue.

"You can't carry me all the way back to the house." She was no featherweight, but tall and muscled.

He didn't pause. "It's only about a half mile."

"That can't be right," she said indignantly. "I drove farther than that!"

"But the road winds around. By the way the crow flies, we're close to the house."

The trees broke away. They were back in the meadow, and when Ann saw the fallen tree with its blackened crown, her brain, so engaged with minor matters like fantasy versus reality, sanity versus madness, and pleasure versus embarrassment, suddenly reengaged.

She'd left something precious back there. "No. I've got to have the lady!"

He stopped. "What lady?"

"I found a painting of the Madonna."

He froze.

"I lost her when I hit you, but while you were gone, I found her again and —" His immobility captured her attention. "Jasha?"

"Where did you find a painting?" He

looked down at her, his face still and smooth.

"When the lightning hit the tree and it fell, well, there she was." And in a day of miracles, that might just be the biggest.

"Was she?" He sounded very odd, choked and almost afraid. "Where is she now?"

"She's back there. Where we were."

He carried Ann back. He let her legs slide to the ground.

Ann searched. She recovered the tile. She showed it to him.

"My God." Jasha knelt beside her, his gaze absorbed and amazed. "I can't believe —" He looked up at Ann, then back at the painting. "You found the icon."

"You know about it?" *Impossible!*

Yet he'd called it an icon, and now that he had, she recognized the stylized method of painting, the use of vivid colors, the Madonna's stiff pose. This was Russian — and so, she knew, was Jasha's family. "Is it yours?"

He gave a short, incredulous laugh. "In a manner of speaking." Gently he took it from her, smoothed his palm across the Madonna's face . . . and to her horror, his flesh sizzled, a curl of smoke rising from the burning flesh.

CHAPTER 8

With a shout, Jasha dropped the icon.

Ann caught his wrists in hers.

A brutal red mark seared his palm and his fingers.

"What happened?" She couldn't believe her eyes. "You must be allergic to the finish."

"Allergic." He yanked his hands away and plunged them into the mud. "Is that what you hit me with? Before?"

"Yes." That mark on his cheek, the vivid flare of red — that was a burn, too. "Why did it do that to you?"

"She did it. The Blessed Virgin. I am not to touch her."

"I don't know what you mean." Ann picked the icon out of the dirt and wiped it with the tail of her shirt. The ragged edge caught on the material. "It's just a painting."

"In Russia, icons are not just paintings.

The revolution is but a weak obscenity compared to the weight of years when icons embodied the Russian soul, the Russian heart, and the Orthodox faith. It's tradition that an icon of the Blessed Virgin and the baby Jesus be given as a wedding gift, and all family icons are kept in the *krasny ugol,* the beautiful corner, decorated with candles and red cloth." He wiped his muddy hands on his jeans, but his gaze never left the face of the Virgin. "More important, icons of the Madonna aren't made — they appear."

"What?"

"Icon painters do not sign their work. So the icons are said to appear, to be miracles."

Ann looked at the picture, trying to see what had hurt Jasha.

The Virgin looked back, serene and un-worried.

"The Madonna refuses to let me touch her," Jasha said. "But you can. She has entrusted herself to you."

"That's —" Ann drew a breath.

"That's what? Superstition? Impossible?" Jasha touched his cheek. "Yet I'm burned. No wonder it hurt like a son of a bitch."

Surreptitiously she touched the mark on her lower back. It felt smooth; if she didn't know better, she would think that nothing was there.

She should have expected her life would take this kind of freakish turn. But after so many years of balancing atop the high wire of normal, of only Sister Mary Magdalene's truly knowing how the infant Ann had been found and the troubles that followed, Ann thought . . . believed . . . hoped she could be ordinary. "I guess I need to change my opinion of what's impossible now," she mumbled.

He laughed sharply, and glanced around. The wind had died; the lightning was fading, the clouds thinning. "The storm is gone, but this is no place to be after dark. Let's get out of here." He slid his arms around Ann again, picked her up, and strode off.

He set a fast pace, and she read his moods very well — it was part of the job description. Right now he was worried. "Jasha, what are you afraid of?"

"That I'll fail."

That made no sense, but he was panting, and his uneasiness transferred itself to her. The last rays of the sun hit the treetops, while in the woods below, the shadows multiplied and thickened. She heard rustling in the underbrush. Wild animals . . . and worse. Maybe . . . maybe things like him.

The wolves.

Jasha and Ann reached the castle in record time — humiliating to think that if she'd run the right direction, she would have returned to the relative safety of a phone and locked doors — and he took her around to the back. Here she could see the garage sitting at right angles to the house, with its four doors for Jasha's prized cars.

And that reminded her — "My poor car," she said.

"I'll call someone to tow it tomorrow."

"If it's still there," she said gloomily.

"Yeah. That was a hell of a storm. Literally." He laughed again, one of those short, bitter laughs that told her he knew something she didn't.

He put her down on the porch at the back door, and held her until she regained her balance. "You okay?"

Her feet were sore, yes. All that running had exhausted her. But she held the icon, and she was alive. Alive as she had never been in her whole life. "I'm fine."

He stretched up to the top of the doorsill and felt along it until he found a key; then he unlocked the door. Using his hand on the small of her back, he pressed her inside, acting as if she would turn and run at any minute.

And maybe he was right. She didn't like

the house anymore; it reminded her all too vividly of that moment when he transformed before her eyes. "Before — how did you get in?"

"There's a dog door." He gestured absently, and reset the alarm system.

"Of course. A dog door. How else would a man who turns into a wolf get into his own house?"

His swift glance assessed her.

The passions and madness had begun to pass, leaving cold good sense and a dreadful suspicion.

His expression gentled. "Ask me."

"Ask you what?"

"The question that is burning in your mind."

There were so many questions. So many. Yet one bothered her more than any other. She shuffled from one foot to the other, tried to decide if she wanted to ask it or remain in blissful ignorance. But one of the many lessons Sister Mary Magdalene had drilled required she seek the truth and face it square on, so she asked, "Did you kill him?"

"Kill who?" He toed off his shoes without untying them and with his bare foot pushed them into the corner.

"Are there so many you don't remember?"

She tugged at the hem of the shirt, trying to cover her thighs with cloth and belated modesty.

His generous mouth tightened in annoyance. "I haven't killed anyone lately, if that's what you mean."

"Before you came in, I heard a shot. And you . . . you had blood on your mouth." She tensed, desperately wanting Jasha to deny the crime, not able to bear the idea that he'd come from murdering a man . . . to her.

"That's the question?" It was almost dark in the small entry hall, and in this light his face was all stone and shadow, with a pale slash of his scar across one cheek, and on the other a blot where the icon had burned itself into his flesh. Only his eyes were alive, watching her with the steady intensity of a predator. "That's all you want to ask?"

"That's enough."

"You amaze me."

She stayed stubbornly silent.

"No. I didn't kill him."

She sagged with relief.

"He was a hunter. He was drunk and he was shooting at wolves."

"That's illegal." *And you could have been killed.*

"That's a lot of things, including stupid,

115

especially when I'm running with the pack." Jasha's grim expression broke into a grin. "I broke his gun and scared him so badly, he'll never stop running."

"Are the other wolves like you?"

"You mean, do they turn? No. They're animals, but they're smart and they're loyal, and although Leader doesn't like it, he lets me run with them without a challenge. And sometimes, like today, running with the wolves is the best way to ease my frustration and my fury."

"Do you mean because of the hunter?"

He rubbed his thumb on her cheek as if cleaning off a mark, and stared soberly into her eyes. "My father always warned us not to turn. He said the change tore down the restraints of civilization and left us vulnerable to the wilderness in our hearts. Today I guess I proved he was right."

She started to place her palm over his heart; then at the last moment, she skittishly pulled back and doubled her hand into a fist. "But I like the wilderness."

"Don't . . ." He caught her hovering hand. "Don't tempt me. It's all still too raw and close, and I found too much pleasure in your body." He kissed her knuckles; then when her fingers loosened, he brought her open palm to his mouth and kissed its center. He watched her as he kissed her wrist, and his lips lingered over the leap of her pulse. Tucking her hand behind her back, he pulled her close.

The press of his body against hers still shocked her with its glory of heat and intimacy, and when he kissed her, the air grew sultry with need so recently fulfilled, and passion so easily aroused.

She tasted him, sinking into the pleasure. Her breasts tightened, and the warmth and dampness between her legs began to grow. . . .

With a gasp, he let her go and leaped back. "You burn me like the icon."

And she stood bereft, trembling and wanting, almost in tears.

Every time she showed her feelings, someone laughed, or someone scolded . . . or no one noticed.

She never got it right.

"Not here. Ann, not in the entry with dirty boots and — don't cry!" He wrapped his arm around her, ushered her into the utility room, and flipped on the light. The floor was tile, coats hung on hooks, and boots neatly lined the wall. There was a counter with a sink and a mirror and a small shower in the corner.

She touched her lips with her fingers.

Since they'd left the woods, he'd been less a lover and more Jasha — businesslike, effective, and brisk. She'd thought that maybe one taste of her had been enough.

But that kiss was anything but businesslike. It was . . . possessive. She should be glad he cared about where they made love instead of simply using her to satisfy his base desires.

She wasn't.

But she was worried about him. "What if the hunter goes to the police?"

"And tells them what?" Jasha pulled towels out of the cupboard and laid them on the counter. "That he shot at a wolf who turned into a man and broke his gun, then turned back into a wolf and chased him, bit him, then turned back into a man who gave him hell and put him in his car?"

"You bit him? But that's evidence against you." She couldn't believe they were holding this conversation.

"No dentist holds the records for my wolf state."

"No, I . . . I suppose not." She was so relieved. And confused. And . . . horny. "So you can change back and forth as much as you like?"

"Yes, but the more times I turn right in a row, the slower I get. It takes a lot of

118

energy." He leaned against the tile counter as if it had been a long day with too much turning, and maybe too long a trip back to the house packing someone as tall as she was.

"And while you're a wolf, you do know what you're doing. You're not out of your mind?"

"Actually, in my opinion, dumb beasts aren't nearly as dumb as we would like to think."

Eagerly she pursued her line of questioning. "You're not controlled by anything like the moon or your moods?"

"That business with the moon is bull. But then, I'm not a werewolf. I'm a —" He hesitated.

"What are you?"

He avoided looking at her while he answered. "I'm like any guy, except I can change into a wolf if I want. Especially if I lose my temper, which I shouldn't have. Not with you. Now, a quick shower here" — Jasha popped the glass door open — "a long soak in the hot tub upstairs, then bed for you. You're tired." He turned on the water. "I need to make sure the house is secure. Cover that broken window by the front door. Check on a few things. Can you take care of yourself?"

She strangled the impulse to claim helplessness. "Of course I can."

"Of course you can. You're indomitable." He pressed his hand to her cheek, held her still, and kissed her hard on the mouth. "Bathrobe's on the hook," he said, and left.

In a sudden hurry, she placed the icon on the counter, stripped off her clothes, and stepped into the shower. Mud ran down the drain in brown streams, and as she scrubbed herself, she moaned with pleasure at the sensation of ever-increasing cleanliness. She had never been the kind of child to play in the dirt; she'd kept her uniform so scrupulously clean the other kids in school, the ones with parents, had loved to throw grass clods at her.

One of the younger nuns, Sister Catherine, had gently tried to get her to really play at recess, to get down in the sand and make roads, or roll in the grass, or swing to the top of the swings and jump out. Ann had tried, but her heart wasn't in it.

Sister Catherine had cajoled her into trying finger paints, then chuckled when Ann grimaced at the mess.

And one evening, when all the other children were gone home or busy with homework, Sister Catherine had swung on the tall swings with Ann. She urged her higher into the air, laughing breathlessly, not like a nun at all, but like an angel about to take flight, and for those few minutes, Ann left her burdens behind and shrieked with answering laughter.

Now Ann found herself standing, her hand pressed on her lower back, staring into space.

The joy had been short-lived.

She brought the bad people. She always brought the bad people.

The lesson had been learned, and learned through blood and anguish. Never again had Ann been so carefree, for when she played, the ghost of Sister Catherine played alongside her.

Jasha thought she'd never been a child.

She had been. A fearfully responsible child, but a child nonetheless. Ann never did anything that wasn't the right thing to do.

Until now.

She leaned her head against the steamy tile and closed her eyes.

One time. Just one time she did something wild and wicked, and look at the damned mess she'd got herself into.

Yet Sister Mary Magdalene would tell her there was no use crying over spilled milk. What was done, was done, and Ann had to deal with the consequences.

Ann stepped out, dried, and wrapped herself in his robe.

Picking up the icon, she washed it free of mud and examined it.

It was beautiful. Perfect. *A miracle.*

There was nothing here to burn Jasha, yet she'd seen his flesh sizzle.

She'd been raised by nuns. She knew very well what such a portent meant.

Somehow, sometime, he had displeased God, and now he was cursed.

A single tear brimmed over and landed on the Madonna's face, and Ann wiped it off.

She didn't understand. He was so normal. More handsome than most men, but not supernaturally so. He had a gift with women, but apparently not a supernatural gift — his fiancée had left him with many a scathing comment about his intensity. He was a brilliant businessman, but only because he worked long hours and knew how to pick his employees, not because his rivals dropped dead of mysterious wolf attacks.

Yet when she'd asked him what he was, he evaded an answer.

Was he cursed?

And if he was, what did that make her? She'd yielded. More than that, when it mattered most, she'd actively and energetically participated.

Worse, she wasn't running away now.

She slid the icon into the robe's pocket.

She was going up to the master bedroom to soak in the hot tub.

Then she was going to snuggle in Jasha's bed.

And for that, she believed she would eventually go to hell.

So she might as well make this a night to celebrate.

CHAPTER 9

Jasha stood absolutely still in the middle of his great room and allowed his animal senses to roam.

First and foremost, he could smell the passing storm, the spice of pine, and the richness of growth. Those odors came sweeping in through the broken window and permeated the whole house.

Within this room, he could smell the odor of the wolf pack; earlier, he'd carried it in with him. The feminine fragrance of Ann's body always lingered in his house; it was a pleasant undertone on every sheet of paper he brought from the office, on the briefcase she packed for him, and on the laptop she used. Yet now her scent was overlaid by her horror at seeing him change; it was that odor that had first spoken to his wolf senses and pointed him to her.

But no one else had been in here. At least — no one human.

He listened, extending the range of his hearing in increments. In the utility room, he heard Ann shut off the shower. He heard the hum of the water heater in the basement. Outside, he heard the brush rustle as the wolf pack circled the house.

All else was quiet.

He looked around his great room. He saw the magazines on the coffee table ruffled open by the wind through the broken window. He saw the paw prints he'd left on the hardwood floor, the shoes Ann had thrown at him, the drop of blood from his chest.

The woman had a good eye and a good arm.

He touched the burn on his cheek.

A very good arm.

Ann was the only intruder in this house today.

But *they* were coming.

His mother had had a vision. She'd been, not unconscious, but speaking words . . . not her own. Or maybe she'd been spouting her own premonitions. Or maybe she'd cursed them all. Hell, he didn't know. He'd never seen her do that before. He hadn't known she had the gift, if it could be called a gift.

The blind can see, and the sons of Oleg

Varinski have found us.

The Wilder family files were intact. His house was secure. Nothing had changed.

But . . . everything had changed. Everything.

You can never be safe, for they will do anything to destroy you and keep the pact intact.

The pact. He knew about the pact. How could he not? On that day when he had turned, his father had sat him down and explained it all. But to a thirteen-year-old boy who'd just discovered he could change himself into a beast of prey, who had just developed the coolest tattoo *ever,* who had a mustache made of five hairs on either side of his lip, the pact had meant nothing.

A thousand years ago? The Family Varinski? The most dreaded name in Russia? A deal with the devil?

Yeah, Papa. Sure. Cool. Now I can stay out all night, because if I can do this, *I don't have to go to school anymore.*

He and Konstantine had had a loud, heated difference of opinion.

He'd gone to school the next morning. As long as he lived under his father's roof, never once had he skipped school, and only once had he stayed out all night long — and Konstantine had made him very, very sorry.

Because his father had been from the Old Country, from Russia, and his sons obeyed him, feared him . . . and loved him.

And you, my love. You are dying.

His mother had presented his father with a death sentence.

Jasha walked to the answering machine, its red light blinking fiercely, and listened to Firebird's voice say, "Papa is off the respirator and doing as well as can be expected. The doctors still don't know what's wrong, but they definitely agree it's his heart. It's, um, a rare condition. They don't, um, agree about it." Firebird's voice shook. "I overheard one of the nurses say it was a mystery and we'd be better off taking him to a witch doctor."

"Of course," Jasha muttered, and deleted the message.

Zorana loved Konstantine. Jasha knew that as well as he knew the stars rotated around the North Star. But three nights ago, on July fourth, due north had moved, and his mother had said things, horrible things. Jasha would never forget the sight of his mother's finger pointing at his father, cursing him with death and eternal damnation.

Her curse had been powerful — and instantaneous.

His father had stared at Zorana. His eyes had filled with tears. And she sprang toward him as he collapsed.

What had she imagined she could do, his miniature mother holding up his ox of a father? But she grabbed him, went down with him, stayed at his side when the fire truck from the county volunteer fire department showed up to take him to the local hospital, then on to Seattle and Swedish Hospital.

Jasha walked to the full-length windows and looked out at the view — at the cliffs along the wild coastline and the ocean, roiling with another incoming storm.

As soon as the doctors had declared that Konstantine was stable, Jasha had assumed the duties of head of the family. He had left Zorana, Firebird, and Rurik huddled around Konstantine's bed, and come here to check that the family's secrets — their assets, their immigration papers, their private information — were still locked in the vault downstairs.

Everything was there, hidden in his wilderness home guarded by the best security system money could buy.

The security system Ann had turned off and left off.

Had she done it on purpose? Had the

Varinskis paid her to come here and betray him? Or, more likely, threatened her if she didn't?

"Hi, there." She stood in the arched doorway. His big, white, terry robe swamped her, and she held the lapels close to her chest. She'd pushed her damp hair back from her pale, bruised face. Red scratches etched her shapely legs, and her blue eyes were wary. But she smiled timidly with that kind of worshipful expression she wore around the office when she thought he didn't notice. "Is everything okay?"

"So far."

"Is there anything I can do?"

She would never betray him. Not without any sign of discomfort. If he was going to say a certain thing existed in this world, it was that Ann Smith was honest. Painfully, completely honest.

Besides, she adored him. He'd known it from the first time she stepped into his office; worship came off her in waves. Her infatuation hadn't affected her job performance, so it had been unimportant, sort of like a space heater giving off a low-level hum of warmth.

She limped to the foot of the stairs, so self-conscious, she tripped on the fringe of the rug. She winced, glanced to see if he was watching, then took a visible breath and asked, "Are you mad at me for coming here? I mean, obviously you weren't expecting me. . . ."

"Or I wouldn't have been a wolf, you mean."

"Yes. That."

He shouldn't have gone out to run with Leader's pack, but he'd been reeling with shock and grief, and he'd thought, *What difference will it make this one time?*

Now he knew.

If only he'd caught her scent sooner . . .

"You asked me who sent me. And you said I was like the devil, and the illegal hunter, and your mother." Ann straightened and looked into his eyes. "What did you mean?"

"I was in a rage." Which was no excuse for what he'd done, but it was the only reason he had.

"You like your mother. Don't you?" Ann's face was forlorn with hope, like a child who'd been disappointed in love far too many times.

Who was she, this woman who had discovered the icon? He didn't know anything about her early life. It had never been important before. *She* had never been important before.

"I do like my mother. She wasn't to blame

for any of what happened. I don't know who was to blame." He spoke almost to himself.

"Then, are you mad about the Ukrainian deal? If you don't want to go through with it, Wilder Wines will be fine. We'll have to postpone our expansion, but not forever. We'll find another company interested in taking our wines overseas."

"I know." And if he needed further proof that Ann knew as much as he did about the company, her assurance gave it to him.

He looked at her. Looked at her hard. Innocent? Yes. Unknowing? Yes.

But for all that, perhaps a traitor still.

She shivered under his gaze.

"You're cold. Go up to bed."

"Are you coming? I mean, to bed? You said you were, but . . . soon?" The wariness in her grew.

What a fascinating woman. She'd discovered his deepest, darkest secret. In a fit of rage and frustration, he'd chased her like prey, caught her, and mated with her without finesse, without a care to the circumstances or to her comfort. Yet while he terrified her, while the sex had been rough and new, nothing scared her like the prospect of being rejected.

"I'll be up as soon as I get some plywood and cover the window." He gestured toward the entry.

"Of course. That's what you've got to do." She turned to climb the stairs.

He'd always felt a responsibility for his young, vulnerable assistant, but it had been the responsibility of an employer for his employee. He wasn't a man to underestimate the significance of the old symbols.

Each of my four sons must find one of the Varinski family icons.

Ann had discovered the icon. Ann had been a virgin. She had bled for him. She had responded to him. She was the key to his family's survival, and he would do anything to protect her.

For them. And for himself.

"Ann."

She looked back, blue eyes wide.

"Nothing could keep me away from you tonight."

CHAPTER 10

Ann heard Jasha come into the bedroom and wondered how every muscle in her previously relaxed body could tense so instantly. She opened one eye and checked to make sure the bubbles — she had used the jets to create a lot of bubbles — still covered her strategic parts. Because even though he had seen everything, and licked it, too, she wasn't ready to pose naked.

Lots of bubbles, but just to make sure . . . she flicked on the whirlpool jets again.

He stepped into the doorway. "So you like my whirlpool?"

"It's nice." Very nice. She was six feet tall, and when she stretched out as she did now, her toes barely touched the other end. The tub was almost as wide as it was long, with jets all the way around, and the rich caramel color matched the grout in the large copper tile surround. When she looked up at the skylight, she saw the last swirls of cloud wiping the night sky clean, leaving the stars with freshly washed faces.

Of course, she'd known all this was here, drooled over the remodeling plans, but seeing made it real. Seeing him strolling across the heated tile floor, his gait unhurried and predatory, made the whole strange day real, too.

Casually, she brought the bubbles toward her.

The currents pulled them away.

A little more frantically, she brought them back.

"Did you find the 'Who needs a man?' setting?" He looked down into the tub.

The bubbles kept escaping. "The 'Who needs a man?' setting? What's the . . . ?" A mental picture formed — her sitting with her legs in the air, getting off in the whirlpool, while he walked in. "No!"

"You should try it." He knelt beside the tub and stirred the water with his forefinger, and the way he looked . . . "The saleswoman gave me to understand it's quite satisfying."

"The saleswoman said that to you?" Ann was shocked at the strange woman's temerity. Shocked . . . and a little pissed.

"I believe she was offering to demonstrate it."

"What kind of professional behavior is that?"

"That's why I refused her kind offer." He looked solemn. "I wanted to wait and see if it works for you."

"I would never . . . I mean, not in yours . . ."

"But in yours?" He chuckled, and shoved the bubbles away so he could see into the water. "Why not? I loved seeing that expression of ecstasy on your face."

"You're *not* looking at my face." And she didn't know what to do with her hands. Put them over her breasts? But wouldn't that look as if she were playing with herself? Over her . . . ? No, that playing-with-herself idea went double there.

"Then why do I know you're blushing?"

"Because . . . oh, darn you!" She sank all the way down to her chin and sort of waved her hands beside her hips like some perverted mermaid. She knew good and well this heat just under her skin had nothing to do with embarrassment and everything to do with Jasha's gaze on her body.

He undoubtedly knew it, too.

Which was why she blurted, "I would never betray you."

The amusement fell away from him so suddenly, she knew his rage was still sim-

135

mering closely under his skin. "No. Not on purpose. But what brought you here?"

"Your engagement."

"My engagement?" He blinked as if he was confused, and flipped off the jets. "That was six months ago."

Dumb guy. What did he think had brought her here now? "When you asked me to shop for an engagement ring, I was so . . . excited." She flushed. Man, this was embarrassing. "I thought you'd finally realized I was the love you'd waited for your whole life."

He kicked off his shoes and socks, climbed into the tub, and sat on the tile surround facing her. With his elbows on his knees, he leaned forward, his eyes fixed on her face. "I'm fascinated."

"But no. You wanted the ring for Meghan Nakamura." Every time Ann thought about the gorgeous, petite, strikingly beautiful woman, her palm itched to slap someone. Jasha, sometimes. But usually Meghan herself.

"Do you know every time you say her name you sound —"

"Sarcastic?"

"No. Disapproving. Like a nun."

Ann sat up stiffly. "I am not a nun."

He ran his gaze along the curves of her

136

breasts, wreathed with bubbles. He smiled. "I noticed."

She sank back under the water. Why had she never noticed his smile was wolfish, with lots of wicked teeth? And why, when she should be scared, did it make her want all of him entangled with all of her? She took a big breath, then in a rush said, "The tub is big enough for both of us."

"Believe me, I've noticed that, too." But he made no move to slide in.

"You got your pants wet. At least take them off!" Because she felt, well, naked, sitting in here naked while he interrogated her.

"How about this?" He pulled his T-shirt over his head.

"I like it." Her voice had changed pitch. Gone higher and sort of wobbly. All because he had a six-pack, a pair of shoulders, a scar, and an inky black tattoo. Which she'd seen many times around the office after he worked out. And seen at very close quarters about an hour ago. But they never lost their allure, and more than that, it seemed he had just made a promise . . . about later.

"Regarding Meghan," he prompted.

She wrenched her attention back to the conversation. "Well . . . I don't sound like one, either. A nun. I don't." She did *not* sound like Sister Mary Magdalene. She did not.

"Of course not. I was mistaken. Tell me more about Meghan and me and you."

"You know what happened. I bought a fabulous diamond. I gave it to you. You gave it to her. Then you told me to contact a wedding planner, and took Meghan to a celebratory dinner." Ann glared, trying to convey her outrage. "Unrequited love is hell."

"So. You love me."

"Out there" — she jerked her head toward the window — "you knew when I was aroused. You said you could smell it."

"Yes, but —" He paused as if searching for a way out of his dilemma.

"You knew I was aroused, but all the women are aroused around you so you didn't think anything of it." She pointed her finger at him. "Right?"

He ran his hand through his hair.

She turned on her side so she didn't have to watch him.

When she thought of the time she spent hiding in a stall in the ladies' lounge and crying . . . and all her friends trying to coax her out . . . and the ugly realization that not only had she imagined she could compete with one of Jasha's beautiful women, but now everyone in the company would know it.

That was the nadir of her whole, empty, loveless life.

She had thought she was going to have to quit the job she adored, leave the man she loved, before the gossip slipped out, and someone stopped Jasha in the hall and shared a good laugh about tall, gangly, plain Ann.

But none of the other girls laughed at her. Instead they took her out to a mall and made her shop. They made her buy the short skirts and the Wonderbra, and Celia, the ringleader of the group, had spoken bracingly of positive attitude and embracing your future and setting goals and making plans. Those women, especially Celia, had figuratively grabbed her by the back of the neck and made her face the fact that she could take action — or she could dream her life away and die an old maid with only a gravestone to mark her passing.

Okay. She hadn't wanted that. But she didn't want this, either, finding out that Jasha was a wolf and that she was the custodian of an icon with supernatural powers. . . .

He slid into the tub with her, and around so that he rested against her back. His arms slid around her, pulling her close, and his words ruffled the tendrils at the base of her neck. "Meghan looked like the hottest woman in the world. But in bed . . . she complained if I made her come, because it made her sweat. She complained I was too intense and wanted sex too often. She considered body fluids — hers, mine — as the enemy. If she had seen me turn — I mean, you know, *change* — she would have complained that I shed on her carpet."

Ann shrugged one shoulder and tried to wiggle away.

Jasha nuzzled her ear. "She would have enrolled me in a puppy-training session."

Ann reluctantly grinned.

"As soon as she stepped in a doggy land mine, she would have put me in a kennel." He rested his cheek on Ann's hair.

He'd never turned on the charm for her before. She knew perfectly well he was manipulating her, and she liked it — too much. "You don't know her at all," she snapped.

"What do you mean?"

"She wouldn't have put you in a kennel. She would have had you put down."

He laughed and turned her to face him. "At the very least, she would have dropped her fingernail file." He ran a knuckle down

Ann's cheek. "*You* nailed me with a damned heavy shoe."

She blinked at his chest. All that remained of the earlier wound was a red scar in the shape of her heel.

"You ran and almost got away," he said.

"I would have if not for your speed bumps."

"I actually put them in to keep visitors out, but I bless them for keeping you in."

Since she'd arrived, she'd been nervous, thrilled, terrified, aroused, and enraptured. And terrified. And aroused some more. She just wanted to stand on stable ground for one minute, to know what he thought. "You said you shouldn't have done it. Chased me, I mean."

"I shouldn't have. It wasn't right, and all my excuses aren't worth a damn. But darling, darling Ann, I'm not sorry." His expression went from whimsical to severe. "Because to have you, I would do it again."

CHAPTER 11

Jasha's words echoed in the steamy silence.

Ann swallowed, for in the depths of his golden eyes, she saw the red of the wolf. He meant it, and everything in her recalled the panic and the pain — and the might of his passion. The Ann she'd been before had imagined sex with him would be highly enjoyable with a bit of conflict — a Meg Ryan romance. She had never envisioned this darkness, this glory, this clawing need and fear and splendor.

"Ann, you've stepped into the middle of a legend. Now you're trapped." His voice was low, gentle, laced with sorrow . . . and satisfaction.

"I didn't mean to." She spoke as softly, but every word trembled with trepidation.

"Yet here you are, at my side. And if I would choose any woman to be with me during this ordeal, it would be you. Would you leave me here alone to face whatever comes?"

"No!"

"I think that's why you were chosen. That . . . and this." He kissed her.

She bunched her fists against his shoulders and tried to pull back, to tell him he'd made a mistake, that she wasn't brave.

But he wrapped his hand around her neck and held her still. He crushed her bare breasts against his chest, and he opened her mouth under his.

This time she found it so much easier to give him everything. Desire rose at once — or maybe it had never completely disappeared. She sucked on his tongue, and gave him hers to suck, as well, and almost drowned in the pure joy he offered.

When he lifted his head, she tugged at his waistband. "Take them off."

"I can't."

"Because they're wet? I'll help you." She reached for the button fly.

He caught her hand right after she made contact with the fly, and the bulge underneath, and pulled her hand away with a grin and a grimace. "No, I mean, if I take them off, I won't be able to keep control."

"Control is overrated." She wrestled for her hand.

"I'll get inside you again, and I've already

ridden you too hard. You're a virgin."

"Not anymore."

"Don't I know it?" That red flare grew in his eyes.

She didn't care. She didn't care if he turned into a wolf right now. "I don't want to just go to sleep!" Not when he'd heated her, softened her, prepared her.

"I didn't say we were going to do *that*." He placed his palm on her chest over her heart and pressed her back against the tub. "Now that we're inside and the security alarm is set, I can make love to you at leisure, without worrying that someone will sneak up, stab me in the back, and take you."

The hunter. He must mean the drunk hunter. "I don't remember you being too worried while we were in the woods."

"While we were in the woods, the wolf pack watched my back." He slid to the middle of the tub, turned the whirlpool on, and lay back, stretching out his long legs next to her hips.

"The wolf pack? The wolf pack does as you command?" She couldn't decide — was she more horrified about the wolves, or the way he smiled and crooked a finger?

"I saved Leader's life. He is grateful. Come here, Ann."

"Why?"

"I chased you down. I screwed you in the woods. Don't you want revenge?"

How could he make such a vindictive word sound so appealing? "What kind of revenge?"

"Straddle me, and I'll show you."

By the time Jasha placed Ann on the bed, she was limp from coming.

And he could have pounded nails with his dick.

Yeah, he deserved it, but that didn't make it any less painful. His wet jeans scraped him like sandpaper, and all he wanted to do was fuck her until he was senseless. He would, too — if he were a true Varinski. If he exulted in his animal nature. But he'd seen what happened when Adrik had surrendered to evil. Their mother and father couldn't stand to lose another son. Especially not now.

So Jasha guessed he'd go take a shower and jack off, then come to bed and sleep with his newfound mate. He looked at Ann, eyes closed, brown hair spread across the pillow.

Fear of the darkness had always made him deny one part of his being, a part he greatly loved — running through the woods, taking justice in his own hands, being at one with the wild.

But this time, he'd given in to the impulse to become a wolf, to run off his frustration and his fury at the curse that now controlled all their lives. With that one impulse, he'd set off a chain of events that changed everything, and forced him to do what he'd never thought he would — cleave to one female for the rest of his life.

Four years ago, Ann had arrived at the Wilder Winery as a file clerk. He'd noted how well she summed up every business situation. He'd kept an eye on her; then when the opportunity occurred, he'd plucked her from among the office staff to be his administrative assistant.

He'd never looked at her as a woman; women he could find easily.

But an administrative assistant whom he could trust with every aspect of his business? That made her rarer than a bloodred ruby.

No choice. He had no choice. A man who took a woman as he had done today had to honor the connection, or know himself to be truly a beast.

So despite his misgivings, it was Ann. He'd made her his mate. And the Almighty made it a covenant, for she was a virgin, and she had found the icon.

She hovered on the brink of sleep, but she whispered, "Jasha?"

"Yes?" He leaned over her.

Her lids fluttered, and she smiled shyly. "Thank you."

She was pretty. He'd always known it; he had a complete appreciation for a good-looking woman. Her complexion was clear and fine; her blue eyes were big and surrounded by long dark lashes. But when she smiled . . . my God, it was like a lamp had gone on in her soul.

Ann was the most kind-hearted, loyal woman he'd ever met — and now she was his. He would keep her forever.

CHAPTER 12

Ann paused in the kitchen doorway. She wore white slacks, carefully chosen for the way they cupped her rear; an orange sweater, carefully chosen for the plunging neckline and the way the loose knit displayed her black, lacy bra and tiny waist; and open-toed sandals, carefully chosen to show off her formerly pristine pedicure, now ruined in her race through the woods.

She observed Jasha as he sat at the breakfast bar, drinking coffee from a heavy ceramic mug. Morning sunshine poured into the kitchen, lighting his sculpted cheekbones, his wide, sensual mouth, his drooping bedroom eyes. He was reading from his open laptop and he had that grin on his face, a grin she hoped would never be turned on her, for his faithful administrative assistant knew it meant he'd scored against an opponent. He filled out his black T-shirt very nicely, with taut muscles and subtle muscles and bulgy muscles. And hey — last night he'd nearly drowned giving her pleasure.

She wished she didn't feel so self-conscious — about wandering around in Jasha's house, about giving off lustful scents, about opening a conversation with a man she'd thought she knew so well. A man who she now knew hid an awful, glorious, damning secret.

She needed to ask questions. Of course. But how to start? What to say? She'd never been in such a situation before, and please God, she never would be again.

Then he glanced up, and she couldn't remember why she wanted to make conversation with him at all. Why talk when they could —

"Come and see what's in our local paper this morning." He turned the laptop and shoved it toward the seat beside him.

She walked across the kitchen, no longer self-conscious, and perched on the stool.

The headline read, CALIFORNIA HUNTER ARRESTED FOR INTOXICATION.

Jasha stood. "I'll get your coffee. Do you want eggs?"

"I'll do it." She started to get up again.

"Read." Hand on her shoulder, he pressed her down.

Californian Eric Lofts was arrested yesterday after he drove to the police department and burst in, claiming he'd been attacked by a Wolf Man while out in the woods. Mr. Lofts claimed the Wolf Man changed from a wolf to a human man who broke his rifle, then back into a wolf to chase him to his car. As proof, he displayed a fresh bite on his neck. Under further questioning, Mr. Lofts admitted he'd provoked the attack when the "Wolf Man" caught him illegally shooting at one of the packs that runs the Olympic Mountains. Mr. Lofts's blood alcohol level tested at .12, and he was arrested for public intoxication, DUI, hunting without a license, and shooting at an endangered species protected by federal law. He has been released on ten thousand dollars' bail.

"They didn't believe a word he said." Ann accepted the coffee and took a sip. Jasha knew how she liked it — French roast served with nonfat milk and a packet of sweetener. They'd spent many an evening at the office drinking far too much coffee as they worked deals with wholesalers or planned their next expansion.

"I told you so." Jasha sounded insufferably smug as he broke eggs into a bowl and whisked them into a froth. "Cheese?"

"Please." They'd done this before, too — prepared a quick meal so they could keep working. "But what about the bite on his neck?"

"They probably think he pissed off someone's dog." He tossed butter into the pan and turned on the burner.

"I suppose." After such a night, and so many revelations, it seemed amazing to find themselves sliding into domesticity. But what better time to ask a few subtle questions?

"Why did the icon burn you?" She winced. She didn't do subtle well.

He cast her a sideways glance. "I'll tell you that story after we eat."

"Will I like the story better after we eat?"

"No, but with some stories, a full stomach helps. Before that, I want to know exactly, word for word, what happened at the office to bring you here." He poured the mixture into the pan and pushed the wheat bread down in the toaster.

"I told you. The Ukrainians are threatening to cancel the deal if you don't respond right away."

"Word for word," he repeated. He put the plate in front of her and kissed her cheek. "Don't look so worried. We'll get this figured out. We always do." He pulled out his stool. "We're a good team. We always have been."

"Yes. We always have been." But this was the same pep talk he always gave her around the office. And they were more than a team now. They were lovers, and their relationship would stand the test of time.

Wouldn't it?

For her intelligence and acumen, Jasha respected Ann more than any other person he'd ever met, so he knew she would draw comfort from his familiar words of confidence.

If the coming battle proved as grueling as it was shaping up to be, she'd use every bit of that intelligence and acumen. She was the ideal woman to stand at his side. She was timid, yes, but she hid an inner strength. More than that, she was loyal. She would never run.

Last night, he'd suffered doubts about her suitability as his mate.

In the clear light of morning, he realized that fate had given him the right woman to keep by his side.

And when they won the battle — and they would, somehow they would — she'd give him strong children. Maybe even a daughter.

He looked at her with an eye for potential breeding.

She was tall and would easily carry his babies. The combination of their genes would produce handsome offspring, and with her astute intelligence and his competitive business sense, the Wilders would come to rule the wine world.

She saw him watching her, and lifted her brows. "What?"

"You're much prettier than Meghan Nakamura."

"For a man with supposedly good taste in women, it took you long enough to notice." Frost dripped from Ann's voice.

"I do have good taste in women." He smiled charmingly and thought, *But I don't understand them.* Because he had no idea what he'd said to make her mad.

She ate her eggs and her toast, drank her orange juice and her coffee, refilled both their cups, then turned to him. "Tell me about you. Why are you . . . like you are?"

This morning, she couldn't yet bring herself to speak of his wolfy state, as Firebird called it. She'd back stepped into disbelief.

"Like I am?" He lifted his brows.

"You know. Part . . . half . . . sometimes a . . ." She knew him so well. She knew he was chuckling at her. "You have a dog door and you don't have a dog!"

"I'll tell you about me, but first — take me through the events that brought you here. Besides the fact that you're infatuated with me, I mean." He chuckled.

Ann didn't.

Perhaps it was a little early in their relationship to tease her. It didn't feel early, but perhaps he needed to remember she'd never been intimate with a man before, and endeavor to make her feel always at ease with him — for there might come a time when her trust signified the difference between life and death. "You know my family is from Russia," he said. "My father's family are Cossacks. My mother's family is Romany. Gypsy."

Ann propped her chin on her hand and studied him. "Really? Your mother is a Gypsy?"

"My parents had to leave Russia. Her tribe didn't want her to be with my father, and my father's family doesn't approve of marriage."

"To a Romany, you mean."

"Especially not to a Romany." He'd heard the story on one chill winter night when he was seventeen, a senior in high school. He'd been accepted to MIT and, like all young men, anxious to strike out on his own.

But when his father had said he wanted to tell the tale only once, Jasha had listened, because the old man loved to tell stories over and over and over.

But not about his past. Never about the Old Country.

"Does anyone else in your family . . . you know . . . ?" She looked anxious, as if she didn't know whether to hope he was the only one or be relieved that there were others.

"All the guys."

"All the guys? Only the guys?"

"It's complicated." And he didn't know how many more shocks she could bear. Although this morning she looked more like the unflappable Ann Smith and less like the creature created of storm and passion.

Which one was the true Ann Smith?

"I suppose it must be. But maybe that's why your mother's family wasn't happy about the marriage."

"Because they're prejudiced against guys who turn into wolves? We could march on the Kremlin and demand equal rights."

Ann still wasn't smiling.

Man, he was giving her his best stuff, and she was not amused.

Yes, this was definitely the real Ann Smith.

While he found humor in the difficulties of life, she waited for him to finish joking, and put him back on track.

But man, how he hated to tell her the truth. "There's a good chance my father's family is carrying a grudge."

"Because your parents got married?" She sounded incredulous.

"Oh, yeah."

"They've been carrying a grudge for thirty-some years?"

If she only knew. "A thousand years is nothing to them."

"Why do you say that?"

"I've got insider information." Sooner or later, he'd have to tell her the whole story . . . but he didn't want to. He suspected that when she discovered what a pile she'd stepped into, she'd want to run for the hills. He wouldn't blame her — but he would have to stop her.

"Now tell me what you know about the Ukrainian deal —"

"I got a fax." Before he could pin her down, she said, "It was waiting for me when I went in three days ago."

"The day after the Fourth of July?"

"Yes."

"Doesn't that just figure?"

"The fax said they'd decided to agree to

our terms, but only if you'd meet with them by the end of the week."

"Meet with them? Where?"

"In your office."

His eyes narrowed as he weighed the possibilities.

Had the Varinskis tracked him? His dad's paranoia had always seemed exactly that — the paranoia of a stern old man with a terrible secret to hide. Yet in all his years in business, Jasha had never seen any indication that anyone from the Old Country cared about his little family.

Yet he never took chances. He'd covered his tracks. He'd hacked into public computers, removed records, made himself an enigma with no past . . . just in case.

"They want to close the deal. They want to meet you in person and get your signature," she said.

To threaten him? To kill him?

To find out his family's location and destroy them?

"What did you tell them?" he asked.

"That you were out of the office at a family function —"

If they'd been fishing for information, they'd pulled in a whale. "What did they say to that?"

"They didn't *say* anything. It was a flurry

157

of faxes, and they made no comment about your activities." She lifted her eyebrows, waiting for his next question. When he said nothing, she continued: "I said I'd contact you, but to please be patient."

"They refused."

"They were very gruff, yes, so I told them I'd bring the contracts and we'd go over them. I convinced them to wait."

He ran his gaze over her. Had they followed her? Had they put a tracking device on her? What else had she inadvertently told them? "Did you bring the whole file?"

"Of course!" He'd insulted his superefficient secretary. She slid off the stool, fetched her briefcase, and spread the contracts and the faxes across the table.

He looked through them. Everything was organized according to time frame. He read them with a new eye, and he heard his mother's voice as clearly as if she sat beside him.

The sons of Oleg Varinski have found you. You are not safe.

CHAPTER 13

The hair rose on the back of Jasha's neck.

He looked directly at Ann, sitting quietly, watching him, and clearly trying to comprehend his thoughts.

If the Varinskis had followed her, she would never have known it. If they ever realized what she'd done, what she was — the finder of the icon, the woman the Madonna had chosen — she wouldn't stand a chance *in hell* of survival.

With more urgency, he asked, "Did they send you anything to give to me? A token of their goodwill? Anything?"

"No."

"Are you sure?"

"Jasha." She sounded exasperated. "You can trust me to know whether I've been given something to bring you."

"I do."

"Then act like it!"

"It's not that I don't trust you. I don't

trust them."

"They're wine distributors." She threw out her hands in a gesture of exasperation. "What's not to trust?"

"You're naïve." She was an innocent in all this, drawn into the depths of an ancient pledge because of her loyalty to him.

"Naïve? About *business?*" She half rose off the stool. "Isn't that another term for *stupid?*"

He'd offended her. He put down the sheaf of papers and looked her in the eyes. "No."

"Oh." She settled back onto the stool. "Okay."

When she backed off, he suffered a pang of regret. After three years of working together five or six days a week, a chase through the woods, and one long evening of making love, she still didn't feel secure enough with him to rake him over the coals. When he took her to meet his mother, she'd teach Ann everything she needed to know about coal raking.

But for right now, he needed to get one step ahead of the Varinskis. Ann was his responsibility, and he had to save her. The world seldom saw such wide-eyed ingenuousness, and he would protect it, and her. "This morning, I thought we'd take a walk down to your car."

She blinked at his sudden change of subject. "Okay."

"See if it managed to hang on to the cliff. Then I can get a tow truck up here and you'll know what to tell your insurance company." His father always said a good lie was the right mixture of truth and seizing an opportunity. And when the old man was right, he was right. "Do you want to change?"

She looked down at her feet. "I didn't bring any walking shoes or jeans. I only have this stuff."

He looked her over. "You look great in that stuff." She did look great, a tall, slender woman with legs clear up to her neck. Last night, after the bath, he'd been restless, holding her in his arms, wanting to do more, knowing he couldn't.

She, on the other hand, had slept soundly, exhausted by the day.

A virgin.

Damn it. A virgin.

The need to have her grew with every moment, tugging at his senses. The scent of her was woman: sweet, heady, seductive. He could almost taste her on his tongue. . . . He *had* tasted her, and the memory gave him a boner hard enough to howl about.

He'd bet if he looked at the icon, he'd see

the Madonna smirking at him.

"You look great in that stuff," he repeated, "but you need something tougher while you're here. Tell you what — my sister's got clothes upstairs in the back bedroom. Do you want to go take a look and see if anything fits?"

"Okay." Ann slid off the stool and headed toward the door, then stopped and turned to face him. "But . . . will your sister mind?"

"Naw. Firebird's really easygoing." Not about her clothes, she wasn't, but he knew good and well nothing would fit; his sister was almost six inches shorter than Ann, and rounded where Ann was thin.

But he wanted Ann out of the room long enough to conclude his search without any more interference.

"Are you sure?"

It must be a female thing, being proprietary about clothes, because Ann clearly doubted his word. "I'll tell you what," he said. "When you meet her, you can ask her."

"I'm going to meet her?"

"Of course you're going to meet her. My dad, uh . . ." How did he tell Ann this? "My dad had some kind of heart seizure. Or . . . something."

"What?" Ann came back to the table and sat down. "When?"

"On the Fourth."

"Why didn't you tell me?"

"I didn't have time. It was one hospital transfer after another and my mother was so . . ." He gestured.

"I'll bet!" Ann took his hand and held it between both of hers.

She was finishing his thoughts for him, and he was grateful. He hadn't realized that talking about his father would recall every fear, every anguish, every frustration. Jasha wanted to howl at the moon. He wanted to get up and hit something, preferably a Varinski. He wanted . . . he wanted everything in his tidy life to be as it had been, and would never be again.

"How is he now?" She squeezed his hand.

"I talked to Rurik this morning." Although neither of the brothers had mentioned the obvious — that if Konstantine died now, he would go to hell.

Men who lived every day with a deal with the devil didn't question consequences.

"When we brought him in, the hospital told us to say good-bye." Jasha recalled the helplessness, the fear, the anguish. He recalled his mother's pinched face, his sister's broken sobs. He found himself squeezing Ann's hand as if it were a lifeline. "Now he's rallied to the point that they're

163

sending him home."

"What are they going to do to fix him?"

"The medical staff can't fix him. They don't understand what's wrong."

"They're sending him home and they don't know what's wrong?" Her voice rose. "Don't put up with that! Make them —"

"They said something about naming the disease after him."

She subsided. "I'm sorry. That's lousy. I really like your dad. He's a great guy. I know I've only talked to him on the phone, but he's always so hearty and funny, and he asks me how old I am and why I don't —"

She blushed so suddenly and so brightly, Jasha experienced the first complete and genuine amusement he'd felt since the moment his mother had given her prophecy.

"He asks how old you are and why you don't marry me?" Jasha weighed his options. But it was too early to say anything, so he stuck with, "On the Fourth of July, he tried to auction me off to the women in Blythe."

"You're kidding."

Jasha enjoyed knowing he'd stunned her. "Named off my virtues, then offered me like a stud bull. Rurik, too."

"Does he do that often?"

"No, mostly he reads the paper, gripes about the idiot legislators who regulate the wine industry, and bellows when the rain falls and splits the grapes. But he wants grandchildren and when my father has a goal, nothing had better stand in his way." Better to prepare her for the reality of Konstantine than to let her be surprised. "After we get stuff settled here, we need to go up and see him."

Ann's eyes got huge and scared.

"You'll like them," he said reassuringly, then gave her a gentle verbal nudge. "And you can check with Firebird about borrowing her clothes."

"Right." Ann stood up and once again headed for the door.

He waited until he no longer heard her footsteps, no longer smelled her scent.

Then he ran his hands over the papers, feeling for lumps. He sniffed them, trying to detect the stench of Varinski on them — had they been in his office?

But everything was as it should be.

He shook the file folder.

Nothing fell out.

Ann's briefcase sat on the table, black, full-grained, pebbled leather, padded handle, detachable shoulder strap, brushed-nickel hardware, and a state-of-the-art lock — all perfect places to hide a homing device.

He started with her personal papers, and

grinned when he shook an envelope and out tumbled a desperate note to Celia from Ann. He didn't read it, but a glance was enough; it mentioned *Mr. Wilder* and *tight buns* in the same breath.

Nice.

He pulled out his pocketknife and split every seam in her briefcase and in the straps, spreading the leather and the lining across the table.

The briefcase was clean.

Lifting his gaze, he stared out the window at the sun-drenched morning. All right. Not in her briefcase, then certainly in her car . . .

The scent of her distress and her faintest gasp of dismay brought his head around.

Ann stood in the doorway, her gaze on the eviscerated briefcase and the pile of her personal papers. She looked down at the size four clothes she held in her hand. With a killing glare, she fled the dining room.

He gazed around at the guts of her briefcase spread across the table.

All right. This looked incriminating. But there was an easy explanation.

He'd better think of it fast.

Rising, he headed after her. Headed after her . . . instinct slammed into him like a speeding train.

Chase the female. Bring her down. Possess her —

No! God, no, he'd done that once.

And how sweet it had been. Her skin was clean and pure, her body hot and deep. . . .

He stopped, his hand on the wall, and took a long breath. Control. Where was his control? He'd never had difficulty disciplining his urges before.

Why now? Why Ann? What was it about her that carried his wild desires so close to the surface?

If he could, he'd turn away from the pursuit, but he had to stop her before she did something rash — he needed to explain.

He half thought she'd go upstairs to the bedroom to fling herself on the bed and cry. But no. He should have realized his Ann wouldn't do anything so simple.

She'd left the house by the back door.

He knew, because she'd left a scent trail of furious indignation — and she'd set off the alarm.

He stopped long enough to punch in the code and stop the shriek of the siren before the cops came out.

Glancing at the hook on the wall, he realized . . . she'd also taken his keys. The keys to his beautiful new BMW M6.

"Son of a bitch!" He ran out the back door.

She couldn't leave him here. Not after what had happened between them. Didn't she know what it meant?

He'd taken her, and she was his.

A growl, not quite human and not quite wolf, rattled deep in his chest.

Before the garage had completely opened, she backed his Beemer out, scraping the top of the car against the custom-built hardwood door. As the wood splintered, as the custom car paint peeled back with a horrible grating sound, he became totally human again.

Human, and unsure whether he was more concerned for her or the car.

Then he decided she was safe, and mourned the Beemer.

She backed up.

He ran out into the driveway. *He had to stop her.*

She put the seven-speed in first, hit the gas, and popped the clutch.

She killed it. She started it at once and did it again. The third time was a charm, and she hiccuped from first to second, her killing gaze fixed right on him.

He braced himself, prepared to jump sideways.

But God bless her, she didn't quite have the nerve to run over his ass. She swerved into the grass, sinking into the mud, then veered back onto the pavement and drove around the house.

Turning, he raced through the house to the front.

CHAPTER 14

That POS. He'd taken her briefcase apart.

Ann had been carrying that thing, treasuring it, since Jasha had given it to her for Secretary's Day the very first year she'd worked for him. And he'd cut it apart because he thought she . . . she . . . she didn't know what he'd thought. But it wasn't good, and he didn't trust her.

Four lousy years she'd worked at his company, three lousy years of it as his administrative assistant, and he didn't trust her.

The asshole.

She cleared the back corner of the house. She hit the gas.

The Beemer hiccuped, then sprang forward so fast the tires squealed on the pavement and she experienced a glorious jolt of adrenaline.

Jasha loved his cars. Right now, he must be cringing.

Maybe there was a time when she'd been less than careful, and the consequences had been deadly. But she'd been a child then, and everyone told her it was not her fault. Even Sister Mary Magdalene had called Ann to her classroom and with great severity told her she was not to blame herself.

So she didn't blame herself, but she'd learned her lesson, and everyone who knew her knew that her name was synonymous with responsibility.

How dare Jasha not trust her?

She hit the front circle drive. All she had to do was drive the hell out of here, and she'd be free of him forever.

And Jasha burst out the front door and ran in front of the car.

That asshole had a lot of faith in her good nature.

She slammed on the brakes.

Justified good faith. Damn it.

She pounded on the steering wheel.

Damn it!

"Listen to me," he bellowed. "I need you!"

"Yeah, yeah," she shouted back. He probably couldn't hear her. The window was closed. But she liked yelling at him.

She reversed and headed for the other half of the circle drive.

He ran across the lawn, skidded in front

of the car again. "Ann, stay with me."

She reversed again and, rebel that she was, contemplated driving across the wide circle of grass in the middle of the drive.

"Ann . . ." He walked toward the front of the car, his hands outspread, a smile placing winsome dimples in his cheeks. "Please . . ."

She wanted something, *anything,* to wipe that smirk off his face.

As if her wish had power, *something* flew past her side of the car and buried itself in his shoulder.

He staggered backward, fell over.

What was it?

Who cares? Get the hell out!

She gunned the engine and drove past him. She circled the drive, and glanced back.

He'd dragged himself to his feet and was standing, weaving as if he were drunk with — she slammed on her brakes. He had an *arrow,* complete with feathers, sticking out of him.

What? Should they circle the wagons?

He doubled over. He ran toward the porch in a crouch.

Good news. This gave her time to get away.

So why was she backing up, reversing, driving toward the house? *Some idiot was shooting arrows out there.*

She needed to run. Run away now. In the car. *She was safe in the car.*

Jasha had collapsed, his torso on the porch, his legs in the driveway.

She drove up next to him. Vaulting out of the passenger side, she grabbed him under the armpits, pulled as hard as she could.

He yelled in pain, but he didn't budge. He was too heavy.

Then she heard a retort. The car's front tire exploded.

Rubber flew; the car collapsed on its right side.

Gunshot.

Suddenly, she discovered the strength to pull Jasha toward the house.

He yelled again, but when she would have stopped, he gasped, "Get me inside." He helped her, using his legs to shove himself along. His jeans caught on the rough stone floor of the porch.

"Oh, God. Oh, God. Oh, God." Somehow her frantic prayer helped keep her moving, keep her mind away from the fact that somewhere out there, some guy had a gun and a bow. Or two guys had — oh, it didn't matter. She just had to get Jasha inside.

And she did. She pulled him across the threshold into the entry, and slammed and locked the door. She ran for the phone.

"What are you doing?" Jasha rolled around to look.

"Calling the ambulance." She shook the receiver. "I can't hear the dial tone."

"He cut the line."

She headed for her purse. *Where was her purse?* "My cell."

"There's no time. Get this arrow out of me."

"I can't take it out. The EMTs —"

"There's no time. If I start to heal, whatever he put inside me will be a part of me, and I can't have that."

"Are you crazy? You won't heal that fast." She shouted at him — not because she didn't believe him, but because she did.

"I've got a knife in my pocket."

"Which you always carry with you." How in the hell had she managed to dredge up sarcasm now?

"Well . . . yeah." He sounded surprised.

"I know." She'd scolded him for losing two others to airport security when he'd forgotten about them. She'd figured it was a guy thing. She'd never figured she'd have to use one of the blades to cut an *arrow* out of his *shoulder.*

She couldn't even believe she was using those words in a single sentence.

Grabbing one of the beautiful cotton throws off the couch, she ran back to Jasha and used it to stanch the blood that oozed out of his shoulder and onto the floor. "How do you know he put something inside you?" she asked. "Besides the arrow, I mean?"

"Honey, if he wanted to kill me, he would have used a rifle and a scope."

Dear God, Jasha had blood all over his T-shirt. His face was pasty white, and that arrow stuck straight out.

"Well, if whatever it is, is nothing deadly —"

"It could be a drug that would make me cooperate with them."

Her imagination immediately sprang into action. "Or a slow-acting poison only they have the antidote to."

He grimaced. "I hadn't thought about that."

"That's because it's ridiculous!" she shouted. "It's something out of a movie! This whole scene is out of a really bad movie!"

"Ann." With his healthy hand, Jasha caught her wrist. When she focused on him, he said steadily, "Dig out the arrow."

She looked away. The arrow was in him. This was her fault.

She brought the bad people. She always

brought the bad people.

"Look at me!" He shook her wrist. "There's no one else I can depend on. Only you."

She looked back at him.

Their gazes locked.

She steadied.

"There's always only you," he said.

"Shit-kicker. Flatterer. Damned, ridiculous, stupid man." She could not do this. She could not. She knelt beside him, pulled the knife out of his jeans pocket. Her hands shook so badly she fumbled and dropped it. "It should be sterilized." She sliced his T-shirt from his neck to his sleeve and laid his shoulder bare.

The arrow had desecrated the beautiful expanse of his smooth skin. Blood — old blood, new blood, stained everything brown and scarlet. She wanted to put her head between her knees. She wanted to vomit. She wanted to cry.

"You can't kill me with a germ." He sounded way too sure of himself. "*You* can't kill me at all. You're going to widen the wound enough to back the arrow out without doing too much more tissue damage."

"Okay." And, *Poison,* she reminded herself. The sharp blade hovered, trembling, over the wound.

"Drugs are most likely." His voice vibrated with pleading. "Please, Ann, do this for me."

Tears sprang to her eyes. She dashed them away — and cut.

The skin was tough. The muscle was like meat. Meat slippery with blood. She used the point to follow the arrow down to the point. It took her a minute to realize . . . "I've hit bone. The point is buried in the bone."

"I know." He sounded as if he were being strangled.

She couldn't bear to look at his face, to see his anguish. If she did that, she'd never be able to finish. "How do I get it out?"

"You pull."

"Oh, come on!" Now she did look at him. His lower lip was bleeding — he'd bitten it through. "Pull it straight out," he instructed. "A hard, fast jerk. Straight up and out. Ann, that's important. If you pull at an angle, you're going to tear more muscle."

Obviously. "I know!"

"Stand up, put your foot next to the arrow, and pull."

This was a nightmare. Her nightmare.

Before she could stand, he caught her hand again. "Listen. After we get done here, if I pass out or go wonky on you, call 911 on your cell, get the paramedics here. But don't go out. Promise you won't go out."

"I won't go out."

"Make sure all the doors are locked. Take the icon and go to the linen closet beside the guest bathroom — there're bottles of perfume. Break one on the floor. It'll confuse his sense of smell."

Dumbfounded, she stared at him. Had the drugs taken effect?

"Why do you think I don't like cologne?" For a man with an arrow in his shoulder and possibly drugs in his system, he sounded quite sensible. "Then go down the stairs to the vault and lock yourself in. Even if they set the place on fire, there's air piped in. You remember the combination to the vault, don't you?"

"Yes," she said faintly. "But I don't think I can drag you that far."

"Honey, I'm the one who'll keep him occupied while you hide."

That pissed her off. "Not while I'm alive, you won't." Standing, she placed her foot on his shoulder. Bending down, she grasped the arrow close to his skin, got a good hold, and yanked as hard as she could.

For a horrible second, the arrow didn't budge. Then it broke free.

Jasha screamed.

She staggered backward. She held it up

and stared. Stared at the iron shaft.

The arrowhead was still in his shoulder.

"No. No. No." She dropped to her knees beside his writhing form. "Lie still!" With her fingers, she probed inside the wound.

"My God. My God." He shuddered in agony every time she moved her fingers.

She felt the outline of the arrow. It was traditionally shaped, a triangle with a point firmly embedded in the bone. "I'm going to have to walk it out."

"Do what you have to." He strained, desperate not to jerk away from her.

She wrapped her palm over the wide base, her fingers over the slick, chipped sides. As gently as she could, she rocked the arrow back and forth. At first it scarcely moved. Then the arc got wider.

Still it wouldn't come out.

She had to get it out.

And finally, she felt the faintest snap as it came free.

He felt it, too. "Hurry. Now!"

She pulled. Her hand slipped. Her fingers skidded across the sharp sides. The corner punctured her palm.

The bite of stone through her tender flesh was instant and agonizing. She jerked her hand away. Tears sprang to her eyes. No mere cut should be so painful.

And he arched off the floor with a silent cry of torment.

"Sorry," she said breathlessly. Sorrier than she could say.

"What the hell happened?" he rasped. "That burned!"

"I don't know. Does it matter?"

"No. I guess not."

Ignoring her misery, she went back in and pulled again. The arrow backed up. Slowly, laboriously, she slid the awful thing free of his muscles, his bones, and his sinews.

As soon as it was loose, he said, "Let me see it."

She handed it to him.

"It's obsidian," he said. "Black glass rock. Did you know that a chipped obsidian edge can be sharper than a surgeon's scalpel?"

"Do I look like I care?" She cradled her cut hand.

"No, that's good. It doesn't do as much damage going in. Yes, for some reason, they want me alive." Carefully he examined the tip. "There it is." He sighed in relief. "You got it out. See?" He held up the arrow. "See that tiny tracking device? It's formed right into the tip, and there's a perforation where the tip should break off in the bone. With my metabolism, the bone would knit and they could follow me wherever I went."

She turned her head away. She couldn't stand to look at the bloody thing. She was sickened, afraid, in pain, barely hanging on to consciousness.

"The important thing is, you don't have to go back in." He sounded encouraging.

Her head shot around to him. "Go back in!"

"If it hadn't come out —"

"Oh, for the love of God —"

"Perhaps not God — God doesn't look favorably on us — but for the love of my family. They're a pain in the ass sometimes, but they would do anything to help me, and I would do anything to save them."

Family? *Are these the kind of sacrifices family requires?* "I should have kept driving."

"But you couldn't leave me." He stroked Ann's arm. "Or her."

"Her?"

"The Madonna."

Ann pulled the icon out of her pocket and showed him. "I *didn't* leave her."

He laughed, but faintly, and closed his eyes. "The entry is a good place for us to stay right now. The board is over one window, the leaded glass makes it difficult to look in, and the siren will sound if anyone breaks in. The local cops are probably pretty sick of hearing my alarm, but out here, they don't have anything else to do, and I put a lot of money into their retirement fund. They'll come out."

She looked around. Yes. She felt relatively safe right now. Going to the wall, she set the alarm.

"Stay low," Jasha said.

"I know." When had she acquired a siege mentality? Outside, it was still morning — how was that possible? — and she thought the sunlight made an attack unlikely.

An attack. She was a modern woman. Why was she worried about an attack?

She looked at Jasha. Because she'd just pulled an arrow out of a man she'd seen turn into a wolf.

This was all a hallucination, because none of it made sense.

But whether it did or not, Jasha looked like hell. Smeared with blood, pale, and sweaty. In shock. "I'm cold," he said, and shivered.

She comfortingly pressed her hand on his chest, then rose, went to the couch, and grabbed a pillow and another throw.

When she returned and lifted his head, his eyes opened, angry yellow and rimmed in red.

But when he saw her, he relaxed. "Thank you," he whispered. "For everything."

Like she had a choice. She shoved the pillow under his head and tossed the throw over him. "Explain to me why I'm not calling 911 right now."

"Because when they arrest the hunter for shooting me with an arrow, he's going to tell the sheriff I'm a wolf. When they question you, you're going to blush and stammer the way you always do when you lie. When I heal as quickly as I do, the hospital's going to think there's something very strange about me. And we don't want anyone thinking there's anything strange about me." He fixed his changeable eyes on her. "Do we?"

"No. I guess not." Sadly, the whole thing made sense to her, and that, more than anything, told her how far she'd come from yesterday. "It wasn't the drunk hunter, was it?"

"It was. The drunk hunter, plus one of my cousins."

She didn't ask how he knew. But she believed him. "Why would your cousin try to kill you? And don't tell me because your parents got married."

"If he'd wanted to kill me, I'd already be dead." Jasha's voice was growing fainter.

"You think these guys are related to the Ukrainians?"

"I think they *are* the Ukrainians."

Her anger rose again. "And you think I'm in league with them."

"No, I think they planted a tracking device on you and urged you to come up here so they could find out where I lived."

"That's dumb!" At least in the real world, it was dumb. In a world where Jasha turned into a wolf and his cousin shot him with an arrow, it made sense.

"I'm still cold," Jasha murmured. "I know it's not comfortable, but would you lie with me?"

She wanted a shower. She wanted to look at the cut on her palm and see whether it needed stitches. She wanted to go home, curl up with her cat, and pretend this never happened.

Instead she made a fist, trying to ease the sting. She wiped at the red smears on her orange loose-knit sweater and her white pants. She thought longingly of the bathroom upstairs, of the soap and the change of clothes. And she said, "Of course." Going to Jasha, she stretched out on his good side, careful not to jar him too much. She covered herself with part of the throw, and placed her head on his shoulder.

He wrapped his arm around her and

kissed her head. "The Madonna has chosen well."

The Madonna? Sister Mary Magdalene always said the Madonna watched over Ann. But in her secret heart of hearts, Ann knew Sister Mary Magdalene couldn't *know.* Sister Mary Magdalene herself had taught Ann that God works in mysterious ways. No mere mortal could know whether the Madonna watched over Ann . . . or whether it was the devil.

Because bad things happened to people when she was around.

Her wishes were curses, and her love was lethal.

Ann went to sleep listening to the beat of his heart — and wishing she'd never met Jasha Wilder, or listened to the urgings of her love.

CHAPTER 15

"Ann. Come on. It's time to go."

Her eyes sprang open. She sat up so quickly her head spun.

"Whoa. It's okay. There's no emergency — the hunters are gone." Jasha looked fine. A little pale, a little tense, but very calm.

She glanced around. Outside, it was day, afternoon by the light. She rested on the floor, tucked into a nest of couch cushions and colorful throws. "What . . . ? How . . . ?"

"You had a shock. You were sleeping hard. So I let you get some z's in, and got stuff ready."

She pushed her hair away from her face and tried to remember her dreams. She'd been running through the forest, faster and faster. She had glanced back and seen wolves behind her. Glanced around, seen wolves all around. She'd been terrified. . . . Then Jasha ran past and smiled, and became a wolf, too. She hadn't been afraid anymore.

But she knew she could never go back. That she had to run forever.

She covered her eyes. "That was horrible."

"It would have been more horrible if you hadn't come back for me." He held out his hand.

"What? Oh." She hadn't been talking about his rescue, but she didn't need Freud to interpret a dream like hers. She knew what it meant; she would never call her subconscious subtle. "Yeah, I'm a sucker for wounded animals."

Sadly, she was. Kresley had arrived on her doorstep, a starving, flea-ridden tomcat suffering from a coyote attack. Until she got to know him, she didn't understand how he'd survived. But unlike her, Kresley was a fighter, and he soon had every dog in the neighborhood whipped into shape. Even the manager's Rottweiler trembled when Kresley swaggered past.

She took Jasha's hand and let him pull her to her feet. And into his arms.

He kissed her, a long, slow kiss that paid no heed to his injury or her misgivings or the possibility of danger. Instead he concentrated on reducing her to the essence of desperation. His hands roamed her back, massaging muscles tense from the hard floor and the prophetic dream. His lips opened hers; his tongue probed deep within. The motion reminded her of the forest, the storm, the all-too-brief thrust of his body inside hers, and the bright lightning of union.

She remembered the pain, too, a warning she'd come too far too fast and now had to pay the price.

"You are a glorious woman," he whispered.

"I look like a giraffe." She'd been told that far too many times to believe anything else.

"And I'm a wolf. We have our Halloween costumes worked out forever. My darling giraffe, have I told you how much I love your long, long legs?"

"The way a wolf admires an antelope?" She couldn't help mocking him. She didn't believe a word he said; he'd easily resisted her charms while she worked for him. It was only now, when they were alone and he needed her, that he paid her lip service.

Lip service . . . in more ways than one, and all very gratifying. "Jasha, why are we leaving? Where are you taking me?"

"We're going into the woods. With this." He put his hand in his pocket and pulled out a thin and tiny silver disk. He showed it to her, stuck on his index finger. "He tagged me like an endangered wolf. He wants to see where I run for shelter. *I* want to draw him out so I can catch him, question him, and finish him."

"Finish him," she repeated

Jasha's eyes were golden ice chips. "Finish him before he finds my family. Finish him before he finishes us."

"So we're *bait?*"

"We have two choices: We can be bait, and turn the tables. Or we can be dead meat. Which do you prefer?"

"I hate those choices."

He waited.

She sighed. "Stick a hook in my ribs, drop me in the pond, and call me a worm."

"That's my girl!" He hugged her shoulders.

Irritated, she wiggled away from him, and picked up a cushion and one of the throws off the floor.

He bent to help her gather up their nest.

She stopped him with her hand on his arm. "You shouldn't do that. You're hurt."

"Not much. Look." He opened his shirt and showed her the wound in his shoulder.

Gingerly, she touched it with her fingertips. It was red. It looked uncomfortable. But it looked and felt like nothing more than a three-inch scar.

And she knew — *she remembered* — she'd had her hand inside. "Is this healing part of the, er, the . . . ?"

"The deal with the devil." He watched her, obviously judging her reactions, seeing too much for her comfort. "Yes, I can heal quickly, and that's one of the benefits. One of many benefits."

"You made an actual deal with the devil?" Her voice squeaked.

He seemed so calm, but she supposed he was used to the strange and miraculous. Or the strange and the . . . seriously strange. She wasn't used to it. No matter what happened, she couldn't get used to it — or wouldn't.

She groped to get a grip on his story. "A deal with the devil. It sounds so melodramatic, like a Faustian play."

"Faust was a lousy bargainer. With a little forethought, he could have got a lot more for the price of his soul."

Mouth open, she stared at Jasha. Snapping it closed, she said, "You should talk. You turn into a *wolf*. Couldn't you have asked for something a little cooler?"

His mouth quirked. "Like what?"

"I don't know. First place on *Dancing with the Stars*?"

"Do you think the devil has his hand in

on *Dancing with the Stars*?"

"He has to. There's no other explanation for Russell and Teresa winning last season," she said bitterly.

He laughed and, when she glared, changed his laugh into a cough and tried to look serious. "If I were making the deal, I'd be more likely to ask for the Giants to win the Series."

"Great. I'm living my own personal performance of *Damn Yankees.*" She piled the cushions on the couch.

He followed suit.

"You, um, can't refuse the deal?" she asked.

"It's not an option."

"No. I suppose the devil might have something to say about that." She glanced at Jasha uneasily. "Wouldn't he?"

"In the past thousand years, I don't think anyone's actually talked to him."

"A thousand years." She tried to get her mind around the vastness of the time passage, and got hung up on the legalities. "So *you* didn't actually make the deal with the devil. It's a family thing."

"Right. My ancestor set the terms, and he didn't know about *Dancing with the Stars.*"

"I suppose not. So the whole family —"

"Only the males," he reminded her.

She bridled. "Doesn't the devil like women?"

"According to my father, women have a tendency to see through Beelzebub's tricks."

"Oh." That was sort of flattering. "Did you have to initial the devil's contract or anything?"

"In this case, it's pretty much sins of the fathers."

"Maybe you could consult our lawyers and void the contract?"

"Lawyers all work for Satan, you know that," Jasha said, deadpan.

She grinned. "If our legal counsel, Bob Rutherford, works for Satan, Satan should buy Bob a better toupee." She touched Jasha's arm. "Really, if you wanted out, what could the devil do?"

"I doubt that any of us have ever seriously considered refusing the gift."

She looked to see if Jasha was joking again. "Gift?"

"Wouldn't you consider it a gift to be able to change into a wolf and run through the forest, free and wild?" Jasha took a breath as if he could smell the limitless fresh air. "Or change into a hawk and soar through the clouds?"

"You can change into a hawk, too?" Seriously cool. She'd always wanted to fly.

192

"No. I'm a wolf. My brother Rurik is a hawk. My other brother, Adrik, is a panther."

"Oh." Her mind worked, and came up with one inescapable truth. "Those are all hunting animals."

"Predators. Yes." Jasha watched her, and only his golden eyes followed her. "For a thousand years, the family hired themselves out to warlords, dictators, kings, and thugs. Whoever had the money to pay, they would work for them. Once they were put on the job, they never stopped until they had done what they were hired to do."

She felt judged, as if Jasha was gauging the depth of her distress and the strength of her determination. "And what were they hired to do?"

"Track people. Find them. Kidnap them. Torture them . . . kill them."

"I was afraid of that." She put her hand to her forehead. "You said that was your cousin out there. And he shot you!"

"Right before I was hit, I caught a whiff of them. I recognized the hunter at once." Jasha shrugged. "He's big on deer urine."

She wrinkled her nose. "Euw!"

"Yeah. There's no explaining a hunter. But the other guy — I've never met him." Jasha's lips lifted in a very wolflike snarl. "He's one of us, though. I know it."

She did not want to hear this. She went back for more pillows, brought them to the couch, placed them, and turned around to find Jasha had planted himself in her path.

"Pretending this isn't happening won't help," he said.

"It helps me," she retorted, then relented. "All right. What does your cousin want?"

"Revenge. That's what they all want. And they won't stop until they get it."

"Revenge for what?"

He sighed. "It's a long story."

"You keep saying that."

"And I was going to tell it to you, but you ran away."

She reminded herself that she'd pulled an arrow out of his shoulder a few hours ago. No matter how much she wanted to, she couldn't hit him hard enough to ring his chimes. In fact, even if she did manage to work up the gumption to hit him, his chimes would probably stay frustratingly quiet.

Jasha was a *big* man. A tall man, broad and heavily muscled. She forgot that, sometimes, until he stood in front of her, as he did now, and looked down at her, as he did now. And inside her, that smoky, sexy feeling rose in her because she had run away, and he wanted her again. "I didn't *run*." She sounded embarrassingly breathless. "I made an intelligent decision to walk away because it was obvious you didn't trust me."

"You don't walk away in the fastest car I own. You were running." He caught her arm when she would have stepped around him. "And I do trust you. I also know if they decided to put a tracking device on you, you'd never know."

"Okay. That makes sense." She looked him right in the face. "Why didn't you tell me that?"

"You sometimes take responsibility for too much, and I didn't want you to blame yourself if you'd led them to me."

"Oh." Oh, great. He'd been thoughtful, and she'd thrown a tizzy.

She would have gone back to their nest and finished picking up, but he placed his hand in the small of her back and guided her toward the stairs. "That can wait. We need to get ready."

"Ready? For what?" Did she want to know?

"My cousin cut the tires on my cars in the garage. He cut my phone lines. If I make a cell call, I know he'll be monitoring to see who I call and where they are." Jasha smiled, all sharp, white teeth and seething charm. "So you and I are going to give my cousin what he wants. We're going to take him on a bit of a hunting trip."

When Jasha looked like that, she remembered whom — or what — she was dealing with. As they climbed the steps, she said, "He's going to hunt us."

"Yes. He'll use the tracking device to follow us, hoping to find my family and eliminate them."

She didn't understand at first. Then she did, but she didn't believe it. "Eliminate them. You mean — kill them? Your whole family? That's not . . . do you really think . . . what is this, *In Cold Blood*?"

"He shot me with an arrow. I think we can acquit him of good intentions." Jasha led her into his bedroom, then into his bathroom.

"But murdering a whole family just because —"

He turned on the water in the sink and thrust her wounded hand under the stream. "Murder is what they do best, and my family wouldn't be the first family they eliminated, right down to the smallest child."

The water ran red. She tensed, waiting for the pain.

She felt only a mild sting. "How will we survive?"

"We will survive. Don't forget — *I* am one

of *them.*" He turned her palm up to the light.

A red streak cut across her palm. The cut was deeper and swollen on one end. She couldn't see anything but pale scars on her fingers, and the lines on her skin no longer completely lined up — but the wound seemed ridiculous in comparison with the pain she'd felt when the arrow pierced her hand. "I don't understand. I really cut it. I know I did." She watched him test the skin, trying to pull it apart.

"My blood helped you heal."

Because he was one of them.

She could pretend he was a friendly wolf. She could applaud his loyalty to his parents and his siblings.

But she couldn't ignore the truth.

When Jasha wished, he turned into a wolf. He was a predator. He was the son and grandson and great-grandson of murderers, rapists, and assassins.

She brought the bad people. She always brought the bad people.

No matter how much she wished otherwise, he *was* one of them.

CHAPTER 16

When Jasha and Ann stepped out the back door, twilight hovered in the air like an essence only they could smell.

"Are they here?" She looked around at the trees that crowded the house and imagined eyes, shining with hunger, watching every step.

"They're gone. I'd bet my cousin's off giving the hunter his reward."

"Paying him off, you mean." The unprincipled rat.

"Giving him what he deserves."

She jerked her head around and stared at Jasha. "Is he going to kill him?"

"I don't know. Possibly. Do you care?" Jasha locked the door, then rested his hand on it, almost as if he were saying good-bye.

"Shouldn't I?"

"The hunter got drunk and shot at wild wolves — at *my* pack, at *my* leader — and ran to the police when he was frightened.

Then he joined with a stranger so he could see me shot with an arrow, and he used a rifle to shoot out the tire on my Beemer."

Troubled by Jasha's rancor, she said, "I wasn't too easy on your car, either."

"I'm not sure he was aiming at the tire. He might have hit you." Jasha looked right at her, his mouth a flat, thin line. "I break out in a sweat every time I think of what he might have done by accident — or on purpose."

"I didn't think of that." She clutched the pocket where she kept the icon.

Was death stalking her . . . again?

"So do I care if my cousin makes him suffer? If he kills him?" Jasha answered his own questions. "No. No, I don't."

But Ann did. Didn't she? She hated cruelty . . . but whose cruelty should she hate now? That of the hunter, the man who preyed on beautiful, sleek beasts who ran wild in the forest? Or the predator who preyed on the hunter? Neither of them was a good man, and perhaps . . . perhaps what happened was nothing more than justice. Certainly there was nothing she could do about it.

"That'll keep the Varinski busy, and no one else will see us go. Do you have the icon? Do you have your cell phone?" When she nodded yes to both questions, Jasha strode off down the driveway into the woods. "Come on, then. We're going to have an adventure."

Before she took the final step into the cover of trees, she stopped and looked back at the castle.

Had it been only yesterday that she'd driven up to the front door and stepped into this legend? Since that moment, there hadn't been one instant when she could have turned back. She knew, because she'd desperately looked for the sign U-TURN ALLOWED HERE.

Or, more fittingly, I'D TURN BACK IF I WERE YOU. Because she was the Cowardly Lion.

She glanced at Jasha, waiting for her in the shadows.

Yes, the Cowardly Lion seemed a very sensible character to be. But Jasha said that wasn't one of her choices.

Bait or dead meat.

She trudged after him.

At once twilight became night. At night, the forest smelled richer; the earth exhaled the scent of last autumn's leaves; the trees groaned and spoke, spicing the air with pine. She couldn't see anything, and she stumbled and cursed.

Of course, what did she expect? She wore Jasha's hiking boots padded with three pairs of socks, and her feet were big, but not that big. She wore a wide-brimmed camouflage hat. She wore his wide-sleeved silk T-shirt, which on him would be tight and on her flapped loosely, and over that, his camouflage shirt. His camouflage pants were held up by a belt cinched tightly around her waist, and bungee cords cinched the bottoms of the legs against the boots.

She'd wanted in his pants, but not like this.

He'd wrapped a bandage around her hurt hand, then put his gloves on her to protect the bandage. He'd turned up the cuffs on his shirt, and he'd buckled a hunting vest, filled with things like compasses and flashlights, tightly around her. Because no matter how tall she was, he was taller. His shoulders were broader. She looked like a little girl wearing her big brother's clothes, and when she thought of her plans for long evenings lounging by the fireplace, wineglass in hand, an adoring Jasha at her feet, she wanted to throw something. The canteen that hung on her shoulder strap, perhaps, or the knife he insisted she carry strapped to her leg.

The most humiliating part was — she wore his underwear. All she'd brought from Napa were lacy thongs, and he had said, "You are not traipsing through the woods in butt floss. Here." He'd tossed her a pair of serviceable cotton briefs.

She'd let them fall at her feet while she stared reproachfully at him.

"It's either that or you're going commando," he'd said.

So she wore the briefs — and cursed the fate that had sent her here.

Of course, she knew fate was innocent. Ann had acted on her own dreams and desires; she was the one responsible for the men's underwear, the trek through a midnight forest, and the realization that merging with a man involved more than flowers and romance. With Jasha, the merging meant that she had adopted his family. She'd longed to be adopted, not adopt! And she'd had to save his life; the Chinese said that when a person saved a life, she was responsible for it. So if they were right, then she faced responsibilities she had never imagined.

She stumbled again.

"Your eyes will adjust to the darkness pretty soon." He put his arm around her.

"The middle of my back feels . . . itchy."

Uneasily, she shrugged her shoulders. "No one's watching us, are they?"

"Unless all of my senses have deceived me, there's only one cousin in the vicinity. He thinks he buried a tracking device in me — and hey, I do have it right here in this plastic bag — and that he's got the upper hand. He thinks my father is weak and my mother is a harlot. He thinks my brothers and my sister and I are all happy, bloated fools." Ann heard Jasha's teeth snap together. "We will show them the truth."

The truth. She shivered. What truth could she show anyone? She didn't have extra-special senses or a clever strategy or unique abilities. All she had was a birthmark, a birthmark she managed to forget about . . . most of the time.

Except now. Right now, for the first time ever, she could feel a faint sizzle under her skin.

Why? What had changed? What had Jasha done to her while she slept?

What had she done to herself?

"You're looking forward to a fight," she said.

"I'd rather fight than wait, but I can do both."

"I'm more of a *Let's negotiate* kind of

person." She cursed the hopeful tone of her voice.

"No one negotiates with a Varinski," he said flatly.

"What's a Varinski? Some kind of gun?"

"The family name is Varinski. When my parents fled Russia, they changed their name to Wilder. They wanted a new start in a New World." He sounded frustrated. Angry. "And they got it, but the Old World has followed us here."

"At least you're not a happy bloated fool." She was really working to find the silver lining.

He chuckled and hugged her. "I *am* happy. Can you see better now?"

She could. Still not well, but well enough not to fall on her face. "Not yet." She liked walking with his arm around her. "Why aren't you a happy, bloated fool?"

"The children of immigrants don't dare become bloated. Our parents have plans for us, and heaven forbid we not fulfill them. Talk of the Old Country is enough to motivate any of us."

"So you're successful because your parents demanded it."

"No, because they expect no less. What about you, Ann? Why are you successful?"

His light tone didn't fool her. He wanted

to know who she was, where she'd come from, who her people were.

And she had no intention of telling him. "I'm successful? I don't think so. I'm just an assistant."

"You're not *just* anything. With the right staff, you could expand Wilder Wines into a worldwide corporation. That's the kind of brain you have. So why *didn't* you go to business school? Why *are* you working for me?"

Now she was sorry she walked with his arm around her. It was dark; probably he couldn't see her expression. But it was equally possible he could smell her discomfort, and she feared he could feel her reserve in the stiff set of her shoulders. "I'm looking for a rich husband, and I thought you were promising. Now I'm not so sure — I'm allergic to pet dander and I don't like camping trips." That came out more curtly than she'd intended. But she wasn't sorry.

She'd told strangers about her past before. Their reactions were always extreme — pity and curiosity. Usually they thought her background gave them the license to interrogate her, and then they edged away, as if bad fortune was contagious, or as if she'd done something to deserve her past.

Perhaps it was true. Perhaps, just perhaps, she had been marked by God as a warning to others to stay away.

Perhaps Jasha wouldn't care. But perhaps he would, and it seemed smarter, or at least safer, to keep her secrets. "I can see now," she said, then told herself she was relieved when he let her go and walked beside her.

The Douglas firs were massive chunks of darkness blotting out the dim light, and the cedars scented the air. When she looked up, she could see the pine tops waving at the chilly stars. Funny, how often she marveled at people who imagined the stars were friendly, concerned with human destiny. As a child, far too often, she'd wished on them and had her wishes ignored. The stars were far away and indifferent, and anyone who believed otherwise was a fool.

She only wished she were still that kind of fool.

"As far back as I can recall, I have memories of walking in the woods." Jasha kept his tone conversational, and he seemed unfazed by her detachment. "Before I could toddle, my father took me in his arms and walked the perimeter of our lands to show me the places where bad people could hide. The next year, I walked our lands all by myself, holding his hand while he carried my brother Rurik. The year after that, he carried Adrik. And finally, ten years later, we took turns carrying Firebird."

She couldn't help but respond to the affection in his voice. "Your dad sounds like a great guy."

"He is. He's from the Old Country, and he's a stern disciplinarian who held us to high standards, but he loves us and never for a minute did he let us doubt that."

When Jasha had told her they had to go out and be bait so he could save his family, she'd realized she should have been grateful to be an orphan.

But when he talked like this, giving her bits of family life that sounded so *Brady Bunch,* an undefined hunger clawed at her insides, and she had to bite back her envy.

Jasha continued. "Before we turned —"

"Before you turned? What do you mean, before you turned?"

"Ah. Well." He sounded as if he was gearing up for a lecture. "When a Varinski's a child, he's just a child. It's puberty that brings out the, um —"

"Beast in you?" she suggested wryly.

"Exactly what my mother calls it." He spoke with humor. "Like adolescence isn't hard enough. Pimples, inappropriate hard-ons, and excess body hair. *Lots* of excess body hair. And a tattoo that appears out of nowhere — and let me tell you, when Miss

Joyce got a glimpse of that, she was one cranky teacher."

They were walking inland and uphill at a steady rate, and she thought if they kept going in this direction, they'd have to cross the highway soon.

"From the time we could toddle, my father taught us woodsmanship. He taught us to be suspicious of strangers. He taught us to track and to know if we're being tracked. He taught us everything handed down from generations of Varinskis, and man, was he tough! He was our Boy Scout leader — the guys in our troop could survive on nothing. And prepared! We were always prepared. He used to set traps for us. One time my brother and I were coming home from school, and I stepped into a snare. It grabbed my feet and swung me in the air upside down. I hit the stub of a branch on the way up. That's what gave me this scar." Jasha stopped, took her hand, and guided it to his cheek.

Ann was well familiar with that pale scar — she had made up Don Juan–type fantasies about that scar — but she couldn't resist inching her fingers along its length, and knowing at least the last day's ordeals had earned her the right to touch his face, feel the texture of his skin and the smooth

208

burr of his just-shaved chin. "It could have taken your eye out!"

"My mother said that, too. She was mad at my father. I never saw her so mad. She laid into him — he let her, too, and then he said, '*Ruyshka,* better me scar his face than the demons of hell cast his soul into the pit.'"

"That's . . . sort of over-the-top." But she wasn't surprised. When she'd spoken to Konstantine on the phone, he'd had a deep baritone and a way of making every phrase seem sensational and dramatic.

"That's the trouble. It's not. He told us over and over the Varinskis would come, and we had to be prepared." Jasha's voice got gravelly. "He would say I wasn't prepared enough. He would say that the long peace had made me complacent, and that I got what I deserved. And I guess he was right."

Shyly, Ann put her arm around Jasha's waist and hugged. She knew he was thinking about his father in the hospital.

"But I'll never forgive myself for the hurt my negligence caused my family. And you." He hugged her back. "And you."

"You didn't —"

"Don't lie to soothe my feelings. You came dressed to seduce me, and you got . . . this." She felt him gesture at their surroundings.

209

"The stars are very romantic," she said.

As if she'd caught him by surprise, he choked, then chuckled. "Papa's the reason I have clothes stashed in the forest. Everywhere I'm going to take you, there's provisions and blankets. You'll be warm. You'll be dry. You won't go hungry."

She was surprised he even brought it up. "I know you'll provide for me." That he wouldn't had never occurred to her.

He stopped. He kissed her. "There isn't another woman I'd want with me on this journey. And — here's the highway."

They stepped out onto Highway 101.

"We'll go south for a few minutes, then turn inland," he said.

"South? That's great." South to her meant towns and freeways and civilization and, eventually, California.

"For now" — he walked back into the woods and came out pushing a small motorbike — "let's give the Varinski a workout."

CHAPTER 17

Six hours later, when the motorbike ran out of gas and the feeble headlight died, Ann didn't know where they were. She knew only that she was sick of hanging on to Jasha's waist, her butt vibrating as the roads turned to trails and the trails turned to tracks, all leading upward.

"That should do it." Jasha sounded satisfied as he helped her off and dropped the kickstand.

She rubbed her rear and stomped her feet, trying to get some feeling back into her legs, and looked around. It was still night, the longest night in the history of the world, and this place looked like all the other places they'd been: wild, forest covered, and dark. Really, really dark. As in never-seen-an-electric-light dark. Her eyes hurt from staring, and she didn't know whether they were open or shut.

"It'll take the Varinski two days to track us

here, and by then we'll be pretty close to my choice of Armageddon." Jasha's deep voice, silken with menace, made her glad he wasn't hunting her.

"You want to choose your battlefield."

"More important, I don't want him to know I have chosen it. I want him to think he's forced the issue." Jasha was only a presence in the dark, but she heard him lift the backpacks off the handlebars.

"What if he's a hawk instead of a wolf? Can't he find us faster?" The farther they traveled, the later the night, the colder it had grown, and when she stripped off one glove and touched her face, it felt stiff, frozen.

"You're beginning to think like a Wilder." A compliment, no doubt. "But I think he's got fur. There's no smell of feathers about him." Jasha sounded intent, weighing the odds, maneuvering like a general with an army of one. "If he is a bird of prey, that's to our advantage. He'll have to cover a lot of ground before he stands a chance of spotting us, and there's still a good chance he'll miss us. Camouflage works well against bird eyes. Here." Jasha helped her into her backpack. "If you can walk one more mile, I can promise you a sleeping bag tonight and a good breakfast in the morning."

One mile didn't sound like so much.

On the other hand, one mile uphill in the blackest night . . .

She would have complained, but walking uphill in his boots kept her conversation to increasingly virulent cursing every time she tripped.

The sharp point of the crescent moon rose over the horizon and pierced the night sky, and at four thousand feet, its tiny bit of illumination looked like a streetlight.

That helped, but not enough.

By the time he called a stop she was both breathless and furious, and rage loosened the restraints she usually placed on her emotions. "Are you sure you don't want to walk a little further?" She tapped the clown-sized toe of his boot. "Maybe enjoy a little run through the forest?"

"Here's water to brush your teeth." He poured her water out of a canteen.

"Trip on some tree roots? Take a header into the brush?" She ignored the cup in his outstretched hand.

He placed it on a rock. "I laid out our sleeping bags on that pile of boughs. Take off your boots and outerwear before you climb in."

"Maybe we could dig a foxhole!" She faked enthusiasm.

"Hush." He slid his arm around her waist, bent her back like a great wind, and kissed her.

She was tired. She was grumpy. She was so, so easy.

She leaned into him and kissed him back, frightened by the return to passion, yet eager to sample him once more. He helped her stand on her own and whispered, "I'll be back soon."

"What?" She forced her knees to take her weight. "You're really going for another walk?"

"Don't wait up." Without a sound, without ruffling the brush, he was gone.

"Spooky," she muttered — but then, up here, what wasn't?

She stood shifting between one foot and the other, trying to decide whether removing her clothes constituted good sense on her part, because the sleeping bag was insulated down to twenty below and she'd be too warm, or bad sense, because Jasha would think she'd obeyed him.

For all that he was a New World American, the old-world autocracy was bred into his bones.

She used to almost swoon at his high-handedness, but now . . . well, now it seemed yielding was another word for surrender.

Then a giant yawn caught her by surprise, almost cracking her jaw, and she decided he could gloat all he wanted. She would be asleep, anyway. She peeled off her clothes, leaving on only the men's underwear and his black silk T-shirt. She roused when, a half hour later, he slipped into his bag and snuggled against her back.

She woke enough to ask, "Where have you been?"

"Catching a rat," he said.

That woke her. "The Varinski?"

He laughed. "No. A real rat. Go to sleep. I'll show you in the morning."

Ann woke to the smell of coffee and cedar, the sounds of birds singing, a holy sense of stillness . . . and something tickling her cheek. Without opening her eyes, she swatted at it — and got Jasha's hand. "I hate you."

"I have coffee." He sounded richly amused and very awake.

"Unless you have bacon, eggs, and wheat toast served on a warm plate with a side of pancakes, I still hate you." She was gloriously warm in the cocoon of her sleeping bag, and she didn't need the nip of the mountain's cool morning air to alert her that coming fully awake would be painful and primitive.

"How about a Baker's Breakfast Cookie?" He crinkled the wrapping near her ear. "You can have a choice between ginger molasses or oatmeal raisin."

"It's bacon and eggs or nothing."

"Okay, I'm eating the oatmeal raisin."

"Give that to me." Sitting up, she fought the bag's zipper down, snatched the cookie out of his hands, and glared. He knew she hated ginger of any kind.

He was fully dressed and looked disgustingly alert. He offered her the cup of coffee, and she stared at his big hands. For a moment, she remembered that first night — the darkness, the sense that this man had stalked her, possessed her, and now demanded she yield everything to him.

Then he backed away, his face long with dismay and alarm. "I never knew you were so cranky when you woke up."

So he wasn't the dark wolf of her imagination. At least — not now.

"I'm not if I've had *more than five hours' sleep.*" And if her butt didn't hurt from the stupid bike.

She hadn't even seen the wolf since that first night, and when she looked back, that seemed the real fantasy. She knew the truth;

216

she'd seen the truth. But she still couldn't completely comprehend that Jasha became Another. This morning, as the sun filtered through the trees and scattered flecks of light across the forest floor, and birds sang their approval, she could easily pretend that this was a camping trip undertaken with the intention of fun in the forest.

A misplaced intention, to be sure, but the intention nevertheless.

Taking a sip of the coffee, she muttered, "Come *on,* caffeine." She unwrapped the cookie and tasted it — healthy, but not too healthy, and it filled the empty space in her belly.

As the food and the coffee worked their magic, she began to rouse enough to survey their surroundings.

They had sheltered in a grove of magnificent old evergreens. Here and there mighty stones poked out of the soft earth. One stone was so close she could lean against it, and she did, and when she did, she looked up . . . and up.

Last night, she'd thought the trees dusted the stars.

In the broad light of day, she realized she was right. These trees — Douglas fir, cedar, western hemlock — had trunks six and eight and ten feet wide, with branches the size of the live oaks in her condo complex. She got dizzy looking up at the tops. "Where are we?" she whispered.

"In the wilderness in the Olympic Mountains." Jasha smiled at her as he cleaned up the Sterno.

Maybe yesterday's shock and last night's journey had combined to make her forget how gorgeous he was. Maybe it was the pure pleasure of watching a man wash something — anything! — that made her breath catch with amazement.

"There's no one for miles," he said. "We'll make a hard walk this morning, then rest for a few hours, then take another hard walk this afternoon to the place where I want to camp. We can have a fire, and I've got a tent stashed there. It'll be like camping out. Fun!"

"Camping out is fun?" Her experience included one trip with the Camp Fire Girls to a national park for a wretched weekend that included a slow, steady downpour followed by a freeze.

"It is with me." With an efficiency of motion, he packed his backpack. "I'll fish, and we'll have trout and huckleberries, and wine — you gotta know I've hidden wine up there — and we'll tell ghost stories around the fire."

Caffeine? Who needed caffeine? The sight of his compelling gold eyes gave her a bracing jolt. His voice was slow and deep and dangerous. His dark hair was ruffled with sleep; the start of a beard darkened his chin and the hollows of his cheeks — and his body! Camouflage emphasized the width of his shoulders and the length of his legs, and she got caught up in the memories they evoked.

More important, he seemed to think she looked good, too. He ran his gaze over her, and he smiled as if the sight of her pleasured him.

She dropped the cookie back into the wrapper and ran her fingers through her hair, trying to restore it to some semblance of order.

"You're beautiful, all mussed from sleep."

"Sure." She didn't believe it, but she liked the way he said it.

He walked over and knelt on the sleeping bag, and his fingers joined hers, smoothing her hair, stroking her scalp, her neck. . . .

She relaxed into his touch, allowing him the freedom of her body if he would only massage away the kinks of tension, take the memories of terror and replace them with slow, sweet passion. He took her cup away, and she let him; then he eased her down on her back.

"Do you know I can see right through your silk T-shirt?" His fingertips stroked her nipples through the thin silk.

"*Your* silk T-shirt." She could barely move her lips.

"The sleeves are so wide, I could see inside every time you lifted that coffee to your lips." His hands slid up her arms and into the shirt, finding her breasts, caressing them so lightly she could barely feel his touch . . . and she could think of nothing else.

"Good view?" She closed her eyes to feel more acutely each pass he made.

"Very good." He lifted her shirt. "Getting better."

Cool air washed her skin, and her already tight nipples grew rigid, almost painful. But the old familiar habits of modesty couldn't easily be broken. So she didn't dare give herself up to passion. Not in the daylight. Not while he watched.

Her hands flew to push her shirt back down, but his hands were in the way, stroking her rib cage, her belly. . . . She pressed her legs together, not sure if she was intent on keeping him away or easing the discomfort passion brought in its wake.

But he made no attempt to go farther. His

caresses grew lighter and more infrequent.

She opened her eyes. He knelt over her, a knee on each side of her waist, watching her as if he wanted to know everything that went on in her head. "What?"

"You're a fascinating puzzle." He lowered her shirt.

"No, I'm not," she snapped back with telling speed. "I'm plain Ann Smith."

"No hidden depths? No skeletons in your cupboard?"

"No." She spread her arms wide. "What you see is what you get."

But he didn't look at the body she offered as distraction. His gaze never left her face.

She worked for the man, had for four years, and she'd learned to read his moods. She prided herself on knowing what he thought.

But right now, she couldn't read his expression. His eyes were shadowed; his face was enigmatic. She knew his deepest secret.

So how was it possible he had become a mystery to her?

CHAPTER 18

With elaborate casualness, Ann stretched a hand toward her coffee cup. "Where did my cookie go?"

Jasha pulled it from beneath his knee and handed it to her. "Hiding, Ann?"

She looked at the slightly mashed breakfast cookie. "It was?"

"No. You are." He was still kneeling over her, still too close, still knowing too much and revealing too little.

"From what?" She looked into his face, but she couldn't sustain the full-frontal contact for long. "Besides the Varinski."

"I don't know. But I can't wait to find out." Jasha rose and walked back to his packing.

She sat up. Her coffee was cold. *She* was cold, and more scared than she'd been when she'd seen him become a wolf, more scared than she'd been when she'd removed the arrow. She'd never thought Jasha would want to talk to her, find out about her background . . . but then, she'd never thought he would want her to meet his family. In fact, she'd been a little vague about what would happen after she seduced him. She'd had this idea that they would have an affair, a lot of good sex, really, really good sex, a lot and often sex, and then . . . and then what? She'd go back to work for him, see him every day, buy his girlfriends flowers, purchase his next fiancée's ring?

Ann shot him a glare. Not in this lifetime.

Or maybe he'd fall madly in love with her, he'd want to marry her, and they'd live this ideal, problem-free life together forever, just the two of them? *Jasha?* The man who called or e-mailed someone in his family every day?

Ann hadn't really thought this through. One of the things that had seduced her was his dedication to his father and mother, his brothers and sister. He seemed the kind of man who could have been Beaver Cleaver's father: proud, thoughtful, a good disciplinarian.

Of course a man like that would think her background was important. She had to give him something, and really, what was wrong with telling him the truth?

Or at least . . . some of it.

She rummaged in the bottom of the sleeping bag until she found her clothes. Then ever so casually and quickly, as she dressed, she said, "I'm an orphan."

He didn't react. Didn't clutch his chest and edge away as if her bad luck were contagious.

"I don't have any family." As she buttoned her shirt, she shivered from the cold.

He didn't glance up from his work. "Really? No family at all?" She could tell he was listening, and listening intently.

"No family at all. I grew up in an orphanage in Los Angeles."

"How did you get there?"

"The nuns took me in." Had he noticed she dodged that question? She'd had a lot of experience.

"You were raised in a convent?"

"Not in a convent!" Her laugh was carefully lighthearted. "It was a Catholic orphanage attached to a convent."

"That explains a lot."

What did he mean by that? Did he know how many hours she'd spent looking in on the nuns, sharing their life, learning their rhythms? Yet despite her desire to be part of a family, any family, she'd always known she wasn't welcome in the convent?

And after Sister Catherine . . . after that,

she was welcome nowhere.

But she could pretend, so she babbled on. "Usually babies get adopted or at least put in foster care, but I was premature, in the hospital for four and a half months. The doctors didn't give me good odds, but I survived, and I finally got out of the incubator and into the orphanage. Sister Mary Magdalene said I was the ugliest baby she'd ever seen."

His eyebrows rose steeply. "That's harsh."

"Sister Mary Magdalene prided herself on not mincing words." An understatement. "But I've seen the pictures. I was this long, scrawny, hairless thing. The doctors already knew my eyesight was bad, and they were afraid there would be a lot of future problems, so no one wanted to take me on." She touched the mark on her lower back, then lay back in the bag to pull on her pants. "An orphanage isn't the best place to grow up, I guess, but we were in a bad part of LA, and an orphanage isn't the worst place, either. I should have been grateful —"

He straightened up and looked at her, amazed.

"I *was* grateful," she said swiftly.

"Really? Who told you that?"

"Sister Mary Magdalene."

"Do me a favor. Don't ever be grateful to

me for anything."

She liked the way he said it, wryly and as if things had returned to normal. Glancing around at the wilderness, she said, "Right now, I can't think of anything I should be grateful to you for."

"The coffee."

"Self-preservation on your part." She sat on the bag and pulled on her socks and tied her shoes. "You knew I'd kill without caffeine."

"Yeah, I'm not the only one who grows teeth and claws. We just do it for different reasons."

He was teasing her . . . until he wanted more details.

But now he knew the almost-biggest shocker, and she could filter the rest through a screen of droll laughter. His wolf senses couldn't smell a half-truth . . . could they?

"Where did you go last night? You said something about a rat?" Completely dressed, she rolled up the sleeping bag.

He had draped a canvas over a hump in the ground, and he pulled it away in a flourish.

He'd created a little cage of twigs, anchored it to the ground, and inside —

She shrieked. "That's a *rat!*" She kept the icon in her pants pocket, and she grabbed it as if protecting the Virgin — or asking the Virgin to protect her.

The rat ran in circles, looking for a way out, digging at the ground, clawing at the wooden bars.

"You brought a *rat* here and it was right there the whole time we were sleeping? A nasty, horrible, bug-eyed, disgusting . . ." She couldn't speak for shuddering.

"Don't like rats, huh?" he said with dry understatement.

"Rodent. Filthy, awful . . ." She remembered them at the orphanage, breaking into the pantry, scurrying around the babies, menacing in their size and their malice. "I hate them."

"I brought it here for one reason." He reached into his pocket.

"You're not going to *kill* it, are you?" She clutched the sleeping bag to her chest like a baby's blankie.

"I thought you didn't like it."

"I don't kill everything I don't like. If I did, you'd be in deep trouble right now." She glared as malevolently as the rat.

"Watch." He pulled out the plastic Baggie containing the tracking device. Taking it out, he wrapped it in a piece of cookie and offered it to the rat on the tip of his finger.

"Be careful!" she squealed.

The rat sniffed, then scraped the proffered meal off his finger and swallowed it whole.

With a smile, Jasha pulled the twigs out of the ground and let the rat go. It ran in circles, then dashed into the underbrush.

Ann found herself on top of a tall boulder, screaming. She didn't remember how she'd got there.

Jasha stood below her, offering his hand to help her down. "I never imagined my calm, unflappable Miss Smith could be such a *girl.*"

"Is it gone?" She tucked her feet under her and refused to take his hand.

"Yes, and in case you missed the point, it's taken the tracking device with it in its belly. Rats have fast digestive systems, but he's not going to stop running for a while, and he's lame. There's a good chance an owl will pick him up, or a cougar, and he'll be in another belly and traveling farther than ever. . . ." Jasha must have seen her horror. "I didn't break his leg. It looks like he caught it on something . . . and why do you care? You don't like rats."

"I know, but I don't want anything to die."

"*Everything* dies. The point is to die in a state of grace." Jasha's lids drooped over his brooding eyes. "The Varinski believes the tracking device is in me, and he'll be after the rat, and not us. Come on. Take my hand. We've got to get going, and in the opposite direction of that rat."

She slid down the rock and into his arms. "So if he's lucky, he'll find a pile of rat poo, and if he's unlucky —"

"He'll find a cougar."

He held her for a minute and looked at her as if he wanted to probe the depths of her mind. "You seem so softhearted, and yet I think that beneath all the uncertainty, you hide a core of steel."

"Yes. But it's rusty steel."

He smiled, as she meant him to. "I don't think so. And I think, before this is over, we'll discover the truth."

The truth? She shivered.

What frightened her more? The thing that pursued them? Or the chance that Jasha would discover that his assistant hid a past and a secret that damned her as surely as any devil's pact?

And if he did find out, how could she explain something she didn't understand herself?

CHAPTER 19

Jasha was right. When Ann camped with him, it was fun.

By seven o'clock, they had reached the campsite, a small, protected grove of trees high in the mountains with a stream nearby where she could wash her face and hands. By nine, he had caught trout, cleaned them, and cooked them over a carefully built fire. By the time the northern sun was finally setting, they settled down with a feast of fresh fish, huckleberries, slightly stale sourdough bread (produced with a flourish from his backpack), and a really good bottle of Wilder Wines's 1997 Sangiovese sipped directly out of the bottle.

Food had never tasted so good, the flames warmed her hands and face while the air cooled her backside, and seeing Jasha across the fire from her gave her a thrill every time she looked up — and she looked up often.

A campout wasn't the way she'd imagined

their affair would progress, but it was pretty darned wonderful.

By the time the stars had started to dimple the night sky, Ann had laughed so much she thought she might be tipsy. That was the only reason she could imagine why she made the mistake of saying, "Tell me about this deal with the devil. Who was the idiot who thought *that* was a good idea?"

An owl hooted. The stream burbled. A tall spiral of smoke slithered up toward the dark heavens, and the trees whispered in the wind.

Yet Jasha didn't answer, and worry seeped into her mind and stained her carefree pleasure.

Had she offended him?

Today he'd been Jasha Wilder, kind, intelligent, thoughtful, needing help, consulting her . . . yet now the fire lent shadows to his face and flame to his eyes, and she remembered, really remembered, that he'd been the wolf that chased her through the woods, held her down, and forced pleasure on her.

He took a drink from the bottle, then wiped his mouth on the back of his hand. His voice, when he spoke, was slow and deep, reciting the story he seemed to drag from the depths of his mind. "The first Konstantine Varinski was a bad seed, a child given to cruelty, then a man who reveled in wickedness. People on the steppes said he was the devil, and that's saying something, because a thousand years ago, life in Russia was brutish and short, and only the strongest survived. After years of vicious behavior, his father threw him out and told him to make his own way in the world."

Ann slid off her log to get closer to the fire, and wrapped her arms around her knees. "Did he throw him into the snow?"

"I can only hope so." Jasha passed her the bottle.

She took a drink, then passed it back. "He was a psychotic? Maybe a serial killer?"

"If you want to put a nice face on it. To me, he sounds like a sadistic son of a bitch. For years, he wandered the steppes, fighting and raping and pillaging, and everywhere he went, the rumor that he was the devil continued to grow." Jasha threw two logs onto the fire, and a shower of sparks rose toward the stars. "Finally the devil himself took note."

A shudder worked itself up her spine.

"Legend has it that the Evil One came to destroy the impostor. But Konstantine knew what he wanted. He offered to do the devil's work for him, and after some negotiation, the devil agreed. To seal the deal, he demanded that Konstantine destroy the Varinski family icon." Jasha stared into the heart of the blaze. "I told you about Russians and our icons, and how an icon of the Madonna is considered a miracle."

Jasha was an American. He'd been raised here. He said his family had no ties to the Old Country. Yet he'd said *our icons.* "Yes. You told me."

"The Varinski icon was not one painting of the Virgin, but four, each portraying a different stage of her life."

"Not one miracle, but four." Ann touched her pants pocket where the icon of the Virgin Mary and her family resided, warm and heavy.

"Exactly. So Konstantine went back to his parents' house to steal the icons. His father was dead. His mother lived alone, and she was a stern old woman. She wouldn't give up the icons to Konstantine, to the man who committed such atrocities. She ran to the church, the icons clutched to her breast. He stalked her like a beast, trapped her in the church . . . and killed her."

Ann had known what the end must be, but still she hunched a little tighter. "He murdered his own mother." She had never had a mother. She'd wanted a mother, she'd dreamed of one, every night she'd wished for one on the evening star — and Konstantine had slaughtered his.

"That is one of the greatest sins. Konstantine knew it."

"He didn't care." Cold air tickled the back of Ann's neck, and she pulled her collar close around her ears.

"More than that, he reveled in the act. His mother's blood would seal the pact with the devil." The flames reflected a red glow on Jasha's skin, and his eyes . . . his eyes looked like a wolf's. "Then he set the church on fire."

"But . . ." In a sudden hurry, Ann unbuttoned her pocket and pulled the icon free. She looked at the cherry red robe of the Madonna, at her serene eyes, at the family that surrounded her.

"Only one thing escaped the fire."

Ann knew. Of course she knew. "The icons. The miracles."

He inclined his head. "Konstantine found them in the smoldering ruins, the four still joined, the colors pristine, the Madonnas serene, the wood and paint hardened by the flames into an unbreakable substance."

Goose bumps rose on her skin.

"But the devil wouldn't be thwarted. If he couldn't destroy the icon, he could diminish it. So while Konstantine drank to celebrate the deal, in a flash of fire the devil divided the Madonnas and hurled them to the four corners of the earth, never to be seen again."

"Is that true?" Turning the icon over, she looked at the back, at the burned, broken edge. The devil's work?

It couldn't be true. Yet Jasha sat before her, his eyes glowing with a rim of red.

"I don't know. That's the story my father told us." Jasha shot her a rueful, very human grin, and took a drink from the bottle of wine. "Adrik always said it sounded like something the Brothers Grimm would come up with while they were smoking mushrooms in the Black Forest."

She laughed, a nervous outburst of laughter that sounded too loud in the ponderous silence of the woods. Quickly, she smothered the sound with her hand.

Up here, it was far too easy to believe that just beyond the reach of the fire, demons watched and danced.

"But the Brothers Grimm never looked far enough into the wild and wonderful. Because I *can* be a wolf, and my brothers can be a hawk and a panther, and my father is a wolf, I guess, although I've never seen him turn." Jasha looked at the bottle as if he didn't remember that he held it. "I guess

I never will now." His grief was visible in the droop of his mouth, his hunched shoulders, his sad eyes.

She wanted to go around the dying fire and hug him, but she'd never learned how to offer that kind of easy affection without having it mean too much to her, and when she got intense, other people tended to get uncomfortable.

"Konstantine Varinski founded a dynasty of men — Varinskis breed only sons — who turn into animals of prey who hunt humans, and laugh as they kill." Jasha almost sounded as if he were talking to himself. "They're demons who can't be killed except by another demon, and each man remains hale and hearty into old age. If they're hurt, they heal quickly."

Ann flexed her hand. Today, impatient with the bandage, she'd removed it, and found the wound almost healed. Healed, except that deep inside her palm, she felt a heat that rippled outward, up her arm, toward her heart.

The Varinski blood was in her.

Jasha continued. "For centuries, the Varinskis have been rich, respected for their cruelty, and feared, first in Russia, then in Europe and Asia, and with the twenty-first century, their influence has spread across the globe. How my family has remained hidden so long, I do not know."

Ann examined the story Jasha had told, and picked at the loose thread. "I don't understand. You said Varinskis breed only sons. But you have a sister."

His gaze flashed to hers. "And I have something else no other Varinski has — a mother." Lifting the wine, he saluted Ann with it, then offered the bottle to her.

She took it. The fire could no longer beat back the night. Perhaps the wine would do the job. "Are Varinskis born out of the mud?" She wouldn't doubt anything now.

"The women wish they were. Varinskis take the women they want — noblewomen, gifted women, artists, and courtesans — get them pregnant, and when the women deliver, they bring the child to the Varinski compound, put it on the turnstile, ring the bell, and run away."

"The women abandon their children?" Ann put the bottle aside, her lovely intoxicated glow completely evaporated.

"What is a woman going to do with a child who turns into a beast when he goes through puberty? Why would a woman keep the child of a man — or men — who cruelly raped her?" When Ann would have argued, Jasha emphatically shook his head. "What

237

woman wants to face the violence of an adult Varinski who discovers she's hidden his son from him? No, the women *have* to get rid of the children."

"That's unspeakable."

"Wherever they go, the Varinskis leave a trail of blood, fire, and death."

"And they're hunting us," Ann whispered. For her, raised in sunny California, where the worst thing that could happen was a bad boob job, the whole story was absurd.

"Only one of them. He may have experience, but this is my territory, and I have the most to lose." Jasha smiled, a cruel flash of teeth, and while he gazed at her, that sensation of being stalked returned in force.

A wolf. She was in the forest with a wolf.

"I am honored to be the first to face the test," he said, "and I will not fail."

"What test?"

Her quavering voice seem to wake him to the night. He glanced around, stood, and stretched. "That's a story for another campfire. It's late now." He smiled whimsically and began to undress. "Want to hit the sack?"

But it was too late for whimsy and seduction. She huddled close to the ground. "No, I'm going to sit here all night with my eyes wide open."

He stripped off everything. Everything. Then casually, as if she wouldn't notice his nudity, he offered her his hand. "The original Konstantine lived a long time ago, and his evil has been in the world since long before your birth."

"But I never knew about it before." She had known only her own horrors, and she'd been careful to keep them at bay.

"You couldn't do anything about it before. Now you can." Reaching down, he forcibly pulled her to her feet and into his arms. "Come on. We'll sleep together. I'll keep you safe."

But he was a Varinski. Who was going to keep her safe from him?

CHAPTER 20

Abruptly, Ann woke from a light doze, tense and straining to hear . . . something.

What?

Jasha held her in his arms, his long, bare body pressed against hers, and any other night that would have been a seduction. But tonight, although they were so close, she was so alone. Alone with her fears and the inescapable knowledge that what she had done could never be undone.

Alone in the woods where nothing — not a single creature — moved.

The hair stood on the back of her neck.

Something was out there.

Jasha put his hand over her mouth to signal the need for quiet. When she nodded, he slipped from the bag.

As he did, she took a long, slow breath, taking in the scents of the night. She could smell the rich odors of humus and pine, but beyond that, it almost seemed as if she sensed a wildness. . . .

And just beyond the ring of trees, a wolf lifted its voice to the stars.

In the light of the crescent moon, she could barely see Jasha — but she knew he smiled.

"Leader," he breathed, and vanished into the night.

Another wolf joined the first, and another, until Ann knew she was surrounded.

A single knife strapped to her leg seemed like a small defense if they decided to take Jasha out.

But his beloved wolves wouldn't do that. Would they?

Her eyes pricked with tears. She sat up, wrapped her arms around her legs, and propped her chin on her knees. She was such a coward, but his story tonight haunted her. He was right; she knew he was. The Varinskis and their evil had been in the world since long before her birth. Yet ignorance was bliss, and not knowing exactly what hunted her had saved her immeasurable anguish.

Or maybe what had saved her anguish was loving Jasha from afar.

Because sleeping in his arms, moaning with the rapture he induced, running with him, knowing his secrets — those things made her frightened for him.

She heard her name, whispered in Jasha's husky voice, a second before he appeared.

He was human. He was naked. He slipped in beside her, wrapped his arms around her, and slid with her down into the bag. "They ran hard to catch us. He's worried. I think he senses a disturbance in the earth."

"What does that mean? A disturbance in the earth?"

"I don't know." Jasha shifted his cold feet to cover hers, to siphon the warmth from her as if they'd been married for years. "I just know — Leader thinks we brought the trouble. He wants to make sure we leave."

"He's a real wolf — and you can speak to him?" His skin was chilly, and she suffered as he turned her to snuggle against him spoon-fashion.

"No. Not . . . no." He spoke softly against her ear, and his breath ruffled her hair. "But I sense his thoughts, or perhaps his feelings, by the way he looks at me, the way he reacts to me. I think he understands me the same way. Do you know what I mean?"

"I guess." She thought of her old tomcat, the way he made his demands known with his loud yowls and the way he slept on her head when he was cold. But for all the long evenings she and Kresley had spent together, their communication never managed to express anything as complex as *a disturbance in the earth.*

Jasha yawned and relaxed, every muscle lax. "I feel safer with the pack watching our backs. If it was just me, I wouldn't worry, but protecting you, the chosen one, makes this more than a game. This is war, and I've got to win." He hugged her to him.

She listened to his breathing as he slid into sleep.

He'd expressed her thoughts exactly. She was no longer responsible for herself. She held the safety of him and his family in her hands, and the Virgin Mary held her responsible.

Ann had wanted to love wholeheartedly. She just hadn't realized the price love would demand.

Jasha knew he'd screwed up last night. He'd carefully planned Ann's seduction. He'd gathered good food and wine, led her to the most romantic spot in the whole world, and zipped their sleeping bags together.

Then what had he done?

He'd scared Ann half to death with stories better told in broad daylight.

Then the wolf pack had come, and that frightened her, too.

So much for that bullshit that girls would cling when they were frightened. Ann didn't cling. She shivered. And when the sun rose, her eyes were wide open. He wasn't sure she'd slept at all.

So today he would regroup, make her feel comfortable again — or as comfortable as a woman who was raised in a Catholic orphanage could be when she traveled with a demon.

He gave her breakfast, another cookie, chocolate chunk this time, and sat down close to her — but not too close. In a deliberately casual voice, he chatted about stuff his mother and sister thought was important. "See the little red flowers right there? The ones in the shape of a heart. That's bleeding heart. Easy to remember, huh?"

"They're very pretty." Ann nibbled on the cookie and smiled at the flower, but her eyes looked worried.

"The ferns are sword ferns, and they're all over western Washington."

"They're in California, too, but there are really a lot of them up here." Her voice sounded calm, level . . . tense and frightened.

"The little birds you see fluttering around are finches. Can you hear the woodpecker?"

"There sounds like more than one." Her gaze shifted between her and Jasha, measuring the distance.

"He's just a busy guy." Ann had always had that wide-eyed gaze of an onlooker. In conflicts, she was quick to step back out, afraid to be caught in the cross fire, fearful of true emotion. She contained her anger, her tears, her joys, in the slender bottle with too tight a cork. Right now, Jasha held that bottle in his fist. He could shake it up, or try to pry the cork loose, but such rough measures might break her. So he tamed his impatience, his need, and said, "Ann, there's no sense in being afraid of me."

She drew a quick alarmed breath. "I'm not!"

"Yes, you are. But I don't quite understand" — he took a breath — "why now?"

"You're a Varinski." She looked at him with the same kind of horror any woman would feel for one of his cousins. "Last night you explained what that really means."

Years ago, Jasha had learned to discipline himself, to change only when it was safe, when he was alone, and only when he desperately needed to throw off the shackles of civilization and run like a beast. But Ann, with her wide eyes and sensual mouth and long, long legs, strained his control almost to the limit.

She was his.

He wanted to take her, prove to her she was his mate, make her understand in the most primitive way possible that she could depend on him for food and water, for safety . . . for passion.

Instead, she shrank from him.

When he'd chased her down, she had been a virgin. He'd hurt her — it had been unavoidable, but he had. He'd also given her pleasure. A lot of pleasure, over and over.

She was skittish still. He would gain nothing by forcing the matter.

Yet he wanted her with a dark torment that tore at his soul and made him wonder if she was right, if the Varinski genes had only been waiting to use the right temptation to take his soul and plunge him into the pit of fire and brimstone . . . and savage pleasure.

"Do you want to know what it really means to be a Varinski?" He scooted over to sit on the log next to her. She leaned away, but he pretended not to notice, and looked earnestly into her eyes. "I told you about the legend. I told you about their reputation. I didn't tell you that when my brothers and I were teens, we sneaked off to the library and searched the Web for the Varin-ski name."

"The Varinskis are on the Internet?" Interest woke in her eyes, chasing some of the shadows away.

"You'd be stunned to see the amount of information about the family. They don't have their own Web site — or they didn't — but like almost everything else on the Net, the info's wrong. Half the stuff said the Varinskis were vampires and the other half said they were werewolves. And supposedly the family is fabulously wealthy, but there were photos of the Varinski 'mansion,' and it was this huge, dark, ramshackle place surrounded by rusty cars." Jasha shook his head when he remembered. "Adrik was always the smart-mouthed one in the family, and as soon as he saw that place, he said, 'You know you're a Russian redneck when you prop up your mobile home with the complete works of Dostoyevsky.' "

"That's terrible!" But she giggled.

A good start. "Then we all joined in. 'You know you're a Russian redneck when you and your cousin Boris Bob can play a wicked "Dueling Balalaikas." ' 'You know you're a Russian redneck when your best coon dog is named Lyudmila.' "

Ann laughed harder and harder.

"After 'You know you're a Russian red-neck when your 'sixty-nine Dodge Charger is painted just like the one on *The Dukes of Kiev*,' the librarian had to throw us out. Again." Sadly, the whole story was true. "And when we got home, we were in trouble. Again." Also true.

Still Ann laughed . . . until a sob interrupted her bursts of merriment. Then another, then another, until she was really crying.

Damn. This wasn't the response he'd been looking for. On the other hand, it was an opportunity. Putting his arm around her, he pulled her close.

She didn't fight, but she didn't cuddle, either.

"What's wrong?"

"I d-don't know." Sobs punctuated her words. "It's just so weird to l-laugh out here, about a story that seems so n-normal, set in a world it seems I never kn-knew." She took a long, quavering breath. "I can't believe someone evil is chasing us. I can't believe the icon came to m-me. I can't believe you talk t-to wolves. I can't believe we could end up d-dead."

"If I have to die, I would rather die with you than with any other woman in the world." He kissed her, a brief kiss on her quivering mouth, then a series of kisses across her wet cheeks.

"I need to blow my nose."

He was ready to seduce her with his best moves — and she needed to blow her nose.

All right. It was daylight; she needed more coffee, more food, and probably some space between her and the place where she'd heard the Varinski legend. He could wait.

Not forever, but he could wait.

He handed her his handkerchief, and she looked at it, then looked at him.

He comprehended her thoughts all too well. She was so private, so unused to sharing her thoughts, her dreams, even her past, she couldn't blow her nose in front of him. Hell, she worried when she showed unchecked emotion.

Yet when she laughed too loud, when she cried too hard, when she gave in to passion, then he caught a glimpse of the Ann she could be, and he wanted her all the more. So he wandered off to finish cleaning up the campground before she caught a glimpse of the wolf that peeked out of his eyes.

She disappeared into the woods, walking toward the stream.

He allowed her privacy, but he listened, too. He wouldn't let her blunder off. His trick with the rat would divert the Varinski only so long, and this morning, when he woke, a sense of urgency woke with him.

Something was watching them.

At first, he thought it was the wolf pack.

But with the coming of daylight, they'd slipped away to sleep in the shade.

No, this was less than knowledge, more than instinct. Something in his gut knew they had at most two more days before the battle.

He intended to keep Ann safe.

The news that she had no parents had taken him by surprise. And yet why? He should have expected it. In a conflict like this, with evil on one side and good on the other, and human warriors marching into battle, of course the shield bearer would be an orphan. Of course he had to try to pierce the shadows of her background and decide — in the end, would she stand by his side? Would she run? Or would she turn traitor?

When she came back, her face and hair were damp and her courage seemed re-stored. "Jasha, what did you do after you saw the Varinski mansion? Did you talk to your father?"

"Not exactly." He finished the packing. "Rurik, Adrik, and I felt as if he'd exagger-ated the Varinskis' importance. We knew the legend was real — we did, after all, turn into animals — but we thought the richest crime family in the world could at least afford a decorator."

"But they're all men. No one cares about their house." She whispered, "Their image is a spatter of blood and the stench of arson."

Jasha jerked his head around in surprise. "That's very wise."

"Whenever I slept last night, and there wasn't much of that, I dreamed about them." She picked up her backpack. "Personally, I'm surprised the Varinskis didn't track you to Blythe from that Internet contact."

"It was early days for the Net." He didn't like that the Varinskis had invaded her dreams. Was she like his mother? No. Ann's subconscious had logically connected the dots. She might have sprung from mysterious circumstances, but everything about her shouted, *Normal!*

Yet after a thousand years, the Madonna had allowed Ann to find her.

What secrets did Ann so thoroughly and prudently conceal?

CHAPTER 21

When Ann and Jasha stopped for lunch in the shadow of a giant yellow cedar, she had questions, and she would not hesitate to ask them. She wanted no more scary stories around the campfire.

She took the piece of leftover sourdough bread and the salami he passed her, and simply held them while he ate.

"If there are no mothers, who raises the Varinski sons?"

Jasha chewed and swallowed. She observed him as he considered her and her question, and knew that he was weighing all the factors — the time it would take him to explain, the distance they had yet to travel, the fact that he'd begun his family's tale and not yet finished it — and she saw him make the decision to satisfy her curiosity. Crossing his ankles, he leaned back against a tree. "The Varinskis keep old women to cook and take care of the babies, but basically, the boys are raised like puppies, tumbling over each other, trying out their teeth. They train, they hunt, they fight each other and the world, and the dominant son takes the name of Konstantine."

"Your father . . ."

"My father is Konstantine." Jasha took another bite.

"On the phone, he's so nice." Ann recalled the booming, accented voice, the hearty pleasure he took in their conversations, the constant, generous offers of his son's hand in marriage. "He makes me laugh. And you're saying he was the leader of that family? That he killed people? He raped women?"

"He isn't proud of what he did, but there's nothing he can do to change the past." Jasha rubbed one hand over his stubbled cheek. "He knows that. He knows the price he'll pay if he dies before he redeems himself."

Ann stared forbiddingly at Jasha. "You told me he adores your mother!"

Jasha dropped his bomb. "He stole her from her tribe, and they've been on the run ever since."

Ann felt her jaw drop, and she crisply snapped it shut. "Your father *stole* your mother?"

"She was sixteen."

"Sixteen! How old was he?"

"There are no documents that prove his date of birth, but we think around thirty-three."

Just when Ann thought the story couldn't get any worse, it did. "The poor girl!"

"Get to know my mother before you say, 'Poor girl.' The poor girl came as close to killing him as it is possible for a mere human to do. And by the way, my mother is five foot one and a hundred pounds soaking wet, and my father's a mountain." Jasha grinned. "She brought him to his knees."

"Really?" Ann grinned back and relaxed. "How lovely."

"She'll talk about it sometimes, tell how he demanded she cook dinner, so she threw a pot of boiling water in his face. When he roared and grabbed her, she stabbed him with her sewing needles. When she tells that story, Papa turns red and mumbles for Firebird to listen to her mother."

"How did they get from bodily injury to falling in love? I mean . . . I assume they're in love?"

"Stupid in love. She . . . I always thought she adored him." He looked at the bread as if he didn't know what it was. "But for sure, he looks at her as if a star has fallen from the heavens and landed in his pocket."

Ann caught her breath. She wanted Jasha to look at her that way.

But instead of a star, he looked at her and saw a woman. A woman he wanted, a woman he meant to have. When they walked, when they spoke, when she slept, when she was awake, always she felt the weight of his intention and his need.

She'd allowed herself to be lulled away from the first shock of knowing he was a wolf. She'd wavered between disbelief and acceptance, but some irrepressible curiosity — or was it a sense of self-preservation? — had urged her to ask about the deal with the devil.

What a fool she'd been. Jasha was a demon from a long line of demons. When she was with him, she knew he would keep her fed and safe from harm.

At the same time, she'd worked for him for four years. She'd studied him with the intensity of a dedicated student. Perhaps she couldn't smell his moods, but she knew them.

He loved the hunt. He loved the running, the forest, the deep dark nights and the brilliant days. Luring the Varinski into a trap was what he was born to do.

And he stalked her with equal skill.

No matter how carefully he tried to hide

his intention, she must never forget what he wanted, and what he intended.

"My parents don't exactly give us the details about the part between the throwing of the water and the falling in love. I think there was quite a series of tumultuous fights that ended in bed." He watched her now, gauging her reaction. "The next thing they knew, they sneaked off to get married."

"And the Varinskis were perturbed," she said with deliberate understatement.

"So were the Romanies. My mother was beloved of her tribe, a beautiful, happy girl with special gifts."

"What kind of special gifts?" Ann asked suspiciously. "Because I'll bet you're not talking about the kind you can wrap in paper and tie with a bow."

"Not exactly. Mama makes plants grow."

"She talks to them." Ann nodded.

"You wish that was true." He watched her as if he understood exactly how *much* she wished that was true. "She works the weather around her."

"She works the weather? As in . . . she controls it?"

"Let's just say, our mountain has a very wholesome microclimate, perfect for growing grapes."

Someone had to be logical. "That's not to

say your mother directs it."

His white teeth bit into the meat. "When Papa and Mama bought the high valley, the winters were too harsh and long to grow much of anything. All the farmers on the lower slopes predicted the weird foreigners would starve or freeze before the first winter was over, but that winter was unusually mild. In the spring, my parents planted vines and a garden." Jasha finished eating and folded his hands across his flat belly. "Everyone in the area grows grapes now, but my parents are the most successful, and the other growers consider my mother a good-luck charm."

Ann tried to remember when pronounce-ments like this had begun to be com-monplace.

"She also has the Sight," Jasha said.

Which made weather working sound posi-tively benign. "The Sight? As in, she has vi-sions?"

"I didn't know that until very recently." His expression became severe. "Very re-cently."

"What did she see?" Whatever it was, he didn't like it.

He looked around at the trees, the stones, the clear blue sky, and shook his head. "That's not a story for out here. Not even in the daylight."

"All right. When is it a story for?" Tearing up the bread, she popped a chunk in her mouth and challenged him with a lift of her chin.

"When we're safe inside with warriors all around."

"And when do you project that will be?"

"When we are at my parents' house. In no more than a week, Ann. Give me patience for no more than seven days, and I swear, your questions will all be answered."

She liked the way he appealed to her, as if she had the right to reject his terms.

But she was a fool in love. She would always do what he wanted. "So your parents ran off and got married, and both families ran after them to break it up."

"You must understand, for my mother's people, who are wanderers and who make their living as peddlers and farmworkers, to have someone who can see the future, who can control the weather — that's invaluable."

"It's *Romeo and Juliet* as written by Stephen King."

He leaned back and looked her over. Then looked her over again, his gaze lingering on the curve of her mouth until she, self-conscious, bit her lower lip. "You have a way of seeing right to the heart of the matter and summing it up in a few words. I've always admired that about you."

"It's my job."

"No, it's your genius."

He had tossed her compliments before, but he'd never really looked at her before. Now he saw her, his gaze so warm, appreciative . . . lustful.

After all that had happened, how could she still love him so much?

In a steady voice, she asked, "What happened next?"

"Everybody — the Varinskis, the Romanies — was in a rage. Unfortunately, the Varinskis' idea was to kill my mother and drag my father back home and beat him until he renounced his madness. Papa's brother Oleg was number two in the pecking order. He was the leader of the expedition — and my father killed him."

"He killed his brother. Like the first Konstantine killed his mother."

"Yeah, the Varinskis are all into keeping that assassination thing in the family."

With every word, with every step, Ann moved further into a world of death and blood, of magic and wonder. She'd fought so hard . . . but always she'd feared that this was her destiny.

"So Oleg's sons vowed to exterminate my father and all of his line. My parents fled to the United States, changed their last name to Wilder, and disappeared into the mountains in Washington." Jasha waved his hand around. "Which gets us to our current situation."

"Not . . . quite."

"Do you know, I used to admire your ability to see the details? Now —"

"Now?" She lifted her eyebrows.

"Now I admire you more."

Smart man. "What did the Romanies do to your parents?" She nibbled the salami and wished for a carrot stick.

"The old woman of the tribe cursed my father."

"With what?"

"His conscience."

"That's brilliant." Ann thought about the ramifications. "That's diabolical."

"He never says anything, but no matter what hour I come home, he's always awake."

"He's afraid to sleep." She knew. "His dreams are like memories, and they haunt him."

"Yes, but why do you say that?" Jasha sounded as if he was accusing her of something.

"I'm a woman. I'm perceptive about stuff

like that." She smiled easily.

"Hm." Again, as he watched her, she caught a glimpse of the wolf within him.

Weren't men supposed to be insensitive? Why wasn't he? Did he smell the truth about her?

Had he seen the ghost of Sister Catherine?

Had he seen the mark on her back?

She reviewed the past few days. When would he have? Not in the woods that first time — they'd been covered with mud. Not in the tub — she'd been very careful. Not when she'd dressed for this trip . . . no. She had to stop worrying about the mark. For all Sister Mary Magdalene's dire warnings, Ann was no different from any other woman.

"What about your sister?" she asked. "How is it possible for a Varinski to produce a girl?"

Jasha smiled, and all sign of the wolf disappeared and slid into a fond expression. "Firebird is our miracle. Mama had the three of us boys, one year after another. Then nothing for ten years — and she delivered Firebird at home in the middle of a storm, the first Varinski girl in a thousand years. We named her Firebird, the symbol of rebirth in Russia."

"That's beautiful!"

"My father hoped it meant the devil's pact has been broken, but that same week . . . I turned into a wolf."

If she hadn't been watching him, she wouldn't have noticed his hungry glance and the slight narrowing of his pupils.

She was sharing a meal with this man, and suddenly, she felt a lot more respect for Little Red Riding Hood.

"I'm done!" She scrambled to her feet.

"You didn't eat." His voice had that deep, resonant tone that made her nervous.

"I was too fascinated by the story," she said brightly. "Let me just wash up and we'll be on our way." She went to the stream. Here the sunshine splashed through the trees, turning the water a dazzling blue. Some long-distant storm had sent a huge tree crashing to earth, and the trunk rested on the rocks on either bank, providing a home for the squirrels and a footbridge for Ann . . . if she chose to cross it.

Rolling up her sleeves, she dipped her hands into the brook. It rippled and sang, never hinting at its icy nature. Perhaps she should take a clue from its deception, and run across that bridge and never look back. . . .

A warning sizzled along her nerves. *Something* was behind her. In a flurry, she leaped to her feet and turned, fists up, ready to fight.

Jasha. It was Jasha. He stood directly behind her, watching with brooding need and very little patience.

Stepping backward, she almost overbalanced into the water.

He caught her and held her a moment too long, a quick, intense reminder of desire.

Her pulse leaped. Her breath caught. She didn't know if he was going to let her go.

She didn't know if she wanted him to.

Then he did.

She blotted her sweaty palms on her pants and pretended not to notice the flare of animal heat from his body. "I would give anything for a bath."

He slowly nodded. "I'll remember you said that."

"In the meantime, I need to finish cleaning up." Calm down. Cool down. Prepare to walk all afternoon beside a man who wanted her . . . and intended to have her.

Why did that make her so nervous? The first time, he hadn't been cruel.

But he hadn't been denied, either. Last night she had held him off, because as he'd explained exactly how ancient and immense was the legend that held them in thrall, each word had been like the rattle of pebbles on her coffin. She was being buried alive by the weight of history and expectation.

"Are we going to live through this?" Her voice quavered with trepidation.

"I promise. I will die before you."

That didn't answer the question, and his narrow-eyed gaze and soft tone did not comfort her.

"Let me finish here." She gestured at the stream. "I'll only be a minute."

He backed away so reluctantly she could almost feel the tendril of his desire slip away. His gaze clung to hers, dragging at her —

From overhead, she heard a shriek of fury. She glanced up, saw a blur of black feathers and two cruel, black eyes diving at her. From the side, Jasha slammed into her. They rolled along the bank. She found herself flat on her face, her nose buried in the earth, with Jasha on top of her, while that banshee screamed behind her head.

"Don't move!" Then Jasha was gone, on his feet.

She rolled over in time to see a giant black bird plunging toward Jasha, long talons extended.

He slammed the raptor with his arm, but it dodged, flipped in the air, and swirled like a fighter pilot to attack him from behind.

Ann found herself on her feet, a fallen branch in her hands, swatting at the bird like a maddened pro-baseball batter. She actually made contact, slapping the bird away as it went for the back of Jasha's head. As Jasha turned and she followed through, the branch smacked the side of his head. He staggered back.

The raptor recovered first.

She saw beady black eyes fix on her. The great black wings spread wide. With malevolent intent, with talons outstretched, the bird dived for her.

She ducked, closed her eyes, raised her arms to protect her face — and heard a scream of fury. Something solid, warm, and strong brushed past her and sent her staggering.

She fell on her rear, and looked up in time to see a giant gray wolf seize the bird in his jaws.

Not Jasha. This wolf wasn't Jasha.

While the bird struggled, flapping its strong wings and ripping with its beak and talons, the wolf violently swung its head back and forth. Black feathers and drops of blood flew.

Before her horrified eyes, the bird changed, growing larger, bare-skinned . . . human.

The wolf lost his grip on the bird/man.

The creature's features weren't quite human — the eyes were still empty, black and shiny. Feathers shaped his neck, his mouth was a cruel beak, and he was huge — taller and more muscular than Jasha. Grabbing the wolf by the nape of the neck, he lifted him off the ground.

Frantically, the wolf snapped at the arms that held him.

The bird/human prepared to dash him on the rocks, and as he did, he smiled directly into her eyes.

She was next.

"Jasha!" she screamed.

Jasha rose up behind them. He caught the bird/human's head in either hand and, in one quick movement, snapped his neck.

Ann would never forget the sound of the bone and sinew cracking, of that life coming to an end.

But before she could get sick, the big, gray wolf sank to the ground, panting, exhausted, bleeding. "Oh, no." She hurried to his side. "Oh, no." She laid her hand on his heaving side.

"No!" Jasha yelled.

She looked up.

A furious brown wolf broke out of the trees and charged toward her.

Ann found herself flat on her back, nose to nose with the huge beast straddling her chest. The wolf snarled, its breath hot on her face, its orange eyes threatening. Even the wolf's scent exuded hostility.

Ann had been here before, but this time there was a difference — and she recognized what it was.

This was a female, the other wolf's mate. And Ann had pissed her off.

CHAPTER 22

Dimly Ann heard Jasha talking to her, telling her to be calm.

She heard the wounded wolf bark.

The female wolf on top of Ann paid no heed to either of the males. This was between her and Ann, the upstart bitch.

"I'm sorry I touched him," Ann whispered. "He's hurt, and I wanted to help."

The male nudged his mate with his head, and gave a whimper.

The female looked at him, at his wounds, and Ann saw her menacing gaze soften. She looked back at Ann, and snarled again. Then she leaped off and nuzzled the male affectionately.

"Stay down, and be quiet," Jasha said.

He didn't have to tell Ann twice.

The male allowed the female to sniff him and lick his wounds; then together they trotted off into the forest.

Jasha stood looking after them. "That was

Leader and his mate. She's upset because Leader was shot, and the run here, and now the bird. That's why she attacked."

Slowly Ann sat up. She was filthy, covered with dirt, scared to death — and like the alpha female, all she wanted was to know her mate was all right. "Are you hurt?" she asked.

Jasha showed her his forearms. Long, bloody slashes bit deeply into his flesh. "They'll heal." He offered his hand. "Are *you* hurt?"

"No." She was bruised and shaken, and a week ago she would have been complaining, but hard lessons had taught her what was worth worrying about.

"Good. Because we've got to move." Jasha scanned the skies. "This isn't the same Varinski who was with the hunter, which means I was wrong. There's one left to come after us. I can't afford to make those mistakes."

He blamed himself. Naturally, he did. This was Jasha, Mr. Responsibility.

Ann took his hands. "Let me wash your wounds." She wasn't so different from the female wolf, after all. She wanted nothing more than to comfort her mate.

"There's no time."

"Jasha, please."

He smiled at her, but his eyes were sober. "I'll heal." He knelt beside the Varinski's body. "I don't understand it. He's not completely human. What do you suppose that means?"

"I don't know." And she didn't care. "Maybe the pact is changing."

Jasha pinned her with a sharp glance. "Maybe it is." He ran his hand over his own face, as if checking his features for anomalies. "I'm going to hide the body. You pack up the camp. We're leaving in fifteen minutes."

"Come on in." Jasha swam into the middle of the pool, his long arms making no sound as they cut through the water.

Ann stood shivering on the stony edge, her arms wrapped around her naked chest. "It's dark."

"That's because it's night."

"Yeah, thanks."

"Come on in," he said again. "It's not cold."

"Liar!"

They'd climbed all afternoon and now they were high on the mountain. She'd never seen stars so huge or a sky so black — or a pool so still and deep and unfathomable. Stony cliffs surrounded it on three sides, one narrow waterfall plunged into the pool, and another plunged out, and she wavered between the embarrassment of posing nude — yes, it was dark, but he possessed that inconvenient wolf vision — and the assured agony of the icy water.

"It's refreshing!" he called.

She put her toe in, then pulled it out. *Oh, God. It's as awful as I feared.*

"You said you'd give anything for a bath," he reminded her. "I came here just for you."

"You knew all along we'd end here tonight." When they arrived, he had dug into a deep, protected crack of a giant boulder and pulled out food, towels, another sleeping bag, a small tent. . . . It was obvious he knew this place well.

"Jump!" he called.

Squeezing her eyes closed, she jumped.

Cold didn't begin to describe it. Frigid, perhaps. And glacial. She broke the surface and still couldn't get her breath to scream.

He caught her to him, laughing. "Swim. C'mon, I'll race you."

"I want out," she gasped.

"You have to swim to get out."

"You tricked me!"

He ran his hands over her. "Yeah, I wanted to see you naked."

So she broke away and swam. She swam

from one end of the pond to the other, back and forth twice.

The afternoon had been a horror of climbing, of cursing her oversized boots, and of being driven by a man obsessed with her safety. She hadn't had time to worry about the dead man or the wolf pack or the icon. She'd barely been able to catch her breath.

And just when she'd caught her breath, she'd plunged into this frigid water and lost it again.

As she started on her third lap across the pond, Jasha grabbed her. "That's enough." He pulled her to the edge and stood her on a rock. He picked up his soap, and began to wash her. "You swim pretty fast . . . for a girl."

When she was warm, if she ever got warm again, she'd be indignant. "I swam in high school. Won the California championship." She would never have thought she'd let a man wash her with his bare hands — shampoo her hair, wash her chest, lift her arms to wash her pits, and lather her breasts — and not feel a thing. But she *couldn't* feel a thing. Her nerves had frozen. Her teeth were chattering.

"Then you ought to be used to water." He turned her to wash her back.

"*Warm* water!" Which she longed for right now.

"I've been in the ocean in California. It's damned cold." He lifted her feet and scrubbed them, then turned her to face him again and started up her calves.

"Swimming pools." As his hand left a soapy trail along her thighs and into the folds between her legs, she discovered that parts of her weren't as cold as other parts. In fact, parts of her could warm up all the other parts with no problem whatsoever.

"Stop squirming. I'm just washing you." But his voice had that tone again, the one that made her heart beat faster.

"You are not just washing me. You're . . . being thorough."

"I want you as clean as can be."

He wanted her to be as aroused as she could be.

Before she could scoot away, he dropped the soap, picked her up, and carried her back until he stood thigh-deep in the water.

"Nooo," she moaned.

"You have to rinse." And he dropped her in.

She swam again, swam hard from one end of the pool to the other — and then, like a shark cutting through the water, he caught her.

He made no sound. She wasn't expecting him. Her startled gasp turned to something else — terror or excitement — when he turned her to face him, and she saw the red glow in his eyes. When he lifted her from the water and put his mouth on her hard nipple, it felt as if someone had lit a candle on her flesh. Every bit of her was frozen except there, and there he suckled . . . and it burned.

Oh, God. It burned, and she caught fire.

She wrapped her legs around him, seeking his heat.

For he was hot. He steamed in the night air. He was a furnace between her thighs and against her belly. He walked out of the pool holding her, still sucking, and knelt with her on the nest of towels.

Had he planned this, then?

He wrapped one towel around her hair, then used another to dry her. He rubbed her all over, and he rubbed her hard. The blood began to circulate to her skin, to her brain, and she knew a crystal-clear moment of fear.

He knew, for he said, "No," and put his mouth to her other breast.

Now she wasn't as cold, for his fire burned just as hot. Her back arched as she tried to throw him off, but he bit down and held her until she stilled. Then he suckled, pulling her nipple deep into his mouth, massaging it with his tongue, and the flood of heat rose in her. With his hand, he explored between her legs, and when he found her dampness, he said, "I knew it," and thrust his finger inside her. One finger, two.

He laughed. "I knew you were ready."

"Damn you!" How dare he laugh? She tried to shove him aside.

She might as well not have bothered.

He kissed her.

This kiss wasn't like the kisses they'd shared in his home, with four walls around them and a roof over their heads. This kiss reminded her that a secret part of him was wolf. This kiss tasted of the wilderness, of danger, of hot lust and cool promise. He took everything she would allow, then took more, his lips and tongue enticing her, and when she resisted, his teeth lightly nipped until she gave him what he wanted.

He had a message for her.

She had been a virgin.

He'd waited for her to heal.

He was done waiting.

He got up on his knees, pulled her to him, her feet off the ground, her legs spread wide.

She flailed, but that was worthless; he held her vulnerable to him. And he was done waiting for permission. Now he simply took. He seated himself, and pushed forward.

He'd had her before, and the circumstances were the same, and yet so different.

This time, she wasn't afraid; she was angry.

This time, he wasn't gentle; he was demanding.

She couldn't see him with her eyes; he was merely a dark outline against the starry sky.

But her body recognized him. The length, the breadth, the heat . . . he was the wolf. He was the man. He burned her inside as his hips drove him deeper and deeper. He touched her inner core, that place of secrets and sensation, and she cried out.

And the son of a bitch laughed again.

Briefly she surfaced to fight him, twisting and turning, but that only heightened the sensations — for him, too, for he groaned and thrust faster, harder, wordlessly demanding all the passion she so carefully controlled.

She couldn't deny him. She moaned now, over and over. Overhead the stars wheeled across the heavens. All around her, earth and wind stood still, waiting.

And climax blasted through her, imprinting her on eternity.

He came, too, spurting into her, filling

her, and desperation and need tinged his voice as he called, "Ann. My God, Ann."

Tears of pleasure seeped from the corners of her eyes, blurring his silhouette.

Gradually he lowered her to the ground and covered her with his body. He kissed her lips, her cheeks, her eyelids. He tilted her neck back and kissed her throat.

He seemed so desperate, it almost seemed he felt more than desire, more than affection.

Inside her, he was still hard, and he thrust again, making her shudder and whimper.

"Yes, Ann." His voice was as dark as the sky and as smooth as velvet. "Come again."

Another woman might think he needed her for more than sex.

Madness, Ann. Madness.

"You're going to get cold," she whispered.

"There's not much time," he answered.

That didn't make sense to her, but then — right now, nothing did. He'd stolen her senses and left her only love.

Slowly, he withdrew from her body.

She sighed as he slipped away, then whimpered when he took a damp towel and wiped her chest and her belly, and ever so gently and thoroughly cleaned between her legs.

She squirmed at his touch, then fought

back a scream when he slid down and used his tongue. Carefully he drew her clit into his mouth. He sucked, and in only a second she came again, and again, and before he was done she was exhausted and shaking.

He rose back over the top of her, and spoke in her ear. "I thought I could wait. I thought the water would be cold enough to tame me. But nothing can keep me away from you, off of you, out of you. You're mine, Ann. No matter what happens, never forget it." He stood. He looked down at her for a long moment, then turned away.

She heard the splash as he dived back in the water. Shivering more from his words and his tone than from the cold, she dressed quickly.

By the time he came out of the water, she waited with towels, and she handed them to him and turned away. She waited until she heard him toss the towels down before she spoke in a low voice. "Jasha, what are you planning?"

"I'm going to take you somewhere safe," he said, "and I'm going to go hunting Varinski."

CHAPTER 23

"Do you have to go now?" Ann asked. *So soon after,* she meant, *while the blood still runs hot in my veins and I want nothing more than for you to hold me.*

But she didn't dare say that.

"You know I do. This afternoon proved that to me. I never smelled the feathers until he was almost on top of us. I underestimated the whole damned family" — Jasha stroked his thumb across her cheek — "because I wanted time with you. I can't be so criminally stupid again. They're hot on our trail."

"How many more do you think there are?"

"I'm sure we've got a wolf after us. I think that's all." He ran his fingers through his hair. "I'm sure that's all."

"How can you be sure?"

"Ann, always take the time to listen to the earth, taste the scents on the wind, take note of your instincts. I didn't take the time, and Leader paid the price. Yet if you listen, the elements won't steer you wrong."

Ann faced Jasha. "My instincts are fine, and they don't want you to go."

He was unabashedly naked, and he enunciated each word, speaking slowly, as if he feared she wouldn't understand him unless he did. "I have to find him. I want to interrogate him, make sure he is the only one, and put him out of commission."

"You're going to kill him, too?" The frigid air was suddenly much colder.

"My darling, softhearted Ann, do you realize that hunter lies dead in the forest because he made the mistake of trusting the Varinski?"

"I know." When she was cold to the core, how could her palms grow sweaty? "But I don't want you to kill anyone. What would happen if someone finds out?" *Will you be like your father, unable to sleep without seeing the faces of the people you've murdered?*

"I plan to disable the Varinski, take him back to the scene of the crime, and sic the sheriff on him. They'll put him in prison, the Varinskis will break him out, and he'll go home a failure." Jasha stood so still, she saw only the glint of his eyes. "But if I have to — I won't hesitate to take him out."

She understood Jasha. More than that, she agreed. If it came to a choice between Jasha and the Varinski, she wanted Jasha alive at any cost.

Perhaps the blood he'd put into her veins changed her. Perhaps it was love, and lust, and mating, that brought forth the savage within. Or perhaps Sister Mary Magdalene was right, and the mark on her back meant she was fated to evil.

"What about the other? Will you take his body back, too?"

"No. He's not all human, and I can't allow him to be found. I left him where the scavengers can find him."

She swallowed. But this was war. "I guess you'd better take me to the place you want me to hide."

He stepped forward, caught her face between his hands, and kissed her, a kiss that branded her, proclaimed to her she was his. Then he gathered the clothes and towels and swiftly led her straight up the hill. He moved silently, a mere shadow before her, and she knew if she weren't here, he would be a wolf. As soon as he left her, he would turn.

Once he stopped her. "You're warm. Sit down."

She wasn't warm, not really, but she knew why he wanted her to cool off. He didn't want her to give off a scent.

She truly was starting to think like a Wilder.

As they climbed, the vegetation thinned until they reached the upper tree line. Here the bones of the mountains stuck through the soft earth and the ground was nothing but windswept basalt. He took her to a crack in the mountain almost deep enough for a cave.

"Listen carefully." He pulled a sleeping bag out of his backpack and unzipped it. "You need to stay under shelter. You'll be out of the wind, but more important, the Varinski becomes a bird. He has extraordinary eyesight. If he's a cat, he can hear everything and stalk like a shadow. But I think they sent a wolf. He'll catch your scent and after he's finished me off, he'll come for you."

"What do you mean, after he's finished you off?" She stood straight and stiff.

"There's always a chance I won't be the winner. He's not their best — they didn't send their best man after corrupt, weak, easy-to-fool me. But he is a Varinski, trained to kill, and he does it easily, without conscience." Jasha gestured her into the mummy bag and knelt to zip it up around her. "Would you rather your lover killed easily, or would you rather I doubted?"

"What a choice." She freed her arms from the bag's embrace, and slid her fingers through his damp hair. "Come back to me. Jasha, no matter what it takes, come back to me."

He kissed her greedily. In a rapid undertone, he said, "Keep still. Keep out of sight. Don't talk, don't snore, don't pray. Be part of the landscape, my darling, and I'll be back for you in the morning."

She watched as he loped down the mountain, and as he disappeared, she saw him crouch, hands and feet to the ground, and suddenly — he was a wolf.

Huddling down in the sleeping bag, she did exactly what he had told her not to — she held the icon pressed between her palms, and she prayed.

Prayed for the success and the soul of a demon.

She woke to hear laughter, if that discordant cackling could be called laughter. Even before she opened her eyes, she knew it wasn't Jasha.

And it wasn't.

But there was no doubt — it was his relative. Like a child out to spook his friends around a campfire, he held a flashlight under his chin.

He had Jasha's bone structure, and Jasha's golden eyes. He had scars, too — a scar across his eyelid, and one from his ear to the edge of his lips. It split his mouth, and his smile, into a lopsided monstrosity. In a heavily accented voice, he said, "Look at what I've found. Cousin Jasha's little toy."

The mummy bag kept her warm. It also kept her arms trapped by her side, and rendered her worthless in a fight.

But what was she going to do? Slap at his face? Call him a brute? She had no defense against him. No defense . . . except her wits.

So she gathered them, and slowly sat up. "Jasha said you were one of the best, and he was right."

"Not like that other fool, that singing bird, that deformed thing that's never human." With great thoroughness, the Varinski cleared his throat and spit on the ground. "He must have been easy to kill."

"Yes. He was nothing compared to you. You've tracked us, you fooled Jasha, and you found me."

She'd hit the right note, for the Varinski preened. "I volunteered for this mission, and before we left, my father took me aside and explained he had to send two hunters to keep old Yerik happy, but he trusted me to make the kill. Of all his sons, he trusted me the most."

"I'll bet he has a lot of sons, too," she said in a tone of admiration.

"My father has thirty-four sons." The Varinski struck his chest. "I have eight sons."

"Already? Surely you're not even twenty-five!"

"Twenty-nine, but I went out on my first woman raid when I was twelve." He squatted before her and showed her a grin that displayed rotting teeth, missing teeth, and a malicious, stupid pleasure in cruelty. "I should make a son on you."

She pulled the knife from her holster on her leg. "I would like that, but doesn't that leave your back vulnerable?"

The Varinski glanced behind him into the darkness. "You think your lover will come for you? No. He is down below, looking for me while I rape his woman." He placed the flashlight on the ground and reached for her.

And from above, Jasha leaped on him.

The Varinski's head slapped the rock hard enough to crack a normal man's skull, but this guy was a demon and a dumbshit, which must make him practically indestructible.

Ann struggled to get out of the sleeping bag, scrabbling for the zipper and, when she couldn't budge it, stabbing the bag with her knife. While she fought the ripstop nylon and mounds of fiber that insulated the bag, she could hear the smack of flesh against flesh, and hear the Varinski curse in snarling Russian. When she finally freed herself from the sleeping bag and stood on her feet, she grabbed the flashlight and shone it around in time to see Jasha bend the knife in the Varinski's hand back on him and say, "Tell me what you know."

The Varinski spit in Jasha's face.

Jasha grinned, and although he had all his teeth shining whitely, the effect was just as gruesome as the Varinski's evil smirk. "A boy's defiance. A piddly bit of fear in the face of death." He bent the knife back farther until the point touched the Varinski's windpipe. "Tell me what they told you."

The Varinski writhed on the ground. His gaze shot toward Ann.

"Don't look at her. She can't save you. She is mine. My mate. She cares only for me, and hopes I kill you. In fact" — Jasha stopped smiling and pierced the Varinski's throat until the blood wet the ground — "I hope you don't cooperate. I hope I get the pleasure of gutting you and watching you writhe in agony as you die."

Ann leaned against the stone, glad for the support, glad for the cool air, yet keeping her flashlight shining into the Varinski's eyes.

He struggled again.

Jasha pressed the knife harder.

Rapidly the Varinski said, "They told us where you did business, and they told us to use the woman to find out where you hide when you disappear. And we did."

"Then what?"

The Varinski growled.

The knife bit deeper.

"We knew we hadn't found the family, and we knew that was what my father and the other elders wanted."

"How many of you are there?"

"Ten!"

"Two," Ann said. "He told me before. There were only the two."

"Good." Jasha smiled, and his teeth looked longer and whiter than ever before. "Whose idea was it to put the homing device in the arrow?"

"Mine!" the Varinski said. "I'm the one who shot it into your shoulder, knowing you would run home to your mama. I'm the one you should fear."

Jasha laughed and leaned back. "You're not very smart, are you?"

In a flash, the man on the ground was

gone, and a wolf stood in his place. The beast leaped at Jasha.

Ann screamed.

And the two wolves met in the air.

They tumbled down the mountain. The sound of their snarling broke the ethereal silence, shattering the silver stars into cold, indifferent shards. Ann ran after them, knife in one hand, flashlight in the other, not sure what to do but sure she would do something.

The flashlight caught glimpses of them as they tumbled. She saw the glint of teeth and heard the deep-throated growls.

They dropped, disappeared over a ledge. She ran toward the drop-off and shone her light down.

Two men were there, two human men.

Only one was alive.

CHAPTER 24

Jasha stood over the Varinski's still body.

He looked up at Ann. Blood dripped from a slash across his throat. Using a fireman's hold, Jasha picked up the body. As he headed into the darkness, he called, "Dawn's coming. Walk downhill. I'll find you."

Whatever that meant.

Ann looked around. She stood on the roof of the world, with nothing around her except giant boulders and the black night sky filled with blisters of stars. The breeze blew, so fresh and thin the air barely filled her lungs. No bird, no wild animal, stirred. No pale ghosts drifted on the wind. She was alone as she had never been in her life.

She brought the bad people. She always brought the bad people.

Maybe so, but Jasha killed them. With Jasha, she was safe, and all of her prayers had been answered.

The life she'd known in California seemed long ago and far away. Everything up here was too big. Life-shattering. She could almost see the shards of her former life scattered around her. With Jasha holding the brush, the colors of her dreams had changed from pastels to bolds.

What was she going to do?

She couldn't run away. She had to stand here on the top of the world and face her fate.

Scraps of the sleeping bag flitted past her on the wind, waking her to the responsibilities of an environmentalist in the midst of one of the world's last remaining untouched wildernesses. She caught the scraps, thrusting them into the intact bottom of the bag. Before she put it into the backpack, she checked the zipper. Nylon jammed it; no wonder she'd had to slash her way out.

As the sky was lightening, she made her way down the mountain, moving north. She didn't know where she was going. It didn't matter; Jasha had said he would find her, and he would. She worried about him, off to create a crime scene: the murder of one hunter by another, then the death of that hunter by a wild-animal attack. Yet she had no doubt he would succeed.

But she wished he were with her.

What an idiot she was. Yesterday, she'd been a pacifist, concerned about the death of every living creature. Then she watched Jasha fight for his life. Now she didn't care that he had killed; she wanted only to know that he was alive and well . . . and hers. When he found her, she wanted to shake him for frightening her, then hold him while he slept, and, when he woke, make love to him as he had made love to her — with the kind of impatience that couldn't wait for permission.

Her feet hurt, and the summer day beneath the trees had turned unexpectedly hot. The cotton briefs had to go, and she discarded the boots and the three layers of socks with a sigh of relief.

She'd always considered herself clumsy; after hiking in boots two sizes too big for her, she would be positively dainty in her own shoes.

She stripped off the camouflage shirt and tossed it over the boulder. She shucked the pants, too, without a thought to who might be watching. Because Jasha had taught her to sniff the air, to listen to the wildlife, no one could sneak up on her without her knowledge.

She slid the underwear down her thighs, taking her time, relishing the wash of air across her skin. . . . Without turning her head, she asked, "You're all right?"

Jasha stepped out of the trees. He was naked. He had bathed nearby, and he was wet, his body still glistening with drops of water. "Yes."

She stepped out of the underwear and leaned her spine against a tree, and smiled at him. Smiled, for the first time, with full knowledge of her sexuality. "Show me."

He came to her, a fierce rush of fury and passion. He claimed her with a kiss, and she allowed him his moment.

Then, grabbing his arms, she pushed him away and down on the flat surface of the stone. Looking down at him, she saw long thighs, splayed to brace himself, a flat belly, and an erection stirring and rising. She also saw his face, stark with anguish and with need.

Only she would fill that need. Only she could.

She stripped off her silk undershirt, then bent over him, pressing her fists on either side of his chest. "I was worried about you."

Worried? Only now, with him here, would she admit that she'd been frantic.

He pushed his dark, damp hair back with his fingers. "You shouldn't have been."

"Why not?" She looked into his eyes, her

lips only a breath away from his. "Because fate has been so kind to me? Because since the moment I left California, I've been in control of my life? C'mon, Jasha! I've learned the truth, and I've learned it the hard way. Life is driven by the struggle between good and evil, and in the end, the only thing we can hope to have is this minute, and each other." She covered him with her body, and pressed her lips to his.

His head fell back, resting on the rock. He let her kiss him as she wished, exploring his mouth with her tongue and her powerful curiosity — she wanted to see what he liked.

From the tensing of the body beneath hers, she guessed he liked it all.

When she pressed more kisses on his cheeks, his chin, his chest, he gave a husky groan. "Are you going to teach me a lesson?"

"Or two." She kissed his ribs, his belly, and caught his erection in both her hands and rubbed him, up and down.

"You remind me . . . you remind me what life is." His anguish had become the anguish of need and glory.

"Let me remind you how good it can be." She took his erection into her mouth, wanting desperately to drive him as mad as he'd driven her that night in the tub, as he had

last night . . . as he had every night since
the day she'd met him. His skin was cool
and damp from his bath, but beneath that,
heat burgeoned up with each stroke of her
tongue. She loved the ridges and silken
textures. When she took him as deeply as
she could, his hips rose, and he groaned and
reached for her.

She lifted her head and swatted his hands
away. "You've had your turns. This is *my*
time."

His hands hovered as if the temptation to
take over could not be fought.

She glared. "My time," she repeated.

He fell back. "You're going to kill me."

"I hope so," she said fervently, and took
him in her mouth again.

He writhed as she stroked his thighs, ran
her hands over his hips, laid her palms flat
on his belly. And she loved the power, loved
having him at her mercy.

But she couldn't restrain herself forever;
the stored-up adrenaline compelled her, and
pleasuring him made her flush with warmth
and damp with passion. Lifting her head
with a gasp, she climbed onto the stone, her
knees on either side of his hips, and slowly
took him into herself, possessing him as he
had possessed her. She was still tight, and
he was still large, but he was wet from her

ministrations, and the tug of flesh against flesh sent sensation in sharp jolts along her nerves. She had no patience; she wanted him all the way inside right now, and sharp cries broke from her as her body opened to him.

He cupped his big palms around her thighs, supporting her, massaging her, while beneath her he held himself perfectly, desperately still. He didn't take over, but she saw his eyes, and he wanted to. Oh, my God, he wanted to.

Where were the soft and delicate desires she used to imagine?

Perhaps someday . . . but now passion was savage, sharp, demanding. She had him contained, but that wasn't enough. She danced the primitive, desperate dance with him, rising and falling over the top of his prone body, her knees pressed into the rough, warm stone. The sun beat down on her head, and lit every glorious ripple of his chest and belly, his stubbled chin, the dark fall of his damp hair against the pale granite.

He was alive. She was alive. Only that mattered.

"Please, Ann." His hands hovered above her chest, almost touching.

Placing her palms over the backs of his hands, she pressed them to her breasts.

He cupped them, kneaded them, taking pleasure, giving pleasure.

In return, she stroked her hands across his chest and over his shoulders, until both moaned in unison. They came together, a great cataclysm that shook the mountains and toppled the last of her resistance.

She wilted down on him, exhausted with passion and the joy that pulsed through her veins.

She loved Jasha; she longed for the moment when he would love her, but even if that day never came, she would always love him.

That afternoon, Jasha led Ann over a rise — and spread out before them lay Puget Sound, with islands dotting the dark blue water and a bank of fog backing out toward the ocean.

He watched as she took a deep breath of delight, and he smiled. He had led her safely through the forest. He had killed the bastard who tried to kill them. And today she'd proved to them both she loved him.

When she had looked her fill, he asked, "Do you have your phone?"

She found it in her pocket and showed him.

"Call Rurik's number. Tell him twenty-one at eight. That's all. He'll know."

She stared at him inquiringly.

That was how at eight that evening, Jasha and Ann found themselves on the corner of Fifth and Union in downtown Seattle climbing into the backseat of a faded 1980s Buick LeSabre.

From the front seat, his brother Rurik turned around and flashed her a gleaming smile. "Hang in there, Miss Smith. In three hours, we'll be home."

CHAPTER 25

"Three bedrooms, two and a half baths, fourteen hundred square feet in two stories," Rurik said as he parked the car in front of the Craftsman-style home.

Ann peered through the windshield at the simple old house that sat alone in the dark, lights shining from every window and on the porch.

"It was built in the 1920s, and when our parents bought the place, I guess it was pretty ramshackle. Mice in the kitchen, rotting floorboards on the stairs, peeling paint, and apparently some god-awful wallpaper in the dining room." Jasha was in the backseat, Ann was now in the front, and he sat forward, resting his hands on Ann's shoulders. "Papa thought it was just fine, because —"

"You know you're a Russian redneck when your Cossack hat is made of a possum," Rurik said.

The guys chortled.

"You know you're a Russian redneck when you have a dancing bear *and* a coonhound," Ann said. "You know you're a Russian redneck when you can't imagine eating your borscht without corn bread."

The two men stopped talking and turned to look at her in blank astonishment.

Oh, no. Had she offended them?

Then Rurik burst into laughter. "Wow, Jasha, you told me your Miss Smith had great legs, but you *never* told me she had a sense of humor."

Jasha had told his brother she had great legs?

"That's because you're too simpleminded to appreciate her humor," Jasha said.

"No, it's because you're afraid she'll fall for my looks and charm."

"Not a problem. She also has good taste in men."

"But she's with you, so we know her *vision's* lousy."

Ann glanced between the two of them, following the repartee like a spectator at a tennis match. The brothers were so . . . normal. So much like the families she'd seen on the sitcoms, like the brothers she'd seen in real life. They gave each other crap and grinned. Watching them made her feel like an outsider desperately wanting to get in.

Families always did that to her. "I see really well," she said primly.

Jasha smacked Rurik hard on the arm. "See?"

"It's going to be a long night for you, then, isn't it?" Rurik smirked and rubbed his bruise, then turned to Ann. "My parents are old-fashioned. Jasha and I have one bedroom. You'll have to sleep in Firebird's room."

"That's okay. I don't mind." Was every woman Jasha brought home having sex with him?

"Does he snore?" Rurik asked solicitously. "Does he crowd? He's a lousy lover, isn't he? I've always suspected it."

Her cheeks flamed, but in the dim light Rurik couldn't see that, so she risked a daring retort. "He's the best lover I've ever had."

"So she was a virgin?" Rurik laughed.

Jasha squeezed her shoulders. "Yes."

Rurik laughed again. Clearly he didn't believe a word of it.

"Anyway" — Jasha glared malevolently at his brother — "Mama and Papa had huge fights about the house. Papa wanted to concentrate on growing the grapes, and told her to stop fussing, woman. So she started

cooking for people to pay for the lumber and paint to fix stuff up. He caved —"

"Of course," the brothers said together.

"— and ever since, she's run the house as she likes," Jasha finished.

The front door opened, and a tiny, dark-haired, dark-eyed woman stepped out.

"There she is," Jasha said affectionately.

She gestured impatiently toward the car, then started toward them.

"You're in trouble now, man," Rurik said. "You didn't tell her what you were doing and she's been worried. Worse, you didn't bring your guest right in. Better go take your medicine."

Jasha leaped out of the backseat and headed for his mother.

Uncertainly, Ann turned to Rurik. "Should I . . . ?"

"Give them a minute." Rurik watched his mother, hugging Jasha, then shaking her finger up at him — he was more than a foot taller — then hugging him again.

On the drive up here, Rurik had been lighthearted, teasing, and he'd looked much younger than Jasha. He was handsome, with reddish brown eyes, smooth brown hair, and a height to match his brother's. Except for the sculpted bone structure, he looked nothing like Jasha. Jasha had introduced his brother as the lead archaeologist on a dig in Scotland.

Now she saw the attributes that made Rurik a leader. His expression was serious, almost grim; worry shaded his eyes, and Ann caught a flash of the steel in him.

"With Papa's illness and the vision and stuff," he said, "having Jasha disappear just about sent Mama over the edge."

Ann was assailed by instant guilt. "I'm sorry. I never thought anyone would be upset."

Rurik flicked her a glance. "From what you two told me, there wasn't a lot of choice. Mama knew that if Jasha disappeared, there had to be sufficient reason. Jasha's as responsible as hell, never acting on impulse, always setting a good example." At that, he pulled a long face. "But with the prophecy, we were afraid sufficient reason might be big trouble. Like death."

What vision? What prophecy? But before Ann could ask, Mrs. Wilder started toward the car.

She was talking before she even opened Ann's door. "— can't believe these boys didn't bring you right in. You must be exhausted and starving." She offered Ann her hand.

Ann took it and was surprised by Mrs.

Wilder's strength as she helped her out. "No, really, Jasha and Rurik have taken good care of me."

"They'd better have. Men aren't good for much" — she shot a glare at Jasha — "but I raised these boys and I expect them to honor my training. Now, I'm Zorana." She led Ann up the steps to the porch, still holding Ann's hand. "This is our home. Make it your own."

Ann had expected a large home with a simple flavor that reflected the country surroundings. Instead, she found herself drawn rapidly through the comfortable living room, where the television played to no one and a computer ran an eye-popping screen saver, and into a cramped kitchen with a large wooden table. The countertops were brown Formica, the refrigerator was huge and stainless steel, the gas range held a stockpot with steam rising, and the whole place smelled like fresh bread and roasted garlic — in other words, like heaven.

A pretty blonde about Ann's age leaped to her feet and ran to Jasha. "You idiot! You couldn't have called?" But she hugged him mightily.

"Hey, squirt, you're positively glowing!" Jasha hugged her back. She'd gained weight, too, but he knew better than to mention that. "Let me introduce you to my administrative assistant, Ann Smith."

Ann stuck out her hand. "It's good to meet you."

"I'm Firebird." She shook Ann's hand and grinned. "Love the outfit. Is that what they're wearing in California these days?"

"In all the fashionable survivalist cults," Ann snapped back, then realized what she'd said. "I'm sorry, I didn't mean —"

Firebird laughed out loud. "Don't apologize! I'm just glad Jasha finally found someone who knows how to walk and chew gum at the same time."

Zorana stood at the counter, chopping things with a knife half again her size, but she paused to survey her children with a keen eye.

"He didn't exactly . . . that is, we're not . . ." Ann didn't dare glance at him, because Firebird was making assumptions about their relationship, and so was Zorana, and all the way here, Rurik had been teasing them, and she knew Jasha would hate being tied to her like that. "That is, I simply work for him."

"Yeah, right." Firebird grinned. "It's true love if he let you wear his camouflage."

"That's enough, Firebird. You're embarrassing Ann." Jasha put his hand on Ann's back at her waist.

Ann found herself stepping into him, as if he would protect her from his own family.

Firebird looked her over. "She doesn't look embarrassed — she looks like she wants to wear real clothes again."

Ann wondered whether that was Firebird's gift — a discerning eye — or whether she just had interpolated Ann's wishes by her own.

"Where is she going to get clothes?" Rurik lounged against the counter next to Zorana. "You and Mama are midgets compared to her."

"Five-six is not a midget," Firebird retorted. "Mama, on the other hand . . ."

Everyone turned to look at the petite Zorana. Ann knew she had to be at least fifty, but her skin was unlined and taut across her glorious cheekbones. She'd rimmed her eyes with liner, emphasizing the slant and the deep brown color. For a moment, Ann caught a hint of merriment, well suppressed.

Zorana waved them off as if they were as unimportant as gnats. "I am big enough to birth giant overgrown obnoxious children who don't know how to offer our guest hospitality." She turned to face them, a full plate in her hand.

"No, really, please, Rurik stopped at a Starbucks so we could grab a scone and a cup of coffee. . . ." No one paid any heed to Ann's protestations.

Zorana's children scrambled into action, and in less than a minute, Ann found herself in the cushioned chair at the head of the table, a shot of clear vodka and a plate of appetizers before her.

Jasha pointed at each thing and named it. "Pickled mushrooms. Chopped herring. Rye bread. Cheeses —" He grabbed a piece and popped it into his mouth.

Without turning around from her chopping, Zorana said, "Don't steal from our guest. I'm filling more plates right now."

Firebird and Rurik grinned at him.

Ann was astonished. "How does she —"

"We don't know, but we suspect the worst," Jasha answered.

Ann remembered what he'd said about the Sight, but surely Zorana saved that for bigger things?

"I'm your mother. I changed your diapers. Do you think anything about you is a mystery to me?" Zorana slapped another two plates in the middle of the long table.

"Hey, Jasha, what did you do to your throat? Cut it shaving?" Firebird hugged him again.

"Let me see." Zorana pulled back his collar and bared the red slash the Varinski had inflicted. Her face went carefully blank. "Hm."

Jasha caught her fingers and kissed them. "It's okay, Mama."

"So you keep saying, but what else are you keeping from me?" She turned to the stove, where a big pot was bubbling. "Jasha, go get your father. You know he's awake. Rurik, you help him — you know how to handle the walker."

"He's out of the wheelchair?" Jasha's smile blossomed.

"We still have it, but you know him. He won't use it." Rurik shook his head.

"He is a stubborn mule," Zorana said. "Like his sons. Only a week since . . . since he was felled, and already he pretends like nothing happened. Firebird, get me the bowls. Hurry, boys, before the borscht gets cold."

Jasha stopped in the doorway and opened his mouth.

Ann knew what he was going to say. She *knew* he was going to ask about corn bread. She pointed her finger at him, just pointed it.

He shut his mouth, turned, and left.

Ann glanced to see if Zorana or Firebird

307

had noticed.

They both had. They stared at Ann in amazement.

"I don't know what that was about, but *I'm* impressed," Firebird said.

Zorana was less impressed and more wary, but her voice was kind when she said, "Drink your vodka, Ann. It'll warm you, and you'll sleep tonight."

"Shoot it," Firebird advised, and put a glass of water in front of her. "It'll make the rest of the drinking go easier."

The rest of the drinking? Somehow, doing shots had never been Ann's idea of a family evening.

But really — what did she know?

At Firebird's nod, Ann threw the shot back, tried very hard to catch her breath, and drained the water in the hopes of putting out the fire.

From the living room, she heard a low rumbling voice, like the growl of a great bear. It got closer and closer, until its owner burst into the room and the sound became a shout.

Konstantine Wilder leaned heavily on his walker. He had an IV in one arm and an oxygen tube in his nose. His complexion was waxy and pale. But he was still massively muscled, he'd imprinted his sons with his features, and he dominated the kitchen. "So you are Ann Smith who I talk to on the phone," he boomed. "Handsome girl."

Ann stood to greet him.

"Handsome girl. *Tall* girl." He smiled, and his teeth gleamed even and white. "Although I like short girls best." He shot Zorana such a lascivious glance, Ann wanted to shield her eyes.

"You say that out of fear," Zorana said.

"Of course, *ruyshka,*" he answered comfortably. "It is a foolish man who does not fear his wife."

"Papa, let's sit you down and you can talk to Ann." Jasha hovered on one side of his father, Rurik on the other.

Konstantine slashed a hand at him and scowled. "I sit when I want."

Ann pushed back her chair and walked to his side. She laid her hand on his white knuckles, straining to hang on to the rail of the walker. "But I can't sit until you do."

His bushy eyebrows rose above his startling blue eyes. "I like you, Ann Smith. You show respect for your elders." He shot a glare around the room. "More children should show such respect." He headed for the chair Firebird held out for him.

The process of putting him in it was prolonged and painful as the oxygen and the IV were placed on either side of him.

While his sons and his daughter adjusted and assisted, Zorana came to Ann and placed her hand on Ann's cheek, and nodded her thanks. Then she hustled back to the stove and started filling the bowls.

Konstantine waved Ann back toward the other end of the table. "Sit in the chair of honor. Eat. And drink!" He slapped his hand on the table. "You have no vodka!"

Rurik brought the bottle to the table. The glasses were lined up on a tray. He filled each to the brim, then carried them from one to another.

Jasha handed Ann a glass, then took one for himself and sat beside her.

Ann stared in fascination at the clear liquid. She drank wine almost every day — it was one of the benefits of working at a winery — and occasionally she splurged and had a Cosmo. But two shots of vodka in ten minutes?

Konstantine lifted his glass. *"Za vas!"*

"Here's to you," Jasha translated. *"Za vas!"*

"Za vas!" Ann said, a beat too late. Again the vodka took her breath away, and as she looked around, the world tilted to the right and assumed a rosy glow. "I had better eat something," she decided.

Jasha pushed the appetizer plate closer.

"Try the herring, the bread, and the cheese. That'll soak up some of the liquor."

Everyone was silent as Ann took a taste. "Wonderful!"

The kitchen exploded into pleased noise, as if they'd been holding their breaths in anticipation of her reaction.

Rurik seated himself next to his father.

Firebird and Zorana served Ann a bowl of borscht. They poured a dab of cream on the top, then stood on either side of her, their eyes gleaming.

She'd learned her lesson the first time. She made a show of tasting the soup of beets, potatoes, and cabbage, and smiling broadly. "Wonderful!"

Once again, they were ecstatic.

Zorana pulled a plate of hot breads topped with garlic from the oven and placed it on the table.

The women seated themselves, and the whole family began to eat.

Ann tried to adjust to the sound level, tried to eat enough to keep everyone happy, tried to observe the family. They were overwhelming, loud, and boisterous. Their smiles gleamed; their pleasure in one another's company was almost tangible. They ate the borscht with gusto and caught up on the events that had occurred since last they'd met.

How odd to see Jasha here in the midst of his family, fitting in so easily as they talked and drank. It seemed as though she'd lost her exclusive right to him — and in the time they'd lived in the forest, she hadn't truly wanted that right.

Now she felt like an outsider, and she wanted to go back. She wanted him for her own.

As Rurik poured his father another shot, she leaned over to Jasha. "Should he be drinking?"

"His doctors would kill us if they knew. He'll kill us if we don't serve him." Jasha shrugged. "A little vodka's not going to hurt that man."

Ann glanced again at Konstantine, and was shaken to the core to find his gaze on them.

He'd heard her. How could he have heard her?

Jasha observed them both. "He's a force of nature."

As if to prove the truth of Jasha's comment, Konstantine used his knuckles to knock on the table.

The conversation died.

"So, my eldest son has returned from a trip into the wilderness. He didn't warn us he was going to leave. He came back with a woman, and a slash on the throat. So, Jasha" — Konstantine fixed Jasha with a keen eye — "tell us why you worried your mother."

Jasha turned to Ann. "Show them."

The icon. Of course. He wanted his family to see the icon. She pulled open her pants pocket, took it out, and cradled it in her palm. The icon felt warm to the touch, smooth, and alive. When she placed the representation of the Madonna in the middle of the Wilders' kitchen table, the colors gleamed against the dark wood, drawing every Wilder eye.

No one breathed; no one moved.

They were so intensely still, Ann felt light-headed, as if all the oxygen were sucked from the room. It was so quiet, it seemed she'd lost her hearing.

"A thousand years . . ." Konstantine leaned forward, oxygen tank at his side, IV in his arm, his gaze locked on the icon.

Zorana tucked her hand into his. "It's your salvation."

"It is at least a beginning." He drew a difficult breath. "It is the first miracle."

CHAPTER 26

Ann looked from Rurik to Firebird to Zorana to Konstantine. A single tear trickled down Zorana's cheek. Firebird clasped her hands on the table and stared at the icon in awe. Rurik shook his head, over and over, as if he couldn't believe the icon sat on the table, the gold sparkling dully, the Virgin's red robes bright, the holy family surrounding her.

Ann dared a glance at Jasha.

He, too, watched his family, taking in their wonder. He smiled at her, and nodded as if in thanks.

Perhaps he gave her the courage, or maybe it was the vodka, but she could no longer restrain her curiosity. "I understand that an icon of the Virgin is a miracle, and I understand that this icon, especially, is a miracle. But I don't understand why this one is *Konstantine's* salvation."

The family looked from one to the other,

knowing what she didn't and silently deciding whether to tell her, how much to tell her. Perhaps . . . whether to trust her.

All her life when she visited her friends' families, she'd experienced that feeling of being left out, of being judged. No matter how much families liked her, they held a reserve between themselves and outsiders.

She'd had it with that kind of bull. She was marked, for evil or for good, but no matter what, Jasha was right. The icon had chosen Ann, and Ann would not fail in her responsibility.

Slowly she came to her feet. She pointed at the icon. "You know, I've spent days being filthy and exhausted, climbing up and down mountains, getting almost raped and killed by a vicious murderer, to protect the icon. I stuck with Jasha instead of running away screaming the way any normal woman would, and I would think that all of you would realize that I'm not some harbinger of doom. I'm a good, clean, trustworthy woman, and you Wilders owe me an explanation, and I want to hear it right —"

Shit. She was making a speech. Every single Wilder was staring at her. Especially Jasha, who knew very well how much she hated giving speeches. She especially hated giving speeches when the only possible ending was to lie down on the floor, drum her heels, and scream like a two-year-old.

She'd definitely had too much to drink. She needed to get away. She needed to get away *now.*

But before she could make an excuse and escape, Zorana said, "Pardon us, Ann, it is difficult to talk about that dreadful day. Yet you're right. You do have the right to know." She looked around at her family, then back at Ann. "On July fourth, I had a vision."

"Oh," Ann said in a small voice. She slid back down in her seat.

"When I was born, among my people, I was hailed as the One — the One who would receive the visions that have guided us for so long. The tribe's amulet was hung around my neck, and never did I take it off — until I left my people. Then I thought the gift was gone from me, and I put the amulet away. For thirty-five years, I saw nothing but that which is here — the earth, the sky, my children, my husband. But that night . . . that night the vision came, and it was powerful, sucking me into a darkness so black my soul was lost to me. I could see nothing, hear nothing. Then . . . a voice. I realized it was my own." Zorana's tone deepened. "I said —"

"Ma!" All four legs of Rurik's chair

smacked the floor. He grabbed her hand. "Don't say it again!"

In exasperation, she shook him off. "I'm not going to have another vision! It isn't words, but the unholy thing, that brought it." She turned to Ann. "The unholy thing was a statue of my daughter."

As if that explained everything.

"What happened to the statue?" Jasha looked around as if expecting to see it on the counter.

"I threw it in the garbage," Firebird said.

"You touched it?" Jasha didn't bother to contain his horror.

"I'm your younger sister, Jasha, and while being related to *you* might make *some* people think I'm an idiot, I am not." Firebird's eyes flashed. "I wrapped it in a towel before I tossed it."

"She's been a little touchy lately," Rurik muttered loudly, and tilted his chair back on its hind legs.

Firebird turned on him, her cheeks rosy with anger.

"That's enough," Konstantine said.

Although the color in Firebird's face died slowly, the squabbling stopped as if cut by a knife.

"Did anyone talk to the kid who made it?" Jasha asked.

"No, because the next morning when River and Sharon Szarvas went looking for him, he was gone." Firebird looked at Jasha.

Jasha looked back.

Their twin expressions of terror sent a chill up Ann's spine.

And Konstantine's look of cold fury made her want to run screaming into the night. Even though he was handicapped by his illness, his ferocity frightened her. She was very, very glad he was on her side.

"So." Zorana leaned back, her hands in her lap, the picture of calm in a sea of violent emotions. "My vision."

Everyone's attention snapped back to her.

"I predicted that each of my four sons must find one of the Varinski icons."

"Four sons?" Ann said. "I thought there were only three."

"I just have the visions, I don't explain 'em." Zorana spoke matter-of-factly. "I predicted their loves would bring the holy pieces home."

Ann's gaze leaped to Jasha.

She was his love?

He hadn't told her about the prophecy. All the time they were in the woods, he'd known what his mother had seen, and he hadn't told Ann.

Now he watched her intensely, as if he

wanted to convey something to her.

Of course. He wanted her to realize that the vision was uncertain and that she shouldn't take it seriously.

Because obviously, he didn't.

Zorana continued. "A child will perform the impossible. The beloved of the family will be broken by treachery . . . and leap into the fire. The sons of Oleg Varinski have found us, for the blind can see."

"What does that mean? 'The blind can see'?" That made no sense to Ann.

"Yeah, Ma, what?" Rurik's voice held a firm tone that surprised Ann. Did an archaeologist really need to sound so commanding?

"I don't know. I just saw these two white eyes staring at me through the dark." Zorana looked at Jasha. "But obviously, the sons of Oleg have found us."

"Or at least me," Jasha said.

"Show your father your throat," Zorana said.

Jasha opened his collar wide and showed them the mark the Varinski had made.

Konstantine examined it. "The mark of a demonwolf. Did you kill him?"

"I did." Jasha's voice was grim.

"Then you'll heal, but slowly." Konstantine bared his chest. The coarse gray hair was thick, except over the mass of white scars over his ribs. It looked as though, long ago, some beast had tried to rip out his heart.

The overhead light was on, and the glow from the living room came through the wide doors.

Yet the night breathed on the window-panes, frosting them with fear, and on the edges of Ann's consciousness, a pale, sad ghost floated.

Ann pushed her glass forward.

Jasha stood with the bottle and walked around the table, pouring another round. Then with a glance at her and one at his mother, he went to the windows and pulled the curtains shut.

At once, the pressure in Ann's chest eased.

Zorana turned to Ann, spoke directly to Ann, as if she needed Ann to understand. "While in my vision, I said that —" She stopped and breathed, as if she fought back tears. "I said that if we do not break the devil's pact before Konstantine's death, he's going to hell and we will be forever separated."

Ann saw the anguish in Zorana's large brown eyes, saw that stern Rurik's hand shook as he sipped his vodka.

Zorana continued. "I said . . . I said

Konstantine was dying. And then . . . then he fell . . . to the ground . . . in the dirt. . . . I tried to catch him, but I fell, too. . . ."

"Hush, *ruyshka,* don't cry." Konstantine caught her hand in his and squeezed it. "The doctors don't know what they're talking about."

Zorana squeezed his hand back as she told Ann, "The doctors make their predictions, too. They say he has two, maybe three years before the end."

Konstantine held up one finger. "They are all quacks!" But he looked wearier all the time.

With a glance at him, Zorana hurried to finish her story. "So, Ann, to have you produce this icon and put it on the table! This is the greatest gift. Nothing in our lives is more precious."

"Where should we keep it?" Firebird reached out to pick it up.

Jasha swatted her hand away. "No! The Madonna burned me." He showed Firebird the red place on his face and his outstretched hand.

"Really, my son? Let me see," Konstantine rumbled. Jasha stood and went to his father, and Konstantine surveyed the red patches. "Do they hurt?"

Rurik leaned in to see, then leaned his

chair back again and grimly crossed his arms over his chest.

"They're like tiny coals under my skin, burning all the way down to my bones," Jasha said.

In Jasha's face, Ann caught a brief glimpse of a beast who suffered.

Had he really been in pain all the time? And he'd never said anything?

She looked down at her palm, at the now-pale scar the arrowhead had inflicted. But hadn't she had a feeling like Jasha's? Not a burning so much as a heat that warned that demon blood slid through her veins? And since she'd witnessed the death of the Varinski, hadn't she noticed, and determinedly ignored, an answering heat that blossomed from the mark on her back?

"Pain is the price we pay for our gifts." Konstantine affectionately squeezed Jasha's chin.

Firebird licked her fingertip, then dabbed the icon like a woman testing an iron.

Nothing happened.

She looked at her finger, then slowly wrapped her hand around the Virgin and picked her up. "It's the Madonna and child. It is so beautiful." Tears sprang to Firebird's eyes and shimmered on her cheeks.

"Yes. I love the colors. I love the scene."

Tears to match Firebird's sprang to Ann's eyes.

Zorana extended her hand, palm up.

"No." Konstantine stopped her with a gesture.

Jasha and Rurik tensed.

"Konstantine, it's all right."

He looked at her, then dropped his hand and inclined his head.

"The visions will come when they will. Trying to stop them will accomplish nothing except to leave us in darkness when we need the light." Zorana looked at her sons. "Do you know why your father stole me from my tribe?"

"Because he was a horny old guy?" Rurik guessed.

Even Konstantine laughed and nodded.

"That, too," Zorana said. "But he took me because he wanted to pass my gift on to his sons. And who knows? Perhaps I have."

Rurik tipped his chair too far. His arms flailed, and he fell backward with a thump that shook the floor.

It was Zorana's turn to laugh.

He stood up, red-faced, dusted off his seat, stood the chair up again, and sat down hard. "Ma, don't joke like that."

"She's not joking," Konstantine said.

Ann glanced at Jasha, who mouthed, "Not me."

Cautiously, Firebird placed the icon in Zorana's palm.

Zorana wrapped her fingers around the icon — and nothing happened.

The men sighed in relief.

But Ann *had* found the icon. She alone had held it, kept it safe. To have other people talk about it, handle it, made her jumpy, as if with each contact, she relinquished possession . . . and that felt wrong. For whatever reason, it was wrong.

Zorana cradled the Madonna in the palm of her hand. "After I had the vision, I prepared the traditional place for the icons." She pointed to the small corner draped in vibrant red velvet. "The *krasny ugol.*"

Jasha translated for Ann. "The red corner, or the beautiful corner. In Russia, red means beautiful."

"Ma, we can't put it there," Firebird said. "Anyone who walks in could take the icon."

Zorana tossed her head in exasperation. "Not yet! When the icons are united, then we will keep them in the *krasny ugol.*"

"For now, put the icon in a safety-deposit box," Rurik said.

"No." Jasha spoke decisively. "The icon is Ann's."

Ann started to agree, but Rurik talked over the top of her. "That thing is a thousand years old! Ann doesn't want to wander around with the icon in her pocket. The responsibility is too much. If nothing else, she could lose it as easily as Firebird loses her car keys."

"Shut up, Rurik," Firebird said.

Rurik's cool indignation forcibly reminded Ann of his profession. He was an archaeologist, and he couldn't bear the thought that any one person should keep such an ancient relic.

Yet he didn't have the right to decide. Only she did. "I won't lose it."

"The icon was given to Ann." Zorana cocked her head and examined Ann. "Isn't that right?"

The kitchen got very quiet. Everyone waited on Ann's answer.

She looked to Jasha, who nodded encouragingly.

"The tree . . . lightning struck the tree, and the tree crashed to the ground. It fell, and in the tree roots, I found the Blessed Virgin. She was looking for me." Ann hated being the center of attention, but this was important. "She put herself into my keeping, and I won't give her up."

The Wilders scrutinized Ann, and for the

first time she realized how dangerous they were. How dangerous they all were. The men changed when they wished, became beasts of prey with fangs and talons. Zorana and Firebird were strong women, alpha women, who would defend their family to the death.

Ann had to do as much for the Madonna. She hated confrontation. But she had no choice. "I'll keep the icon."

Rurik came to his feet. "All right, I'll concede that you found her." He leaned his fists on the table and, with ice-cold logic, said, "But that doesn't give you the right to keep her, no more than any discovery I make as I excavate this Celtic tomb gives me the right to keep it."

"No, but *this* gives her the right." Jasha also stood, stripped his shirt off his shoulder, and showed them the small white scar. "The Varinski shot me with an arrow. We didn't know why. He could have wanted to poison me, or drug me so I would bend to his will. Ann didn't hesitate. She cut me open and removed the arrow — and the tracking device that would have led them here."

Jasha made her sound like a heroine. "I was scared," she whispered.

"She was scared to death," Jasha agreed.

"She's not like us. She hasn't been raised to face violence. She grew up in a Catholic orphanage. She's an innocent. She's been protected from the violence we understand so well. But she saved me. She saved all of us." He stared Rurik down. "If she wishes to have it, the icon is hers."

Zorana stood, the icon in her grip. She turned to Rurik.

Ann scrambled to her feet. She didn't know what Zorana would do: she knew only that she needed to be standing.

Zorana said, "The icon is Ann's."

Rurik nodded, a stiff, swift nod.

Zorana came around the table, placed the icon in Ann's hand, then curled Ann's fingers over it. Taking Ann's cheeks in her hands, Zorana stood on tiptoe and kissed her forehead. "I am grateful. Thank you, and welcome to my family."

Then the whole family stood, even Konstantine.

One by one, they walked past Ann, and hugged her and kissed her forehead, all solemn and kind. Firebird, Rurik, Konstantine . . . Jasha.

Jasha, who kissed her lips rather than her forehead.

That night, as Ann lay in the upper bunk in Firebird's bedroom, she began to comprehend what the icon meant to the Wilders, to their family, to the love that bound them together. Any one of them would die for the icon, for to them, it represented their father's salvation.

And Ann — Ann had gone from having no one who cared if she lived or died, to having five people vitally concerned about her safety and happiness. At last, after twenty-two years of loneliness, she had the family she'd always wanted. This was wonderful. This was the fulfillment of her dream — wasn't it?

Yet if they were responsible for her, then she was responsible for them.

And what would happen if Ann, who took her responsibilities very seriously, failed them? What would happen to her then?

CHAPTER 27

Jasha watched his mother as she hustled around the kitchen, cleaning up the breakfast dishes. He also kept an eye on Ann, who sipped her coffee as if she hoped the caffeine would cure her hangover — or help her wake up from a nightmare that included a miraculous icon, a family of demons, and a deal with the devil.

"What do you two want for supper?" To Ann, Zorana said, "We keep farmers' hours, and have our big meal in early afternoon."

"That's great," she said.

He'd donated more of his clothes to her, but this time no camouflage. Instead she wore one of his blue dress shirts with the cuffs rolled up, and a pair of his jeans with one of Firebird's belts cinched around the waist. And although the shirttails drooped over her fine ass, she still looked so cute he wanted nothing more than to take the clothes right back off.

She put down her cup. "Is there anything I can do to help?"

"Yes, you can tell me what you like to eat."

"Anything you fix will be fine."

"You've been in the wild for five days. You must want something," Zorana coaxed.

"Ma, *I'd* love a rhubarb custard pie," he said.

"You know you're the only one who likes rhubarb custard pie and you scarf down the whole thing." Oblivious to any irony, Rurik finished his third poached egg and another piece of toast.

"I fail to see the problem," Jasha answered.

Ann watched them with her blue eyes wide.

Jasha wondered if their all-American normalcy comforted her, or whether she saw it as a camouflage for their true, beastly nature.

Yet his father sat in the living room in his recliner watching *CSI* reruns. His sister was sleeping in. And his brother was a pain in the ass.

"Ma, make lemon meringue," Rurik said.

"We can have both, but we should let our guest decide what she wants first." Zorana's words were a reproof to her sons.

"I'm not being selfish. Everyone likes lemon meringue," Rurik said piously.

Jasha snorted. He knew Ann would never profess a preference. Her manners were too good, her desire to please was too ingrained, and that nun, Sister Mary Magdalene, had taught her to be grateful.

He hated grateful.

Zorana wiped her hands on her kitchen towel. "Lamb? Ann, you like lamb?"

"Very much."

"That is appropriate for the meal, yes?" Zorana asked her sons. "For we are celebrating your father's salvation."

"That's perfect." Ann broke into one of her rare smiles.

And Jasha was transfixed. Even around the office, one of Ann's smiles was an event. She didn't realize how hard her coworkers labored to make her smile, or that her pleasure gave everyone a lift to their heart.

In her most loving voice, Zorana said, "It is because of you, Ann, that we can have this celebration."

"It was luck that I found the icon," Ann said.

"No. It was fate," Zorana answered.

Ann's smile drooped, and as if she was in pain, she reached around and pressed her hand just below her waist on her right side.

"Did sleeping in a real bed make your back hurt?" He grinned at her. "Want to go out and sleep on the ground again?"

Hastily, she removed her hand and sat up straight. "No. Really. I'm fine!"

"Don't tease her, Jasha," his mother said.

No, he shouldn't tease her, especially now that he remembered — since they'd started this trip, she'd made that gesture fairly often. *Did* her back hurt? She looked guilty — was she concealing something from him? A pulled muscle, or a burn?

During the trek through the wilderness, all Jasha's concentration had been focused on Ann, on keeping her alive, on wooing her as she deserved. He'd always known how smart and efficient she was; now he saw the beauty that shone from her and the bravery that lurked at the core of her being.

He got up and poured himself a cup of coffee.

She thought she was a coward because she was afraid.

He thought she was a champion because she fought despite her fears.

She would never tell him if she'd somehow hurt herself, or worse, if he'd somehow hurt her. He would watch to see if he could discover what was wrong.

He carried the coffeepot over and refilled her cup, and when she lifted her face to his to thank him, he kissed her.

Two nights ago, he'd given in to his lust. He'd possessed her because he had to, because he knew there was a chance he would die, and he had to know her one more time. Yesterday, she'd turned the tables and claimed him, tormenting him with her desires, making love to him in a glorious celebration of life.

So why had he spent last night restless and horny?

Because he'd grown used to having her beside him, to waking up when she stirred, to holding her in his arms and wanting her. Always wanting her. If he lived to be 150, he would still want her.

None of the sex, no matter how good, had convinced Ann that she was his. Even when she was surrounded by his family, she was isolated.

And he couldn't bear her loneliness. "Ann," he whispered, and because he couldn't resist, he put his free hand on her throat and kissed her again.

She restrained herself, embarrassed by their audience, until in a rush her resistance collapsed. She melted against him, and she kissed him back.

"Get a room!" Rurik said.

Ann pulled away, blushing.

"I wish," Jasha said fervently.

"But before you leave, pass the coffeepot," Rurik said.

Jasha handed it to him, and looked up to find his mother watching them.

She wasn't having a vision, but she was definitely seeing more than he liked. His parents might have met through an abduction, and married under a cloud, but for them, that proved the good sense of traditional values — they wanted their sons to choose their mates wisely, and treat them with respect.

He was ready to do that, for he respected Ann more than any woman he'd ever met, he trusted her, and never had he imagined wanting a woman like he wanted her.

Even better, she wanted him just as violently.

The first chance he got, he would ask her to marry him.

She'd like that. It would be a good marriage.

Firebird shuffled in, still in her turquoise bathrobe.

"It's about time." Jasha made a show of checking his watch. "It's after eight. What happened to my baby sister who always bounded up at five in the morning?"

Firebird pushed back her lank hair and glared. "I'm not feeling so hot. *Okay?*"

"You want breakfast?" Zorana asked.

"No." Firebird collapsed onto a chair. "But thank you, Mama."

Rurik jostled her with his elbow. "Hungover?"

"No," she snapped.

She couldn't be hungover. Last night, Jasha hadn't been paying much attention, but he'd noticed she barely touched the vodka to her lips. Probably it was that time of the month. . . .

Ann smiled again, right at Firebird. "Morning sickness is a wretched business, so they tell me."

Firebird stared at Ann with a stricken expression.

Ann tried again. "Jasha didn't tell me you were expecting. When are you due?"

"Expecting? You mean, like, pregnant? Don't be silly. She's having her . . . that is, Firebird isn't . . ." Jasha got a good look at Firebird's guilty face. He waited for his mother to scoff.

Instead, Zorana shook her head and looked down at the floor.

The realization hit him, and hit him hard. Instant fury roared through him. "You're *pregnant.*"

"Oh, no," Ann whispered.

"Could you say it a little louder, Jasha?"

Firebird snapped. "I don't think Miss Joyce in town heard you."

Firebird didn't deny it. She was pregnant. His baby sister was pregnant.

"Son of a bitch." Rurik got to his feet and stared at Firebird in disbelief. "You've got to be kidding."

At least Jasha wasn't the only one who didn't know what was going on. Because it was obvious the women sure did. Even Ann, who had just got here, realized Firebird was pregnant.

No. Not pregnant. *Knocked up.*

Jasha stalked toward Firebird. "Tell me who did this to you, and I'll get him."

"I'll help you." Rurik stood shoulder to shoulder with Jasha. "We'll bring him back. We'll make him —"

"Marry me?" Firebird's eyes flashed. "I don't *think* so."

"He ran out on you." Jasha's fists clenched.

"No. I ran out on him. He doesn't even know." Firebird held up one hand — like that would stop them. "And that's the way it's going to stay. I'm not marrying him. He's not getting custody of my child, and he's not getting visitation rights. I appreciate the offer, but he's an asshole. So, you guys, just put a sock in it."

"He . . . ," Jasha said.

"You . . . ," Rurik said.

"I'm allowed to be as stupid as any other twenty-year-old and go to bed with the wrong guy." Firebird flicked a tear out of the corner of her eye, but she didn't break down. Firebird never broke down. "Don't tell me you guys didn't do dumb things when you were my age, because I remember that time when Rurik and Paula Hecker, the pecker checker, ended up in La Grange in jail for public intoxication and lewdness —"

"Sh!" Rurik shot a glance at his mother, whose narrowing eyes warned of trouble. "I paid you to keep quiet."

"And I did! You just didn't pay me enough to keep me quiet while you lectured me." She turned on Jasha. "And you can't tell me that you and Ann have a platonic relationship. I see how you watch her when you think no one is looking, like a wolf, and I heard you prowling the hall last night. If I hadn't been in the bedroom with her, nothing could have kept you out."

Startled, Ann looked at Jasha.

He scowled at his sister.

And Zorana scrutinized him.

Firebird continued. "So don't berate me as if you were —"

"Your father?" Jasha said.

"Yeah." Firebird subsided and muttered, "As if you were my father."

"That's enough, Jasha." Ann got up, went and sat down next to Firebird, and hugged her shoulders. "Will your father be very upset?"

Firebird rubbed her forehead. "He's old-fashioned, and he thinks I'm still a virgin. He'll be like Jasha and Rurik, only worse." She lowered her voice. "I'm not sure he won't throw me out."

"He adores you." Rurik put his hand on Firebird's shoulder.

"All the worse," Zorana said.

"I know. Do you think I don't know?" Firebird placed her hand on her belly. "I was going to tell him that night . . . you know, *that* night."

"How far along are you?" Jasha couldn't take his gaze away from her hand, shielding the baby, protecting it.

"Almost six months," she said.

"Six months?" he shouted.

Firebird and Zorana shushed him.

"Tone it down, Jasha," Ann said sternly.

"How could you be six months?" he demanded in a whisper.

"It's her first child," Zorana told him. "A woman never shows as much with the first child, and Firebird has been careful to dress right."

Rurik rounded on his mother. "So you've been in on this?"

"Don't you talk to Mama that way," Firebird scolded. "She guessed while we were at the hospital, and it's not as if she could do anything about it."

A new voice spoke from the doorway. Konstantine's voice. "Maybe Firebird's child is the fourth son of the prophecy." He stood there, leaning heavily on his walker, his bushy brows lifted high.

All eyes turned to him, horrified, but no one moved.

Then Firebird came to her feet. She rushed to him and wrapped her arm around his. "Papa, you're not supposed to be up by yourself!"

"I have to go to the bathroom, and all my family's in the kitchen shouting at each other. What's an old man to do?"

Jasha should have been quieter. He meant to be quieter.

Konstantine lifted one trembling hand and cupped Firebird's chin. "So you are going to make me a grandfather?"

"Yes, Papa." For the first time, Firebird's eyes filled and overflowed.

"I should tell you never to darken my

door again."

"I know, Papa." She wiped her cheeks on her sleeve.

"And I would, but I have to go to the bathroom first." He glared at Jasha and Rurik. "Maybe one of the big lugs who call themselves my sons could give me a hand."

Rurik rushed to his side and helped him turn around.

Zorana sighed in relief and went back to her cooking.

Jasha hugged his sister and murmured, "Congratulations, little one."

Ann sagged in her chair. The tension in the kitchen evaporated. The crisis was over.

For now.

CHAPTER 28

Ann didn't think she was hungry, but at one that afternoon, when Zorana placed the filled platter on the table, her stomach gave such a huge growl, everyone heard it and laughed.

"What a compliment!" Zorana stood with her hands clasped before her.

"It smells so good!" Ann tried to explain.

And it did. After days of wandering and deprivation, the smells of lamb encrusted with garlic and herbs, golden brown potatoes, and carrots made Ann's mouth water. The sights of a green salad fresh from the garden and a huge plate of bright red, freshly sliced tomatoes brought tears of pleasure to her eyes. The garnet wine sparkled in the glasses. And she had managed, but only barely, not to drool on the three pies that lined the counter, waiting to be cut — rhubarb custard, lemon meringue, and a golden, cinnamony apple.

"This feast is in honor of you, for what you have done for my family." Zorana's lips trembled as she looked across at Konstantine, seated at the end of the table. He looked better this afternoon. Not well, but better. "You have given us the first glimmer of hope in our long night."

The family, even Rurik, slapped the table and said, "Hear! Hear!"

Ann didn't know how to respond. Her delight in their praise seemed a sin, yet all day she had soaked it in, settling into the family, catching the rhythm of their teasing, their fights, their silences.

"If she hadn't cut that arrow out of me, you would have never seen me again," Jasha said.

"Shut up, Jasha. Until you said that, I really liked her." Rurik grinned at his brother.

The two guys arm-wrestled briefly, then shook hands in one of those prolonged male rituals that indicated affection without sloppiness.

When Rurik caught Firebird watching them and shaking her head, he wrapped his arm around her and touched her belly. "You'll give us a boy, won't you? One girl every thousand years is all this family can stand."

Firebird laughed. "What will you do if I have a girl?"

"Spoil it as horribly as we spoiled you," he said.

"Then she will be blessed." Firebird pressed his hand in hers.

These Wilders were different from any family Ann had ever seen. They loved one another, and they showed their love through touch. There was an old-world charm about their affection. To Ann, the constant contact was an invasion of her personal space; nevertheless, she sort of liked it. It certainly explained why Jasha had a reputation around the office as being touchy-feely.

While the family feasted, Zorana sat next to Konstantine, leaned close, and quietly spoke to him.

He nodded, and when the plates had been emptied and pushed away, he lightly tapped his wineglass with his knife. "Today I found out my daughter, my sweet little Firebird, is going to give me a grandchild. I am very happy" — he placed his hand over his heart — "yet I find myself furious with the beast who seized her, seduced her, and took her with no thought of the future. She will not tell me who he is so that I can take appropriate measures, and I have no choice but to let him go unpunished."

Firebird looked down at her plate and played with her fork.

"Today my wife, my Zorana, came to me and said that she believes another such beast exists." He looked right at Jasha. "And he lives under my roof."

Ann choked on the last bite of salad.

"This beast I have taught better. This beast has no excuse," Konstantine said. "Come here, Jasha."

Ann opened her mouth to object.

Jasha covered her hand with his, and shook his head. The kitchen was absolutely silent as he went to Konstantine's side and knelt beside the chair.

Tubes were taped to the old man's arm and ran up his nose. His complexion was pale, but his words were stern. "Did you take this girl against her will?"

"Yes."

Konstantine lifted his arm and slapped Jasha hard across the face, and for all his feeble appearance, the blow was sharp and sure.

Ann leaped up. "What are you doing?"

Rurik and Firebird caught her arms and held her in place.

Jasha didn't move except to shake his head as if to clear it.

"He's from the Old Country," Firebird

told Ann softly. "He used to take unwilling women, and he stole my mother —"

"But that's no reason to hit his son!"

"And he taught his sons that they should always control themselves." Rurik also spoke softly.

Konstantine took a deep breath. His complexion, already pale, turned gray. "Was she a virgin?"

"Yes."

Ann lunged again, wanting to claw her way forward.

Firebird spoke in her ear. "Today, he found out I was pregnant by a son of a bitch. Not to mention he has adopted you as his own. He's angry with Jasha, and he's protective of you."

Konstantine slapped Jasha's other cheek, and the sound echoed through the house. "How *dare* you disrespect everything I taught you? Have you no honor? How dare you violate an innocent girl?"

Ann wrestled herself free and bounded forward. "How dare *you* hit him? You have no right!"

"Ann. It's okay." Jasha still knelt beside his father, the marks of Konstantine's fingers clear on his cheeks.

Konstantine looked up at her. "You are the daughter of my heart. I would do the

same to any man who took you. But Jasha
— it is worse that it is Jasha, for he is truly
my son. I have every right to discipline him.
I taught him better."

"Well, he's my —" What was he? Ann
didn't know, but she blundered on. "He's
my *mate,* and I tell you, don't lay a hand on
him again."

Konstantine cocked his head and examined her. "Your mate, is he? How do you
know that?"

She shrugged, a large, helpless roll of her
shoulders. "I simply knew the first time I
saw him that he . . . was the one."

"That he gave you no choice — you forgive?"

"I think . . . that it was inevitable."

Konstantine's gaze moved beyond her to
Zorana, who sat, her fingers woven together.
"I am glad for that." His gaze returned to
Jasha. "But I am sorely displeased with you.
What were you thinking?"

"I wasn't thinking. I was angry. I wanted
her. And she . . . ran." Jasha glanced up at
Ann, and what she saw in his face frightened
and thrilled her.

He still wanted her. If she ran, he would
still give chase.

Konstantine continued. "So you, like a
beast with no brain or heart, pursued her

and raped her."

"No!" Ann took Jasha's hand. "I . . . he made me . . . different. I didn't know before, but after . . . I . . . ."

Again Konstantine's gaze shifted to Zorana.

Their eyes met.

Ann caught a glimpse of red glow in his.

As if suddenly attacked by shyness, Zorana's gaze dropped, and a half smile tilted her lips.

Something had passed between them. A memory of a time long ago.

Jasha kept Ann's hand in his, and took Konstantine's with his other. "Papa, I deserve to be slapped, and I thank you for your care of Ann. But honestly, if I had it all to do over again, I would do exactly the same . . . as long as, in the end, I could have Ann."

"All right." Konstantine shoved at Jasha's shoulder, then shook his finger in his face. "But you are not an animal. Remember that. Instinct can be your friend — and your enemy. Use your brain, boy, and don't let your *erkek* point the way."

As Jasha came to Ann, everyone was smiling, not at them, but about them. Taking her hand, he led her outdoors.

She went willingly, wanting out of this

house stuffed with so much kind interest she was afraid she would suffocate.

Jasha walked to the stone bench under the broad-leaved maple, sat down, and patted the place beside him.

She sat down and stared straight forward, shoulders hunched, hands gripping the edge of the cool stone.

"So, I'm your mate, am I?"

"I suppose." She'd thought if she left the house, she'd be less embarrassed. Instead her face flamed hotter. "But I don't even know what that means."

"I do."

He was going to say she loved him, and that was true, but she didn't need him to smirk about it. "It's not what you think."

"But it is. Who better to know than me?" Taking her chin, he turned it toward him. "Ann, *ruyshka,* I want to marry you."

Stunned, she stared into his golden eyes for the briefest second. Then she came off the cool stone in a fiery red wrath. "How dare you? I know I'm an orphan who was thrown away in a Dumpster —"

"The Dumpster. You never said anything about the Dumpster!"

She hadn't said anything about a lot of things. "I know I'm nothing more than your secretary —"

"Administrative assistant."

"And I'm too tall and my hair's brown and my boobs aren't very big. But at least they're real, and so am I, and I won't let you make fun of me!"

He stared at her as she stood over him, fists clenched at her side, vibrating with indignation.

"I am not making fun of you."

"Maybe not. But you're not telling the truth, either." Not telling the truth about loving her, she meant.

"I like brown hair. I like tall women. They're easy to dance with." He stood up, right against her, and wrapped his hands around her waist. "I like you. You're wonderful to make love to. I admire you. You don't have any relatives, but you've collected friends around you and made your own family, and they adore you."

"Pfft!"

"Do you think I haven't noticed the way they talk about you? They're always pointing out your good qualities. And I know damned good and well if Celia realized what had happened between us in the woods, my dad would have had to stand in line to knock me ass over teakettle." Jasha brought her close so that his body warmed her, and he tilted her head to rest against his shoulder. "Ann, why is it so hard to believe I want to marry you?"

Because he didn't know who — or what — she truly was. He didn't know what happened to people who cared for her. For all that he was a demon, he didn't realize that she was the worst kind of murderer — the kind who watched people die for her, and did nothing more than cry about it.

And yes, he could embrace her and seduce her until she melted against him. But she knew exactly why he wanted to marry her — because of Zorana's prophecy. Because he thought he should, or because he thought to bind her more closely to him and his family. She wanted to be loved, but she damned well wouldn't be used.

"I love you," he said.

She'd heard him use that impatient tone of voice before — with his fianceé when she'd thrown one of her tantrums.

She removed first one of his arms from around her, then the other. "I liked it better when you didn't tell me lies."

"What makes you think I'm lying to you?" He did incredulous very well.

"You'll do anything for the sake of your family," she said bitterly. "But do you really think I'm so dumb that I'll believe a man who discovers he loves me after I found the icon that would save his family? Come on, Jasha. What if some other woman had found it? Would you still love me, or would you oh so suitably fall in love with her, instead?"

"My father expects us to marry, yes. My family expects it. But I know what I know. We've come through fear and pain and struggle together, and because of all that, in only a few days we've grown closer than most people do in a lifetime. We trust each other, Ann. What's more important than that?"

"Love."

"I said I loved you."

"And I said I didn't believe you. That tepid admiration you feel for me is not love."

"My dear Ann" — Jasha spoke through clenched teeth — "I would like to point out that you wouldn't recognize love if it dragged you off into the forest, which at this moment seems like the only way to get through to you."

She turned her back on him. "You're right. I wouldn't recognize love. But I know it's not synonymous with convenience."

"All right, Ann." His voice was crisp and businesslike. "I thought we had established more confidence in each other than this. I realize now I'm going to have to work harder to make you believe that I would never let you down."

She couldn't stand to see him angry. And she didn't understand herself. All her life she'd told herself she would be practical about marriage. She'd promised herself she'd be happy to be part of a family. Now she was rejecting him not because he turned into a wolf, and not because of the responsibilities of being the icon finder, but because he didn't truly love her? Why wouldn't she take what he offered?

Because she wanted to know she was more to him than his other women.

"I grew up begging for scraps of affection from nuns, from other people's parents, and I deserve better than that. I'm not going to take the icon away, but I don't care what your mother's prophecy said." She faced him. Faced his irritation and his impatience with a lift of her chin. "I'm not going to be the wife you have to marry to save your family."

"All right. You're not going to believe me. Do you believe this?" He caught her wrists, yanked her toward him, and kissed her.

His passion was like a blast from the furnace of hell, a mixture of sex and fury. She shouldn't respond; right now, she didn't even like him. But it seemed liking him had nothing to do with the blistering sensations he roused in her, the ones that made her fight to free her hands, then wrap them around his shoulders and yield to him.

By the time he lifted his head, she was clinging, weak-kneed, and reckless. She would have gone anywhere with him, done anything for him. . . .

"Jasha!" Firebird yelled from the porch. "Ann!"

Jasha lifted Ann's chin, and red rimmed his golden eyes. "Remember that kiss when you're telling yourself you're not interested in my kind of love."

"Jasha!" Firebird yelled again. "Ann!"

He glanced toward his sister. "We'll finish this discussion later," he said to Ann.

"Why bother?" Ann muttered as she followed him toward the house.

"Come in here. Quick!" Firebird disappeared inside.

Jasha looked back at Ann.

One thought swept through their minds. *Konstantine.*

They both raced toward the house.

Inside, everyone stood in the living room, staring at Rurik.

Rurik held the phone, a mixture of awe and disquiet on his face as he spoke sternly into the receiver.

Firebird grabbed their arms and squeezed.

"He got a call from the site in Scotland, and he's gone all air force captain on them."

Ann didn't understand the tension that held the family so taut with anticipation.

As soon as Rurik hung up, Jasha asked, "What is it?"

Rurik looked at Jasha as if he didn't recognize him. "The tomb . . . my team excavated far enough to see the gleam of gold. There are traps, but also, they think there's a huge cache of treasure."

"Way to go!" Jasha stuck out his hand, and again they did the elaborate handshake.

"I instructed them to wait for me to return before they try to spring the traps and go for the gold. But one thing's clear — we've found the tomb I was looking for, the tomb of a great Celtic conqueror." Rurik's voice became quiet, slow, and dark. "A tomb that dates back a thousand years."

"A thousand years." Now Ann understood. "Definitely not a coincidence."

"Exactly." Rurik's brown eyes grew still and deep and satisfied. "This guy knew the first Konstantine Varinski."

CHAPTER 29

A limo picked Jasha and Ann up at the airport and drove them through the summer heat, past the miles of grapes, past the other wineries, and down the long, treelined drive to the tall French-style château that housed Wilder Wines.

It was afternoon and the height of the tourist season, and Jasha noted with satisfaction that the parking lot was full of cars and buses. Tourists lined up for the tasting tours, while on the shady, well-tended grounds, other tourists sat at picnic tables indulging in the decadent premade lunches and glasses of wine.

His family might be going to hell — literally — and his romance might be faltering, but by God, the business was booming.

The château's main floor held the tasting room, the deli and sales counter, storage for the vintages they were selling, and a packing and shipping center. In the basement, the tour guides explained how wine was made, and displayed the great stainless steel tanks awaiting this year's pressing. The top two floors housed the winery offices, so the limo deposited Jasha and Ann at the back door. Together they took the elevator up to the plush reception area, two professionals in suits and her with a briefcase. A briefcase that held the first icon.

They didn't talk.

At first, Jasha hadn't noticed they weren't speaking. He'd been too busy congratulating his brother for his clever combination of intuition and research. He'd helped Rurik get plane tickets, driven him down to Seattle, and dropped him off at the airport. Then he'd come home and sat in the living room with the rest of the family, wondering what Rurik would find. Some pure, historical data?

That would be a disappointment to them, of course, but a huge boon to Rurik's career, and would bring him more grant money for more excavation.

But Rurik hoped to find information on how to break the deal with the devil. Or even . . . discover another icon.

All that evening, Ann had talked; she'd asked questions; she'd expressed awe and wonder. In the morning, as they prepared to return to California, Jasha noticed stiffness, but put it down to a slow resumption of her business persona.

It was only gradually he had noticed — she wasn't speaking to *him.*

And why not? Hadn't he proposed to her? Hadn't he told her he loved her?

He supposed she'd been indignant because he hadn't gone down on one knee, offered her roses and jewels and a life on a cushion. But he'd done that with Meghan and she hadn't been impressed, or at least not impressed enough to marry him.

Thank God.

Besides, Ann was an eminently sensible woman. She surely understood that in this case, his family required his whole attention.

You'll do anything for the sake of your family.

He should have done more than show her how easily he could seduce her. That sure as hell hadn't been his smartest move. But when Ann, gentle, kind, sensible Ann, squared her stubborn chin and told him his love wasn't enough, she drove every battle tactic from his head and he wanted to show her exactly what he did feel.

Unfortunately, she seemed to think his lust for her was no different from his lust for other women.

He snorted.

Startled, Ann glanced at him.

The elevator doors opened, and Ann walked out ahead of him.

He stood still and watched.

She moved like a Spanish dancer, sinewy and graceful.

Yesterday, his father had tried to slap some control into him, but all Jasha wanted to do was bound after her and take her down. He wanted to roll on the floor with her, kiss her until she released that deeply passionate nature she hid so well, then undress her and . . .

Take her for granted? Hell, when she was around, he had trouble keeping his mind on business at all, much less on the business of survival.

Was that love?

Yes, but not the kind that made him turn his back on all he'd loved before. Instead, it was the kind of love that made him bring Ann into the middle of his pack, where she would be safest, and keep her there.

"Mr. Wilder! Miss Smith! We didn't know you were coming!" The pretty young receptionist got to her feet so quickly Jasha suspected she'd been reading a book in her desk drawer.

"Surprise," he answered.

Ann placed her hand over Nicole's as it hovered over the phone. "Let's keep it a surprise."

They headed down the hallway, past the windows of the conference room where wine salesmen and wine buyers met. Shawn, their lead salesman, stood talking to the buyer for Austin Liquor, showing him Wilder Wines's gold medals. Shawn indicated them as they walked past. He had no qualms about using his good-looking boss and his long-legged assistant as a symbol of Wilder Wines. When they married, Shawn would view it as an advertising triumph.

When they married . . .

Ann was trying to keep their professional life on a businesslike basis.

In the normal course of events, Jasha would completely approve. Office romances were the death of a business relationship. And when it came to business relationships, there were none he treasured as much as the one he had with Miss Ann Smith.

Or at least . . . he had.

Now he just damned well wanted her to fling herself at him like she'd done on that rock in the forest. Or leap up to defend him as she'd done when his father gave him hell. Or at least stop retreating every time he advanced.

He needed to think ahead, stay one step ahead of Ann in the way she thought and the moves she would make. If he was canny, he could keep her so occupied with business that she didn't notice he'd taken over her life.

Celia Kim, Jasha's production manager, walked out of the copy room, her head down as she flipped through charts. She dodged them with a scowl, then did a double take. Her face blossomed into a warm smile. "You're back! Did you, er, get everything cleared up?" She looked meaningfully between Jasha and Ann.

As code went, that was the worst Jasha had ever heard.

"Everything's fine," Ann said in a clipped tone.

"Very cleared up." He smiled charmingly, presenting his usual competent façade . . . and a little more. "I enjoyed having Ann at my home. In fact, I took her up to meet my parents."

"Really?" Celia drawled the word, imbuing it with every meaning.

Ann frowned with austere displeasure.

"Yes," he said. "We're going to be working long hours for the next few weeks until they're cleared up some more."

Celia simpered like a girl. "I'm so glad!"

Ann kept walking toward their office suite.

"Although it's a little icy today," he said in an undertone to Celia.

"I'm surprised," she answered. "She's always adored you."

"Passion has caught her by surprise."

Celia glanced between him and Ann. "In a good way, I hope."

"A very good way." Actually, he'd used passion to push Ann into a corner, and he hoped he could find a way to save her pride before more trouble loomed on their horizon.

As Ann reached their office, Celia hurried forward and called, "I wouldn't go in there if I were you."

Ann tried the knob. It was locked. She looked back inquiringly.

Celia mouthed to him, "Jordan and Sophia."

The head vintner and one of the women from receiving.

Jasha flushed with a surprising rage. "Really?" In the suite where Ann labored in the outer office and guarded his privacy, where they had spent long hours in his inner office talking and working? "I don't think so." He strode to the door, unlocked it, and caught the two lovers in an embrace that left nothing to the imagination.

They both jumped and stared, and Jordan stammered, "Look, Jasha, I can explain —"

"Not if I don't listen. You two get dressed, clean out your lockers, and pick up your checks. I'll call the cleaners to wipe off Ann's desk." Jasha shut the door with a thump.

"I knew this was going to happen." Ann leaned against the far wall in the corridor. "I should never have left."

"This is not your fault," Celia answered sharply.

"Celia's right." Jasha took Ann's hand and led her back down the hall toward the cafeteria. Celia followed. "I understand irresistible passion" — he kissed her fingers — "but those two can suffer from it somewhere else, and not during working hours."

"He's a creep and she's" — Celia glanced at Ann — "also a creep."

He'd noticed that before. When Ann was around, everyone used their exotic vocabulary sparingly. She had that effect on people — they were on their best behavior.

"Why has this place gone to hell in six days?" he asked.

"Ann keeps an eye on things," Celia answered. "Because she does take responsibility for everything. She watches everything. She works all the time."

"Ann, I should give you a raise." He smiled his best winsome smile.

But it was wasted, because Ann didn't look at him. "You certainly should."

She didn't want to talk about irresistible passion; she didn't want to meet his eyes . . .

"Let me get us something to drink." Ann twisted her hand free. With a glance around at the empty cafeteria, she placed her briefcase on the chair next to him and headed for the coffee center.

Celia looked between the two of them.

He shrugged and smiled ruefully, trying to defuse the tension, knowing full well if Celia sensed trouble, the entire company would be on alert watching their boss and his secretary.

Damn civilization. Damn proper workplace behavior. He wanted to go back into the forest with his mate and show her the way of the wolf.

But then they would come out again, and again they'd have to deal with the winery and their obligations and his family. They needed to get this settled, and settled in such a way that Ann wore his ring on her finger and slept in his bed every night.

He sat at one of the tables and indicated

the chair across from him. When Celia had seated herself, he leaned close. "Meeting her away from the office made it impossible to resist her. She wore this beautiful dress —"

"I helped her pick it out."

"Good work." Come to think of it, he remembered that dress. Black-and-white, with one big button . . . he'd seen her walking down the stairs, and with each step, her long leg had slid through the wrap.

"What else?" Celia asked eagerly.

"She was so shy and so sweet — oh, I can't talk about it." He leaned back in his chair. "It was perfect."

"Except the part about the wine deal going sour."

"We didn't talk about it a lot." He smiled at Ann as she placed a cup before him.

"What's happened since we left?" Ann asked, still with that businesslike tone.

"The Ukrainian deal is definitely off. They sent some really ugly faxes, but when we couldn't get ahold of you guys, we didn't know what to do." Celia had clearly had a rough time.

"I'll need to see those," Jasha said.

"They were the wrong company to take us international." Ann handed a cup to Celia. She put the briefcase on the floor between her and Jasha, and slid into that chair.

"True." Jasha stared into the milky depths, then up at Celia. "I liked them because they spoke Russian and I didn't need an interpreter, but really, interpreters are cheaper than prima donna CEOs."

Celia grinned and he saw the tension slide out of her shoulders. "Yeah, I thought that, too."

"I wish I'd known that before I chased you up the coast, Jasha." Ann's tone was sharp to the point of sarcasm.

A fairly new development for Ann.

What a hell of a time for her to get comfortable enough to talk back to him.

"We had a nice vacation anyway." Jasha cradled the cup as he spoke to Celia. "I introduced Ann to my family. We all talked about the wine business, and we've decided to keep expanding across the US. What do you think?"

Celia leaned back, suddenly so relaxed that she smiled with disproportionate pleasure. "Great! I recommended that strategy last year, and I still think it's a sound policy. Less risky, with huge potential for success."

"I remember your report." He hadn't liked it at the time. "After Ann and I get caught up, let's go over it together."

"Let's!" Celia glanced at her watch. "Damn. I've got a teleconference. Good to see you two back . . . together."

With a sense of a job well-done, he watched Celia leave. She had gone from being Ann's advocate to being his, and perhaps that was unfair to Ann, but in this battle between him and his lover, he needed all the ammunition he could amass, and if that included commandeering her best friend, well, that made the last fifteen minutes a brilliant maneuver.

He turned to Ann. "I would hope your office is clean, but if it's not, you can come into my office and help me with the mail." Alone in his office. He could close the door. Lock it. And allow no one to come in until she had confessed her love, agreed to marry him, and yielded to him. Yielded everything.

Without a hint of a smile or the scent of infatuation, she stood and picked up her briefcase. "Of course, Jasha."

He caught up with her and took her arm. "I want you to bring in someone who can do your work."

She turned a cool gaze on him. "Why would I do that?"

"Because I want you to concentrate on finding out the exact identity of the person behind the Ukrainian wine distributor."

"I thought you were certain it was one of Oleg's sons."

"Yes, but I want to know how he found me. I want to know how much he knows about me . . . and I want to know about the Varinskis. Their weaknesses, the size of their organization. I want to know names and most important, I want to see faces. Since that time my brothers and I looked up the Varinskis on the library computer, I've never bothered to worry about them. That was a dangerous oversight."

"Yes. It was. What were you thinking?"

"I was thinking they'd paid us no heed for thirty-five years, and it would be better not to call their attention to us by waving a defiant fist."

"All right." Her eyes narrowed and her pace picked up. "I'll get Geekette to make me untraceable while I'm doing the research. Where do you want me to set up my computer?"

"In my office."

She stopped short.

He kept going. "It's the only place in the building that's secure enough." Still she didn't join him, and he turned to face her.

She stared at him, her eyes narrowed, as if trying to see a way out of a trap that tightened around him.

His tactic was to close the jaws on her while she was unaware. "Ann, if you don't want to marry me, that's fine. My ego can handle it." A reminder that the question hung between them, unanswered. "But you know you are the only person I can trust to do this research. You're the only one who's smart enough, *and* you're the only one who knows the special circumstances well enough to comprehend the danger." He used a heavy hand with the trust issue.

Slowly she nodded, but still she waited.

Waited for the other shoe to drop. Smart girl. "And since you'll be moving in with me anyway —"

"I will not!"

"— so I can keep you safe —"

"I'm not moving in with you!"

"— the information you find will be protected, too."

Her chest rose and fell as she took deep breaths, seeking an answer he would listen to.

"If you don't want to move in with me, I suppose you can turn the icon over to me for safekeeping."

Ann stalked past him, so stiff she looked as though she could shatter if he touched her. "You're a jerk, Jasha Wilder."

He watched her walk down the corridor,

and he smiled with all his teeth.

He had a strategy, and Ann didn't stand a chance.

CHAPTER 30

When Jasha touched Ann's shoulder and said, "It's time to go home," she jumped so hard she cleared the chair.

"I'm sorry. I thought you heard me the first time." Jasha frowned at her. "Where were you?"

"In Russia in a tangle of deeds and papers. Boris Varinski is your man, head of the fake Ukrainian wine distributors." She stretched her arms over her head. "Did you know Yerik and Fdoror are on trial in Sereminia for racketeering and murder?"

"Good ol' Yerik and Fdoror." The first part of his strategy was working. She excelled at this type of research, she was enjoying herself, and most important, she was talking to him. "Who are they?"

She pointed at the photos on the screen. "Yerik. Fdoror. Sons of Oleg. So's Boris. Oleg was a busy boy. Well, all Varinskis are busy. Do you know how many Varinskis have been born in the last thirty years?"

"No."

"No, of course you don't. Because in the Ukraine, the Varinskis can apparently do whatever they want, and what they want is to not leave any records of births or deaths or crimes committed. The only thing I can really look for is the money trail, and it's buried beneath a tangle of false ownerships and fake deals. It's only in paperwork from the last few years that I can make any sense out of what's going on, and that's because it seems as if the younger guys are none too good at keeping a low profile."

Jasha used his hands on her arms to lift her from the chair. "That's good. A little incompetence goes a long way to helping our cause."

"Don't kid yourself. Boris and the rest of Oleg's sons are brilliant at what they do. You wouldn't believe the number of crimes informally linked to them. They make the Mafia look like a bunch of Tibetan monks."

He closed the laptop and slid it into his case.

"I think their weakness is their incredible vanity. The younger men don't worry about keeping their secret from the public. There have been *weird*" — she made quotation marks with her fingers — "animal sightings, and apparently, sometimes when they go on raids, the women are fighting back and winning."

He led Ann down the hallway, down the elevator, and out the door to his car, just delivered from his house and already running.

"They really are Russian rednecks, and the *Deliverance* theme is playing in the background," she said.

He laughed. "You have a way with words." He put her in the passenger seat, placed the computer in her lap, and shut the door.

By the time he'd come around to the driver's side, she'd disentangled herself from her fascination with his family and was staring at him accusingly. "I need to go to my condo and get my car, and Kresley."

"Kresley." Shit. He hadn't thought about her cat.

"Kresley." She nodded, then watched him to see whether he would object.

He wasn't crazy. "Sure. I can't wait to meet the little fellow." He put the car in gear and drove out of the parking lot.

"He's not so little. Actually, he weighs twenty-one pounds."

"Now *that's* a cat." If he had to have one of the varmints in his house, he was at least glad it was a decent-sized animal.

She directed him to a gated community in the Napa hills, then to a two-story building divided into six units. She had the upper left; as he climbed the stairs, he discovered an incredible curiosity about her home.

She hurried ahead of him, almost like a woman running away from her lover. Certainly his lust rose as he watched her legs, and he allowed his mind to wander ahead, into her apartment, into her bedroom, where he would slowly remove her clothes one by one. . . .

Then she unlocked her door, and he realized she hadn't been running away. She had been running to . . . her cat.

"Kresley!" She rushed toward the couch, toward this enormous fuzzy orange pillow.

Then as she picked it up, the orange pillow unfolded and became a cat with drooping legs and the same lethargic air that all cats had right before they realized they had an urgent appointment and started dashing frantically around.

Kresley blinked at her, then started making a noise. At first, Jasha couldn't figure out what it was. Then he knew — that was the sound of a twenty-one-pound cat purring.

"He's immense!" Jasha said.

"Isn't he? He's so beautiful." She rubbed

Kresley's head and under his chin, and spoke right into the droopy cat's face. "He's my big, beautiful boy."

Kresley jumped as if startled. Lifting his nose, he sniffed her lips. His eyes got big.

And he started growling low in his throat.

"Kresley!" Ann said.

The big cat used his paws to push at her chest. He leaped out of her arms and backed away.

"Oh, Kresley." Ann sighed. "I suppose he's mad because I left him alone."

"Really?" Now, that was a pet! "You can leave him alone for six days?"

"No, I had my neighbor downstairs, Mrs. Edges, come in and feed him and sit with him. She's a nice woman, a widow, retired from the navy and the post office." Ann dumped her purse on the end table.

He looked around.

She had decorated her living room in tans and browns. Orange accents provided the necessary pop, and the place felt warm and welcoming.

Which was more than he could say for her. She was eyeing him like a piece of couch with a broken spring.

"Can I help you pack something?" he asked.

"No." She turned and headed into the

bathroom.

"Okay," he said to the closed door. He wandered around, checking the rest of the place out.

Her kitchen was small and well organized. Not surprising.

Her bedroom was quite a bit more exotic, with billowing bed-curtains over a queen-sized bed, and that was a revelation. Why, he didn't know. He'd already figured out that her well-organized exterior hid a romantic, passionate interior. Off the bedroom was a great little bathroom that she'd painted a warm, pale peach with aqua accents. Very soothing. He could imagine her relaxing in the tub filled with bubbles, her hair piled on top of her head, her pretty toes lifted and pointed . . . and if he kept imagining stuff like that, her toes wouldn't be the only thing lifted and pointed.

Hands in his pockets, he wandered back into the living room, where the cat sat on the couch, staring malevolently at him. This cat was going home with him, so he approached slowly and extended his hand for Kresley to sniff. "Nice kitty. Good kitty."

Kresley started that deep-throated growl again, a growl that quickly grew into a full-blown threat.

Ann came out of the bathroom, holding a

handful of the kind of feminine products that let him know he was *not* a father, and he was *not* getting any tonight, something he'd suspected more from her behavior than from her scent.

"Kresley, what is wrong with you?" she asked.

"Cats have a tendency to do that — they sense the wolf in me." Jasha took a few steps back.

Kresley followed.

"They react instinctively," Jasha added.

"And with good sense." She stood watching. "Is he *stalking* you?"

"I believe he is."

"Well, he can't do that." She dropped the tampons on the table, walked over to Kresley to pick him up — and Kresley turned on her.

If Jasha hadn't lifted her away, her own cat would have savaged her.

"Kresley!" she wailed.

"He smells me on you." Jasha didn't say they had a problem. With Ann, he never had to state the obvious.

Her voice trembled as she said, "I'll see if Mrs. Edges will watch him until he gets used to you."

"That might be a good idea."

■ ■ ■ ■

Ann shut the laptop and studied the bright morning sunlight for a long moment, then looked across the office at Jasha. "You know, everything I find out about the Varinskis makes me realize what a formidable foe they are."

He raised his head from the papers he was signing. He put down his pen and folded his hands. "Time for a summary?"

"There seem to be well over a hundred of them, with numerous false identities. The older men are brilliant, setting up false corporations, laundering money, and always, always pursuing, torturing, and assassinating. The younger guys, for the most part, seem significantly less competent, but perhaps that is because they're young."

"More likely undisciplined."

"Hm. Yes, that's possible." Or maybe demons who lived to a great age matured later than normal men. Although Jasha had seemed mature from the first moment she'd laid eyes on him. And handsome. And smart. Too damned smart.

They'd spent the last five days together. *Every damned minute.*

In the morning, she woke up in his house,

in his bedroom, in his arms. She'd been having her period, so she used that excuse ruthlessly — she'd used it so she wouldn't have to have sex, and even more satisfactorily, she'd used it as an excuse to be bitchy.

Her aptitude for bitchiness surprised even her.

She ate breakfast with him; then they drove to the office — separately, thank God, because she'd been sensible enough to insist on having her own car. But once there, she did research on the laptop in his office. All day. Every day. With him talking and walking and breathing . . . always there, always watching . . . there was never a moment when she wasn't aware of him.

He had told her he knew her scent.

Well, now she knew his. And liked it far too much.

At five, she escaped to feed Kresley, but that wasn't really an escape. Kresley didn't like her anymore. He didn't attack her again, but he watched her warily, and when she petted him, he growled. She tried explaining he could go to Jasha's with her if he'd stop that, but he wasn't buying it.

Then it was home for dinner at one of the top restaurants in Napa.

Deliberately, Jasha showed her the contrast between their time together in the forest and their time together here. They dined on the most spectacular meals, and always by candlelight. Celebrities stopped by their table and chatted, and one night, he'd taken her dancing. At the beginning of the evening, she'd been too self-conscious to dance well. But by the end of the evening, it seemed she had always been in his arms.

She wasn't stupid. She knew he was showing her that no matter the circumstances, he could provide for her, and well.

Yeah, yeah. She was determined not to be impressed — but she was.

After dinner, they went home and watched some television or read . . . and went to bed together.

As a strategy, *every damned minute* seemed pretty successful. No matter how hard she tried to hang on to her resentment, he kept charming her. She kept forgetting about Zorana's damned prophecy that had made Jasha give her an insulting proposal of marriage, and remembering only how pleasant he was to be with, and how knowledgeable, and all the reasons she'd fallen in love with him in the first place. Plus as the discomfort from her period faded, she had those additional memories. . . .

Everything about their mating had been primal, exhilarating, violent in its lust, tender in its passion. His hands on her breasts, his weight on her body, the slow thrust inside, the quickening beat . . . last night she'd dreamed of it, and him, and woke up on the verge of orgasm. She'd lain there trembling, trying to calm herself before he woke up. She knew him. If he realized how horny she was, he'd take advantage.

But apparently she'd succeeded in hiding her arousal, because the bastard hadn't stirred.

The one time she could have pretended she was asleep and dreaming and not responsible, and he hadn't come through.

Face it. He was undependable.

But she'd paid him back. She wore suits to the office, suits with skirts demurely hemmed at the middle of her knees, and pleats at the bottom, and sometimes a slit at the back. Today she wore a black jacket and a pencil-thin skirt, and under the jacket she wore a hot-pink satin blouse. She'd caught him looking at her legs with a hunger that gave her a little of her own back.

Oh, and she always put makeup on the mark on her back. Just in case.

At least that part of the week had been fun.

"What do you suggest?" he asked.

"Huh?" She stared at him. Was he asking if he should propose? Or if he should seduce? Or what restaurant they should go to tonight?

"Should I call Boris and talk to him?"

"Oh." Thank God she'd said nothing dumber than *Huh?* "The Varinski you killed said they hadn't tracked your parents, and I think we can assume that's true. But somehow they've nailed you and your brother —"

At the mention of Rurik, his eyes got that red glow deep inside.

The discovery at Rurik's dig had hit the networks even before Rurik had landed in Scotland — the opening of a thousand-year-old tomb filled with gold had fit every news editor's needs on a slow news day. And when *someone* blew the tomb sky-high, and Rurik and the photojournalist Tasya Hunnicutt disappeared, the reporters had gone mad with excitement.

And continued, "So taking the initiative and making the call might impress these guys. They're certainly into posturing."

"Animals — and men — spray to mark territory. I have the better stream right now, because I can tell Boris *I* killed his sons."

"Yes." She loved it when they tossed ideas back and forth; she always had. These ideas were so much more important than any they'd ever dealt with before, and she knew he valued her input. "He knows his killers haven't checked in, but he may not even know they're dead."

"Depending on whether he has surveillance on me, he may think we're all dead. So if you agree it's a good idea, I'm going to call Boris."

"I agree, but it's the middle of the night there right now."

Jasha picked up the phone and smiled with that toothy grin that always presaged trouble for his challengers. "All the better."

CHAPTER 31

Boris cut the connection and clutched his wiry hair in his hands.

Two Varinskis were dead.

And one his own son.

He had lots of sons; one more or less didn't matter.

But Gavrie had been the Varinskis' best tracker, eager and willing, good with electronics, yet he knew how to use a wolf predator's most important tool, the nose. He hadn't been too bright, but he'd been a powerful warrior. Yet why would the boy need those skills?

The sons of the degenerate Konstantine couldn't defeat a true Varinski.

Yet somehow this spit-wad son of Konstantine's had defeated Gavrie and left his body to be found and desecrated by the American police. Boris was no closer to knowing Konstantine's location so he could kill him and all his spawn — and reverse the decay of the great Varinski family.

True, he had given Jasha news to break a brother's heart, and he knew he'd shocked the boy, but he also knew the boy didn't believe him.

For good reason. Rurik still lived.

But not for long. Not for long.

Boris wanted to roar, to go out in the great room and kick Varinski ass, but what good would that do? Most of the boys would sit there, their mouths hanging open, not understanding his fury. The ones who did understand would snigger and mock, and his son Vadim would watch him coolly and try to judge if now was the time to strike Boris down.

Power was slipping between Boris's fingers — and why?

Because of Konstantine and his bitch Gypsy. Because Konstantine betrayed his family. Betrayed everything the Varinskis stood for — murder, terror, and profit. For how could a family remain united when brother killed brother in defense of a mere woman? For the sake of . . . love.

Boris spit on the floor, then shouted for one of the women to come and clean it up. While she worked he paced, paying no attention to her flinching and her moaning.

At first, when Konstantine had killed his

father, Boris and his brothers thought only of revenge. Boris had marshaled the forces of the Varinskis to track Konstantine and his wife — Boris spit on the floor again — to kill them both. Kill them hideously, slowly, painfully.

But Konstantine was too clever for them. The couple had disappeared off the face of the earth.

That had led to trouble. Boris's brothers and nephews had rumbled that Boris had failed them. Boris had had to assert his dominance through treachery and struggle. Thirty-five years ago, his mind and his reflexes had been clever and quick, and within a year he'd been firmly in command.

By then Konstantine's trail was cold, as was Boris's mind.

Let the traitor go. He didn't matter. What did matter was moving the Varinski operation into the modern world. Faxes, computers, tracking devices — the old leaders didn't like them, and old men don't change easily, but Boris was young. Boris had the chance to remake the family into a modern corporation with tendrils of terror that encompassed the whole world.

Even now, Boris thought it was a good plan.

Except that slowly it became obvious that

the devil was displeased. The deal was un-
raveling.

First one son was born with a limp. Then
another was missing a finger. Then one
turned, and he was not a wolf, or an eagle,
or a tiger. He was a ferret, a small, sneaky,
disgusting rodent with sharp teeth and
beady eyes.

Never in a thousand years had such a
change occurred.

Boris killed him, of course, before anyone
knew.

But it was only the beginning. Within five
years, other sons turned, and they were
snakes, and weasels — predators, yes, but
not noble predators.

They made Boris shudder in revulsion.

Not all of the boys born were lesser beasts.
But more all the time, and some of them,
once they changed, never quite changed
back.

Worse, for the first time, the ravages of
time struck at the Varinskis. The boys' teeth
rotted. The old men's fingers grew stiff.
Uncle Ivan sat in the corner, blind, with a
white film over his eyes, and that was the
scariest thing of all.

For Uncle Ivan saw things, things no one
else could see. Last year, in the dead of
winter, he had said things to Boris. . . .

Ivan's bent old fingers scrabbled to grab the front of Boris's shirt. With surprising strength, he pulled him close, and with breath that smelled of rot and a voice deep and unlike his own, he whispered, "For a thousand years, the pact with me has held firm. But now, Boris Varinski, it is failing. Every day hell's fire comes closer, for Konstantine and his whelps continue on this earth. Eliminate them, and you save the pact. Fail, and I will torment your soul through eternity." Ivan's eyes glowed, not red, like a true Varinski's, but blue like a coal.

Boris shuddered and pulled away — and knew he'd been handed an ultimatum from the devil himself.

The final straw occurred when Boris took a pack of the young ones hunting. They tracked their prey, a couple with a young son they'd been paid to remove, and during the fight, Boris was shot in the leg. He howled with pain, then laughed, then came home to mend.

The wound had healed, but not as quickly as wounds had in the past, and it left him with a twinge in his hip.

A twinge. A twinge! Varinskis did not suffer twinges. They healed at once. It was part of the pact — or the pact as it had been.

After a month, Boris went on a solitary hunting trip — for a doctor. He'd found one in Minsk. The weary young doctor obviously had never heard of the Varinskis, or didn't believe, or didn't care, because he took an X-ray and curtly told Boris he had arthritis.

Arthritis! He, Boris Varinski, the leader of the Varinskis, had arthritis! His grandfather had lived to be 127. It was said the great Konstantine himself lived to be 150.

And Boris . . . Boris was only 53.

Boris had killed the doctor, of course, and his only pleasure was seeing the man's futile struggles, seeing his eyes bulge and his cheeks turn purple, then black, and the light of life fade from his lying, stupid face.

Then Boris had gone home, secretly took his medicine, and told no one.

But always Vadim watched him, his eyes alight with malice.

Did the boy know? How? It wasn't possible that he had followed Boris . . . was it?

Lifting his head, Boris stared out into the yard where weeds grew above the fence and broken vehicles littered the ground, and his brain raced along the familiar track.

The Varinski troubles had started when his uncle Konstantine had grown soft and let that Gypsy bitch possess him.

So it followed that when Boris destroyed Konstantine and his whole family, then the devil would be pleased once more. Then the sons would become as they were before — whole, cruel, and noble. Then Boris would be well without twinges of age that foretold his downfall. And Vadim would slink back into the pack, his gaze downcast and his air respectful.

Yes. That was what would happen.

And now Boris knew how to bring Konstantine out of hiding.

Picking up the phone, he made a call to the Varinski stationed in Napa Valley.

In his office, Jasha sat on his weight bench and worked his biceps over and over until his mind cleared of anger and he could think once more.

Ann was right. Jasha had caught Boris off guard.

But Boris had caught Jasha off guard, too. In his heavy accent, he had said, "So I hear your brother has disappeared from Scotland. Perhaps he has met with an accident, heh? So dangerous, this archaeological excavation, and so unfortunate when bad things happen. Of course, should we come across his body, we'll ship him home to you. After all, you're relatives."

Jasha didn't believe him; they hadn't heard from Rurik since the explosion, but his brother was not so easily killed.

Yet the fact that the Varinskis were tracking Rurik's activities meant they'd wormed their way much further into the Wilder secrets than Jasha had realized.

He needed to increase security at his home and his winery.

Ann stuck her head in the door. "How did it go?"

Most important, Jasha needed to keep Ann safe at all costs. "I've got to make another call, but I'll tell you about it later."

He watched as she nodded and backed out to give him privacy.

Tell her about it later?

Hell, he'd be lucky if she was speaking to him later.

CHAPTER 32

At five o'clock, Ann slipped the laptop into the case, turned to Jasha, and said, "I'm going to spend some time with Kresley. I'll come to your house later." She always called it *your house* — it was a small defense in the battle between them. She didn't expect Jasha to say anything except, *Okay, I'll meet you at home.*

Calling it *home* was his return volley.

Yet tonight, when his gaze met hers, his eyes were narrowed and rimmed in fire.

"What's wrong?" She thought she knew. The phone call to Boris had left Jasha intense and quiet. She recognized that attitude — he had instigated a plan he considered necessary, but of which no one else would approve.

She didn't realize *she* was the one who wouldn't like his plan.

"Go to your condo and pick up your cat, and bring him home," he said.

His tone made her bristle, but she kept her voice even and reasonable. "Kresley doesn't like you."

"We'll learn to get along." He looked her straight in the eyes. "And he'll be happier at my house than in your empty condo."

"Empty? Condo?" She took a step closer to him. "You're kidding, right?"

"I told you we'd talk about this morning's phone call."

"With Boris." She stood tense and still.

"Yes. With Boris." Jasha stood as if standing would calm his restlessness. "I woke him out of dead sleep, but he's like any animal. He revived at once. He asked what had happened to his son. I told him I killed him and ate his heart. He shrugged it off, said the boy was the least of his sons, and told me how much he admired my ruthless brutality. He suggested a truce."

She'd done the research. "Varinskis don't make truces."

"I know. I know so much better than you. My father taught me what the Varinskis say and what they really mean, and what tactics they use and when and why." Jasha rounded the desk, striding rapidly toward her. "I won't have you stay alone again."

"So you had my furniture moved to your house? *Today?*" Her outrage grew until she felt as if *her* eyes glowed red. "Why didn't you ask me?"

"Don't give me trouble about this." He caught her arms in his hands.

"Give you trouble about this? This? You didn't ask me, you didn't tell me, you just had my furniture moved, and you're acting as if *I'm* unreasonable?" She'd always known he was high-handed, but this!

"You spend every night at my house anyway. What difference does it make if you keep your furniture there?" He wasn't ridiculing her. He was serious.

She could feel the furious rush of blood staining her cheeks. She clenched her fists, and she struggled to lift her arms so she could box his ears. "What difference does it make if I have my own home, the first home I've ever had, with my own furniture where my own cat can be comfortable? I don't know — why don't you move in with me and see whether you feel displaced?"

"I'm sorry. I didn't think about your condo being your first home."

He did look sorry, and that really fried her. How dare he feel sorry for her?

"I would stay with you if it was possible," he said, "but there's no way to be secure in your home."

"What do you care? The icon is in your

safe." And that pissed her off, too. Maybe it wasn't strictly her icon, but everyone agreed — at least, she and Zorana agreed — that it was her responsibility.

"It's not the icon I'm worried about. It's you."

"Let's talk about what's really important — your place is nicer," she mocked him.

"Not nicer. Larger and easier to guard."

Now, in addition to feeling sorry for her, he was being patient. "Oh, please. As if the great Jasha Wilder would stay in my little condo with —"

He kissed her.

He hadn't kissed her since the day he'd proposed, and this stealth attack caught her off guard. All the days of being with him, yet being alone, caught up with her, and she kissed him back. Kissed him with her heart and soul open and vulnerable. Kissed him passionately and lovingly.

When he drew back, he made the mistake of smiling with the smile she'd seen him practice on so many women. "Believe me. I love you, and I want you to marry me. Please."

A month ago, she would have killed to hear those words and have him smile like that at her.

Now she just wanted to kill. "You think

you treat me like you treat every other woman in the world, and that'll be enough? I don't think so, buster."

"I do not treat you like I treat other women." He slid his hands over her rear and lifted her into him, letting her feel his erection. "Other women don't keep me hard twenty-four hours a day."

"Am I supposed to be flattered?" She injected disdain into her voice, but the sensation of him against her made her nipples ache and her body reach for him.

She was so easy. And he knew it, because he was a wolf.

Great. Just great.

"No, you're not supposed to be flattered. But you should be flattered that I still say I love you. I may have proposed to another woman, but I never told another woman *that*." In direct contrast with his irritated tone, his hand moved with slow sensuality up her spine, and his fingers whispered lovingly to the soft hair at the base of her skull.

"I wouldn't be flattered even if you meant it."

She saw the rush of blood to his cheeks, the narrowing of his eyes. She'd finally made him lose his temper.

"What about me? All you want from me is safety."

"What?" Why did he think that? "That's not true!"

"First you thought you wanted some dream man, some noble cavalier to rescue you from your loneliness. Then when I turned into a wolf, when you found the icon, when you realized we were fighting for lives and our souls, you wanted to run away — until I proved I could protect you. Then you were willing enough to be at my side."

"How can you say that?" She tried to elbow her way free.

He kept her close. "Finally, when I told you I loved you, you were afraid to believe me. Fine. Don't believe me. Tell yourself my kind of love isn't the kind you want. Just let me do what I do so well, and protect you from harm."

He was bitter, he was annoyed, and worse — parts of what he said were true.

It was the true parts that made her angrier than ever. "All right. I'll move in with you — until the danger's passed, however long that takes. But I won't marry a man like you."

"What do you mean, a man like me?" Jasha's face grew cool.

"A man who arranges things as *he* likes. A man who doesn't trust me enough to tell me his secrets."

"Am I the only one with secrets?"

She stiffened under his direct stare.

"That's what I thought." His hand still caressed the nape of her neck, but her impression had changed. Somehow, the gesture was less tender and more blatantly sexual. "And you do know my secrets."

"If I knew your secrets, maybe this move wouldn't have taken me by surprise. Maybe I would have —"

"Volunteered to move in with me?" He found nerve endings that sent sensation to the hollows of her elbows and knees, to the sensitive places at the tops of her thighs. "If I thought there was a chance you would display that kind of sense, I certainly would have had you arrange the move. After all, that's the kind of work a secretary is supposed to do."

His calm insult caught her by surprise, and cut her to the quick. He never called her a secretary, he always thought well of her, and he always insisted that she turn the rote phone calls over to the receptionist.

Her upsurge of loathing surprised her more. "I have never hated anyone like I hate you." Right now she meant it — but perhaps she really hated only herself.

Jasha walked to his office door. He shut it. Locked it. And when he turned around, the blaze in his eyes made her take a step back. "Since you hate me forever anyway, I might as well prove how very much you also love me."

He paced toward her, and just the way he walked, with the slow, long stride of a predator, made her realize his intentions, and her heartbeat accelerate. "Jasha, no."

"Why not? What are you going to do?" As he circled her, he stripped off his tie. "Despise me? Hate me? Refuse to marry me? You already do all those things. So what have I got to lose?"

She thought she felt him brush her earlobe, but when she swung around, he stood off to the side, taking his belt out of the belt loops. "Don't take off your clothes," she said. "Nothing's going to happen."

She might as well have saved her breath, for he asked, "Do you know how very much I love to watch you walk in this skirt? But of course you do. You wore it to tease me."

She caught his scent on her left side, felt a wisp of his breath on her ear, but when she turned, he paced behind her. "No, I didn't."

He laughed in disbelief. "You've worn skirts every day this week, just to get even with me for keeping you at my house. Don't you think I recognize a good strategy when

I see one? And it worked, too. You've got such a long stride, and the slit on this skirt —"

She jumped as he ran his hand up her thigh.

"The slit on this skirt shows such a beautiful expanse of pale creamy leg. But I have to wonder — what kind of panties are you wearing?" His voice dropped to a husky whisper. "Bikini? Thong? A sensible cotton number, perhaps?"

Her mouth grew dry, and she shifted her legs, suddenly uncomfortable, needy, and far, far too bare in her thong.

"Do you know what has been my fantasy this week?"

"I don't care." She so cared.

"The weight bench. I could see you straddling it, bent over, and facing away from me, while I —" He caught her around the waist, moving so quickly she didn't have time to scream. He propelled her backward — the movement was almost like dancing — until the bench struck the backs of her knees and she overbalanced.

He caught her on the way down, spun her away from him, and lifted her skirt at the same time.

She found herself standing at the end of the bench, bent from the waist, her hands gripping the sides.

His fantasy was almost reality.

He groaned with delight, and stroked the bare globes of her rear. "Ann. My God. You're going to kill me."

"Only if I can get my hands on you." But her eyes closed as he moved the thin string of her thong aside and caressed her, his fingers exploring her clit, then slipping inside her, exploring her depths, then sliding slowly up her crack.

Her hands gripped the bench so hard her fingers turned white.

My God. It was broad daylight; her legs were spread; he could see colors and textures, all the contrasts that made her a woman. Worse, he didn't wait for permission to do whatever he liked. He truly was the autocrat she called him — and all she wanted to do was tell him to hurry up.

He pulled the thong down, off, and that was a step in the right direction. He urged her forward, making her spread her legs to straddle the weight bench.

She heard his pants drop. Then he stepped up behind her, as close as he could get. He pressed himself against her, and used his dick to stroke her.

The skin was silky hot, the size large and rigid, and she wanted him to stop messing around and . . . "I hate you," she whispered again.

"And?"

She rubbed herself against him like a wolf in heat. "And . . . Jasha, I need you now."

"That's it. That's exactly what I wanted."

His quiet exultation made her want to turn on him, shriek at him.

But she couldn't, for he thrust himself inside her.

The head, the ridges of his cock rubbed her inside and out. The sudden intrusion made her tighten almost to orgasm. As he pulled back, her body released him only reluctantly, and he groaned.

Then he thrust again, and thrust again, and she met each lunge with an eagerness that demanded its due.

She wanted to come. She needed to come. She craved that sweet release, those moments when nothing but pure pleasure filled her mind, and she and Jasha were one.

Yet climax remained tantalizingly out of reach. No matter how hard she tried . . . she bent down farther, put her cheek to the weight bench, and gave herself up to the motions, the sounds, the scents.

"Please," she heard someone say. "Please." She recognized her own voice, chanting its plea.

But before she could reclaim her dignity, his hand slid between them. His fingers softly bit at her clitoris, and climax jolted through her, bringing her alive and wild with the glory. She shuddered and spasmed, and when she could contain it no more, she screamed with a pleasure that couldn't be contained.

And he was there with her. He moved her hips back and forth as he pounded into her. Waves of scent rolled off him: pleasure, release, satisfaction, and yet more pleasure.

She truly did hate him, but he was right — she loved him, too, and if she wasn't careful, he would absorb her. For as she came to rest, she realized — she could identify his moods by the shifts in his scents.

When had that happened? When had he marked her so completely?

He slid out of her, and she crumpled onto the bench, gathering all her strength, and all her courage.

"Ann." He grasped her waist and helped her sit up, helped her tuck her skirt under her. Sitting beside her, he took her hand. "We can't go on like this. We've got to talk. We need honesty between us."

"I was thinking exactly the same thing." She risked a glance at him.

He looked tired, worried, and satisfied, all

at once.

She thought perhaps she looked the same.

He didn't understand why she held him away, and everything between them had become twisted, complicated, confused. She had to tell him the truth.

For the first time ever, she would tell someone — no, show someone — her secret.

"I didn't refuse to marry you just because your mother said we ought to," she said. "I had reasons of my own."

"I would never marry to fulfill my family's expectations. If I was willing to do that, I would have been married at twenty. But please — I'm fascinated to hear the reasons of your own."

She brought the bad people. She always brought the bad people.

"Do you know what my first memory is? I was tiny, three or four, and I was in the bathtub. One of the volunteers was bathing me, and all of a sudden, she screamed and pointed, and screamed again." In a move so bold she didn't recognize herself, she stood and walked to the west window, where the sun beamed into his office. "I still remember the words she screamed. *Fiend. Monster.* I didn't know what those words meant, but I remembered them so clearly." Ann still remembered how terrified she had been.

"The girl was so frightened, she ran away. That was the first time I knew."

"Ann, I've seen you naked," he said patiently. "There is nothing monstrous about you."

"You haven't seen this." Ann turned her back to Jasha, lifted her skirt, and pointed to the mark. "I've made sure of it."

He strolled over, curious, yet sure of himself and what he knew. "I saw it just now, when we made love. It's a tattoo. I couldn't tell what it was, but I had other, more pressing matters that held my attention." He grinned at her, a sexy quirk of the lips that made her glad she'd taken the opportunity for one last chance in his arms.

"Look closer." With her thumb, she rubbed the makeup off the mark that made her special. That made her different from everyone else.

He leaned forward to scrutinize her, and she could tell — he was on the verge of making a risqué joke.

Then he observed the outline, the shape, and maybe, maybe he saw the thing that set her apart from the rest of humanity.

His eyes grew wide, and he took a compulsive step back. "What . . . ? How . . . ?"

"I've had it since the time I was born. Sister Mary Magdalene didn't like to talk about it, not even with me, but she told me a few things. She told me she thought that mark was probably the reason my parents abandoned me in the Dumpster like I was garbage. She told me I could never tell anyone about it, or the bad people would come and take me away."

"That's ridiculous." But he bent again to look. His finger hovered over the top . . . yet he didn't dare touch the thing that marked her.

"No, it's not. The bad people did come."

His gaze jerked to her face. "What happened?"

"Sister Catherine was a young nun. A nice, young woman who worried about me. She told me I was the most solemn nine-year-old she'd ever met. So she told me jokes. She hugged me. She tried to teach me to play." Ann lowered her skirt and turned to face him. "One evening, she wanted me to sneak out, leave my homework, so we could go and swing on the swings. She was so pretty and so smart, and I wanted to be just like her . . . so I went. And we swung. And the bad people came. . . ." Ann found herself staring at the square of sunshine on the carpet, and the old anguish, the anguish she'd tried to put behind her, rose from the depths of her soul. "They came for me. When she realized they wanted to steal me, she told me to run, and she fought them for me. She died for me, right before my eyes."

"Ann." Jasha put his arms around her, but gingerly, as if she were injured . . . or as if he was afraid of her. "That wasn't your fault."

"That's not what Sister Mary Magdalene said." The vision of Sister Catherine's broken body and her crimson blood burned Ann's memory like a brand.

"I don't like your Sister Mary Magdalene."

"She's not lovable, but she did tell me the truth. She told me the bad people wanted me, to use me and my mark. She told me . . . she told me that God had a service for me to perform, and to pray that I was strong enough to perform it." Ann remembered the years of obedience fueled by fear, and a slow fury unfurled in her gut.

All her life she'd done what she was told.

First she'd lived in an orphanage with no chance of adoption — because of her mysterious mark.

Then she'd taken a secretarial course, moved on to a job at Wilder Wines, and willingly placed herself in Jasha's service, working her way up to the position of his executive assistant — because she loved him.

She had always, *always,* lived under rules passed down to her by a higher power, making sacrifices to give others peace of mind, and she'd done it without a thought to any kind of return.

And she'd received what she anticipated, because no one had ever bothered to try to make her happy. At least, not without an ulterior motive.

Her eyes narrowed on Jasha.

She was done trying to please him. She was done being a martyr — for anyone or anything.

She pulled out of his embrace. "If the service God wants me to perform includes marriage to you, I won't do it. I won't sacrifice myself for God or for Sister Mary Magdalene or for your family or for you."

"You love me."

He wasn't a quitter, not even when he knew the truth; she'd say that for him. "Yes, I do, but there's one thing our adventure has taught me — I deserve the same kind of total loyalty and total love I'm capable of giving."

"Why do you think I won't give you that?"

"Not *won't,* Jasha — *can't.*" Ann was very sure of herself. "You can't because you're balanced on a knife's edge, throwing all your heart and mind into breaking the deal with the devil. And because we both know Sister Mary Magdalene might be wrong."

"What do you mean?" His face and body grew still as if expecting a blow.

"I mean you don't dare marry a woman who might unwittingly be in league with the devil." She caught her jacket off the chair and flounced toward the door.

"Ann, don't run too far."

She turned back and looked at him.

"Because don't you know? In the wild, wolves mate for life." And his eyes glowed red.

CHAPTER 33

Driven by anger, concern, and confusion, Jasha sought answers the only way he knew how — by going right to the source. Picking up the phone, he dialed the Convent of the Blessed Virgin in Los Angeles. "I'd like to speak to Sister Mary Magdalene."

The person on the other end, a severe female with an attitude that clearly declared he was impertinent, said, "The mother superior is busy. May I take a message?"

"It's about the orphan Ann Smith."

The voice changed, became terse and concerned. "I'll see if she'll speak with you."

He wasn't surprised when the nun came to the phone right away.

"Is Ann well?" Sister Mary Magdalene's voice was thin, old, and deep-South Southern.

"She's fine." And *he* was furious. "Do you really care?"

A long pause followed his terse query. "I

do care. Every day since Ann graduated from high school and left, I've prayed for her well-being."

"And for her wicked soul?"

"There is nothing wicked about Ann's soul," the sister said sharply. "She's kind and sensitive, and let me tell you, mister, I've taught a lot of children, and she's one of the few I can say that about."

He'd just had his knuckles figuratively rapped with a ruler.

"Mr. Wilder, you're Ann's employer, is that right?"

"She's told you about me." So Ann was still in contact with the convent.

"So you are Ann's employer." The nun wanted her questions answered, and clearly she had the experience to get her own way.

"I am."

"Then listen to me, sir. My concern is now and always has been that through her own kindness and innocence, she'll fall in with someone who will want to use her for their own evil purposes. And, sir, if you are one of those, I warn you, an angry old nun is a formidable foe. Now, why *are* you calling?"

Okay. Maybe he'd read the situation wrong. "I'm calling because today I found out about the mark on Ann, and I want to know —"

"You're her husband?"

"I am trying to be, but she won't agree." She wouldn't agree for a lot of reasons, but now he'd realized everything in Ann's life went back to that damned mark.

The hesitation on the other end of the line was long and thoughtful.

He scrambled for the right words to convince her of his good intentions, and the best he could come up with was, "Sister. I love her."

"Very impressive. No man has ever told *that* lie for his own gain."

Wow. A cynical nun. In exasperation, he asked, "How do you expect me to prove my good intentions over the phone?"

"Proving your good character will be enough. Tell me, Mr. Wilder, what did you see when you saw the mark?"

"I saw a rose in bloom with a snake coiled around it."

"And?"

"And . . ." He felt stupid admitting what he'd seen. He felt as incredulous as Ann must have felt when she'd seen a wolf turn into a man. "And the snake opened its eyes and looked at me, then closed them again."

"That's all?"

"Isn't that enough?"

"It is."

He'd passed a test. He didn't know what test it could be, but he'd passed.

"Did Ann tell you what I do?" Sister Mary Magdalene asked.

"You're a nun? You're a teacher?" He groped for more.

"I'm now the mother superior of this convent, and administration and prayer takes up my time, so I've given up teaching."

Clearly, she was proud of her promotion.

"But when I taught, I taught history and church doctrine, not only because the task of guiding children is a rewarding one, but because history is my passion." The tone of her voice changed, became more intense. "Specifically, the study of the eternal struggle between good and evil."

He cast his mind back to school. "I don't remember reading about that in the history books."

"I didn't teach the children the stories I know. If they realized how closely the battle raged to their own front doors, and how evenly matched the odds, it would scare them half to death."

"Yes." In the background, he heard the rising noise of children's voices. Class must have just let out. "I suppose it would."

"I don't know if she told you, but Ann was found in a Dumpster."

"She did tell me."

"Then she trusts you quite a lot." Sister Mary Magdalene took a breath. "Dumping a baby isn't unusual in this part of Los Angeles. Not unusual anywhere, really. The difference was that she had been premature, she'd been in there for days, and the wino who found her was so frightened of her he wouldn't touch her. He told the other street people about her, and the mark on her back." She shut a door, and the sound of children died away. "He said it was the mark of a witch."

"That's the mark of a witch?"

Sister Mary Magdalene's voice developed a teacher's intonation. "No, actually, a third nipple is a mark of a witch. Ann does not have one."

He almost agreed, but caught himself in time.

"As was wont, word got to me about the find. I went down to get her. Actually, I thought to pick up a tiny corpse, because this was during one of our rare cold snaps, and babies don't survive without heat. When I got to that alley . . ." Sister Mary Magdalene's voice wobbled in remembered disquiet.

He found himself leaning forward in his chair. "Steady, Sister."

"A bag lady, one of our schizophrenics and a woman dear to me, had rescued the baby, wrapped her in a newspaper, and taken her to the community fire to keep her warm. As I walked into that alley, a beggar I had never seen before was attempting to take Ann." Jasha could almost see Sister Mary Magdalene clench her fists. "The beggar and Mary were playing tug of war with the baby, while Mary screeched that he wanted the baby for a sacrifice. Before I rescued her, they'd dislocated both her shoulders and the newspaper had caught fire."

In his mind's eye, Jasha could see the scene — the screaming baby, the shrieking woman, the nun parting the chaos like Moses parting the Red Sea.

"The man didn't fight *me* for the child. Instead he performed a rather hasty disappearing act. We put out the fire, I called the ambulance, and I thanked Mary."

"Tell me where she is now, and I'll thank her more." He tapped his pen on the desk.

"She didn't survive. Within a week, she was found with her neck broken."

He stopped tapping. "My God."

"Precisely, Mr. Wilder. When I unwrapped

414

the baby, I saw what all the fuss was about. There to the right of her spine was a tightly closed rosebud surrounded by a small, coiled snake."

"A rosebud? But it's —"

"In bloom. I know. As Ann grew, her birthmark changed."

Jasha leaned back his chair and covered his eyes with his hand. To hear this story while the sun shone so strongly seemed obscene. This story should be told at night at a teenage girls' slumber party right before they watched *Night of the Living Dead.* It was not a story to be told about Ann with her sweet mouth and her wide, blue eyes and the way she looked at him as if he were a hero . . . or she had, until that day in Washington when he'd claimed to love her.

She'd said he was lying, that his love was nothing more than expediency.

As always, she'd seen the truth.

He'd been willing to settle for fabulous sex and a great relationship.

But she wanted more. She wanted it all.

"I knew she was a special child, but it took me years to discover what the mark meant." Sister Mary Magdalene's voice turned tart as she anticipated his questions. "And no, I can't do most of my research on the Internet. The church doesn't put its ancient texts on the Internet. And no, I couldn't travel to view the texts because I wouldn't leave Ann alone."

"What could happen to her in a convent?"

"I didn't keep her isolated, Mr. Wilder. She attended school with the other children, went to play at their houses, joined the Camp Fire Girls and the swim team. But I didn't tell anyone about her birthmark — a secret is only a secret when it's kept by one — so I couldn't trust anyone to make sure that Ann was kept safe."

"Right." A whole different picture of Ann's early life was emerging. Sister Mary Magdalene wasn't the ogre he'd imagined, but a holy woman doing the best she could in extraordinary circumstances.

"My first clue as to the meaning of the mark came when she was three. We had a worker in the nursery, a young woman, a former drug addict we employed to help with the children. I sent her to bathe Ann, and from the bathroom I heard a shriek of terror. She ran out, babbling that the snake had struck at her."

"My God." He *had* to stop saying that.

"When I went in, Ann was in the tub, wide-eyed and frightened, but not crying — Ann seldom cried — and when I looked, the snake was moving. It circled the rose quickly as if agitated. When it saw me, it settled down and closed its eyes."

Now he knew why she'd asked what he'd seen when he looked at the birthmark, and why his answer had satisfied her.

"Later that week, the woman came to work and asked to care for Ann. She said she must have imagined that the snake had moved."

"Bull."

"Exactly. So I watched her. I caught her sneaking out of the orphanage with Ann in her arms. She had returned to her depraved ways, and she'd struck a deal to sell Ann for quite a lot of money."

Jasha became aware that he was gripping the edge of his desk hard enough to cut into his palms.

"If that woman had collected, she would have had the cash to buy enough smack to kill herself a hundred times over. As it was, later that week after I threw her out, someone did the job for her."

"She was killed?"

"A fall from one of the tall buildings in downtown Los Angeles. There wasn't enough of her left for an autopsy."

Jasha flinched. "How did she get up there?"

"No one knows." The nun's voice grew

quietly enthused. "But that incident gave me the clue I sought. Unfortunately, in the seven years it took me to reveal the truth of the mark, we had another incident."

"Sister Catherine."

"Yes. Sister Catherine. That tragedy almost broke me, for perhaps if I had told her about Ann's mark, she wouldn't have . . . well." Sister Mary Magdalene's voice was heavy with sorrow. "Such supposition is foolishness. I did what I thought best, and perhaps there was no good way to handle the matter."

Should he have been watching the Varinskis from afar? Would they have noticed him, guessed his identity, and come looking for his family sooner? Or would he have been prepared for their attack? "Second-guessing the situation will get us nowhere, Sister."

"You're right, and of course, the real tragedy wasn't Sister Catherine, who died in a state of grace, but Ann, who has lived to blame herself."

"She believes the mark brings the bad people," he said softly. The memory of Ann's anguish still broke his heart. "Why is it on her? What does it mean?"

Eager now, the nun explained, "I found its purport in an obscure text I borrowed from the Convent of St. Agnes in Kraków, Poland. The rose, of course, is Ann, the innocent, the one who must be protected until she could do the task which God put her on this earth to do."

"But the snake . . . in biblical mythology, the snake is not exactly on the side of the angels."

"The snake is used by God as God wishes. To push mankind out of Eden and into the world to prove itself, or as an ample protection for one of his chosen."

"I see." But he didn't know if he agreed.

"So God uses us all in the battle between good and evil. There is a Russian saying I like — 'God sits high and sees far.' "

"I've heard that." From his father.

"And perhaps you've seen that in your own life, Mr. Wilder."

Jasha thought of his mother and her prophecy, of the lightning strike that brought down the tree and revealed the icon to Ann, of the love that united his parents . . . and bound him to Ann. "Yes, I have."

"I have a saying, too. Pray as if all things depend on God, and work as if all things depend on you. So I prayed, and I worked, and I did what I thought best — I blocked any chance for Ann to be adopted, because

I believe that Ann's birthmark attracts the evil ones. I believe she has a special role in the battle between good and evil."

"She has accomplished at least part of it when she found a thousand-year-old icon that is precious to my family."

"Did she? And are you protecting her, and it?"

"The icon is locked up in a safe in my home. And I go almost everywhere with Ann."

"Good, for the Satan worshippers and the demons, they want to destroy her."

Not all of the demons wanted to destroy her. *He* wanted to keep her safe. Because he feared the sister was right.

"Ann deserves the love and devotion of a good man. Are you a good man, Mr. Wilder?"

"Very seldom," he admitted.

The nun chuckled. "Then you had better love her with all the passion that is in you, for she deserves nothing less."

"I know. And . . . I do." Of course he did. But he heard Sister Mary Magdalene's voice echoing in his mind.

Ann's birthmark attracts the evil ones.

He found himself on his feet. "Sister, I have to go. I have to —"

He dropped the phone and ran out the door.

God couldn't be so cruel as to show Jasha love, then snatch it away.

CHAPTER 34

Ann walked into her condo, her beautiful condo that she'd taken such care to decorate, and the place was so empty it echoed. Echoed with her footsteps on the hardwood floors, echoed with memories of her delight in her first home ever . . . echoed with Kresley's yowls from behind the closed bathroom door.

Hurrying over, she let him out, and he stalked past her, so offended all his fur stood on end. He looked around for his food bowl, for his couch, for his toys, and when he saw nothing, he growled and stalked around the living room in the epitome of feline fury.

"I know, sweetheart. I know." The place was too empty, yet the air was stifling. She went to the sliding glass door and pushed it open, stepped out on the balcony, and looked over the manicured grounds.

Her home. This was her home, with a

swimming pool and live oaks shading the grounds and air conditioners humming in all the units. She'd been gone every night for the last two weeks . . . and Kresley was madder than hell.

Turning away from the vista, she wandered into the condo and looked into the bedroom, stripped of everything, the bathroom, stark and naked, the kitchen, empty of pans and hanging racks.

She went back to the living room, sat on the floor against the wall by the gas fireplace, and closed her eyes to hold back the tears.

She had walked out on Jasha in a dramatic exit worthy of an opera diva.

And what good would that do her? She had no furniture and nowhere to go except to the safety of his house. Because no matter how hurt and angry she might be, she knew perfectly well she was in almost as much danger as the icon. No matter how much she wanted to pretend otherwise — the bad people always *did* come.

She knew Jasha well enough that no matter how stunned and frightened he might be by her birthmark, and by the horrors of her past, and by her cowardice, he would still want her where he could keep an eye on her.

That had been Sister Mary Magdalene's strategy, anyway. Keep the marked child close in the confines of the convent and away from families who might wish to adopt her and use her in a cult, or sacrifice her to Satan. Because that had been the learned sister's real fear — that Ann's mark would attract the Evil One and his minions.

Instead, it had brought the icon and a family of warmhearted demons who took her to their collective bosom. And Jasha. The mark had brought Jasha, and no matter what she did, no matter what she said, he was there. There in her dreams, in her heart, in her body . . .

The thrusts, the motions, the sounds, the scents of sex — everything made her think of him, made her want him again, and again. As the memories made her damp, she pressed her legs together, trying to preserve the pleasure for another few fleeting moments.

Where did all of this leave Ann?

The same place she'd always been. Sitting alone in an empty room, unloved, unwanted, and feeling *really* sorry for herself.

Kresley stalked over to her, growling. He sniffed her, and she thought she was going to cry if he rejected her again. Then he shoved his way into her lap, and curled up, a heavy weight she welcomed, a warmth she craved. She scratched his throat; he arched his throat and purred, and he was loud enough to sound like a small motorcycle.

"Dumb cat," she muttered, and bent to bury her head in his fur. "So you've forgiven me, huh?"

He licked her face with his sandpaper tongue, and she laughed a wobbly laugh.

The loud knock on the door made her jump.

Who dared to interrupt her own quiet pity party? Jasha?

No. He wasn't much for knocking. He was more about barging in, or calling on the cell and making demands and giving instructions, as if she were some simpleton who needed his guidance to get through the day, when in fact she'd been alone and taking care of herself for —

Whoever it was, he knocked again, and this time he was clearly impatient.

Scooping Kresley up in her arms, she walked to the door and looked through the peephole.

A tall guy dressed in coveralls with the mover's logo on it stood holding a clipboard and scribbling on it.

Of course. The paperwork. Jasha probably wanted her to pay the bill. What an asshole.

She opened the door.

The mover barely glanced at her when he said, "Hi, Mrs. Smith, I'm Max Lederer. I just need your signature on these papers that say you inspected the condo and we did no damage."

"I . . . haven't looked around at all." Could he see the marks of the tears on her cheeks?

"You want to do it while I wait?" He glanced at Kresley, who for a change was absolutely still and silent.

"Sure." She shifted Kresley in her arms and held out her hand for the clipboard. The forms said CANTU MOVERS, followed by the list of rooms.

Max pulled a pencil from behind his ear and used it to point at the form. "Just go through each room and see if there's any problems, and if everything is okay, check the box that says *walls, pull-ins, fixtures,* whatever. If there are problems, jot down some notes, and I'll go over it with you." Max had a great build, blond hair, a tan, and a slight accent.

Ann would bet he attracted women in droves. He smelled sour, but then what did she expect? He'd been moving furniture all day, and it was the Napa Valley in July. And . . . he was barefoot. How weird.

He must have seen her looking, because

he explained wryly, "I wore new boots to work, and now my feet hurt."

"And I don't have any Band-Aids to offer." Because without getting her permission, that jerk Jasha had had her condo emptied. Not that she would have given her permission. And not that he wouldn't move her back in fast enough when he figured it was safe for her to live alone. "Okay, Max, I got it. If you want to wait in here, I'll run through it." She'd start in the bedroom and go from there.

But as soon as Max stepped across the threshold, Kresley started growling, the same deep-throated, threatening growl he'd used for Jasha.

"That's one helluva big cat." Max had that *I hate cats* look on his face.

"Are you the one who shut him in the bathroom? That would explain why he's so hostile." In fact, with the noises Kresley was making, she didn't trust him not to attack Max and then, the way her luck had been running, she'd be slapped with a lawsuit.

"I'll put him away." As she started toward the bathroom with the big cat, her cell phone rang.

Behind her, she heard a snap as Max shut the front door, and a snick as he turned the lock.

Ann froze. Now she knew why Kresley was growling.

She brought the bad people. She always brought the bad people.

And this time, she truly *had* brought him. She had let him in.

Chapter 35

Ann turned.

Max grinned.

She'd seen that grin before, in the woods when the other Varinski prepared to attack. But unlike before, she had no knife strapped to her leg, and no icon to protect her soul.

Her heart leaped into a gallop. Sweat trickled down her spine. And the cell phone stopped ringing.

Jasha probably thought she didn't want to talk to him. She'd told him she didn't want to talk to him.

What had she been thinking?

She was alone, with nothing and no one to depend on but herself.

Max started toward her, his bare feet making no sound on her hardwood floor.

The phone started ringing again.

She bolted into the bathroom. She tossed Kresley at his cat box. She slammed the door, turned the lock — the stupid little lock that wouldn't keep out a flea. All Max had to do was stick a screwdriver in the little hole and —

He kicked it open.

The door slammed back against the wall, ripping the lock through the trim.

He filled the doorway, still grinning, still stinking, savoring each moment before the kill. He took one step in, then another, the sound of his laughter singing the melody of her death.

She grabbed the towel rack. With the strength of fear, she wrenched it off the wall. She swung it at his head.

He caught it in one hand.

She kicked him in the nuts.

He doubled over. His grin disappeared.

He wasn't having quite so much fun anymore.

He grabbed so quickly she didn't see his hands move, yet suddenly they were around her neck, and she couldn't breathe. She tore at him with her nails.

He didn't flinch.

She could see his handsome face, and he was grinning again. Distantly, she could hear the racket of glass hitting the floor. Then she could hear nothing but the sound of her heart frantically trying to beat. She could see nothing but explosions of red and a fog of black.

Suddenly she was free. She slammed against the wall, gasping for air, holding her throat.

Max staggered backward, her cat attached to his head. She saw Kresley's claws swipe, and swipe again, ripping Max's face.

Max swore, a vicious stream of Russian profanity. He grabbed the cat, tore free, and flung it as hard as he could against the wall.

Kresley hit, fell to the ground, and lay unmoving.

Max had killed her cat.

Time stopped.

The earth shifted.

Ann took a long breath, and as air filled her lungs, scalding fury filled her being.

Max started toward her, bleeding from deep scratches across his forehead, his nose, his lips. "You're going to pay for this. . . ."

Incandescent with rage, she leaped to meet him. She slashed at his chest.

. . . And he staggered backward, stumbled, fell into the empty living room with a thud that shook the building.

Time started again.

The earth settled on its axis.

He sprawled on the floor. He groped at his chest. Four long slashes ripped his uniform, and blood oozed sullenly from the cuts.

She lifted her right hand before her face and caught a glimpse of the long, sharp, wolflike claws.

They vanished even as she stared.

He saw them, too, and a low rumble started in his chest. Slowly he came to his feet and stood, shoulders hunched, head outstretched, and his eyes . . . his eyes glowed bloody red. In the guttural tone of a speaking beast, he said, "Abomination! No woman may take part in the pact. I'm going to *kill* you. Abomination!"

He started for her.

And Jasha — the wolf Jasha — leaped through the open sliding glass door and into the room.

In a single smooth move, Max tore off his coveralls and became a wolf, large, pale, broad-shouldered, with a sharp-fanged grin.

Ann flung herself backward, out of the way, as the two beasts clashed. Fur flew as they ripped at each other, tearing at each other with tooth and claw.

She couldn't stand to watch, but she couldn't stand to look away. She scooted backward, toward Kresley's still body. She touched the still-warm cat, sinking her fingers into his fur. Her throat swelled from

Max's throttling, and her heart thumped so hard she wanted to faint.

But she didn't dare. She needed to keep her gaze on Jasha, always on Jasha, as if she could project her power into him. Because he was fighting for her. Fighting to the death for her.

The icon was safe. He didn't need her to be alive for that to be true. So . . .

Dear God, he meant it. He loved her.

The two giant wolves rolled and snarled, their white teeth flashing, first one on top, then the other. Sparks snapped off their upraised fur. Scarlet blood spattered the wall, and a metallic odor filled the air.

They hit the wall hard. The glass in her window shattered. They bounced off.

She heard a snap and a yelp.

Then . . . nothing. Not a sound.

As she slowly stood, transfixed by the horror of two wolves, one dark, one light, lying unconscious on her floor, while dual transformations took place.

The big blond wolf became Max, naked, bloody, his head skewed at an odd angle.

And Jasha . . . she dropped to her knees beside him. He'd taken a horrible beating. He had bruises and gashes all over his legs and arms, and his chest reminded her of his father's — it looked as if Max had tried to take out his heart.

She pressed her fingers to the artery in Jasha's neck, then dipped her head in thankfulness.

He still lived.

In a flurry, she leaned over Max and checked for signs of life.

He was dead, his neck broken.

Good.

Jasha's clothes. Where were Jasha's clothes?

She ran onto her balcony.

There, flung on the ground below — his pants, his shirt, his shoes.

"Dear, are you all right?" Mrs. Edges stood below, looking up. "When I saw your young man flinging his clothes off, I was pleased for you, but once he leaped up there, the thumping was so loud, I called the police because I was afraid he was killing you."

"No, he was killing a guy who was trying to kill me." She thought about Max. When the police showed up, she could explain one naked man, but not two. "And rape me."

Mrs. Edges pressed her hand over her heart. "Look at the bruises on your neck! Are you all right?"

"Jasha saved me." *Again.* Jasha had saved her *again.* "Would you toss me Jasha's clothes, please?"

"Of course, dear."

Ann leaned over to catch the rolled-up bundle of his pants, shirt, and underwear.

Then Mrs. Edges said, "Stand back!" and his shoes came flying over the rail.

"Thank you, Mrs. Edges." Ann hurried inside.

"No, thank you," Mrs. Edges called. "It's been a long time since I've seen a young man like yours, at least not in the flesh."

She must have seen him before he turned.

Ann stopped just inside the door.

Jasha was sitting up, his back against the wall, spattered with blood. But his eyes were warm, golden, amused. "I'd say that's TMI from Mrs. Edges, wouldn't you?"

She rushed to him, almost hugged him, drew back at the last minute. "You're hurt. You're so hurt."

The bruises were coming up fast, and in great purple blotches. "Yeah, and remember, demon bites don't heal worth a damn."

"Then you can go to the hospital." Thank God.

"And you, my darling. And you." He stroked the swelling on her throat. "When I think how close I came to losing you . . ."

"Don't." She caught his fingers. "I'm all right."

435

"We're going to have to come up with one fascinating explanation about the wolf bites and scratches I got killing the guy who tried to murder my fiancée."

In a burst of inspiration, she said, "You had run through the grounds to save me, and . . . and someone's mean German shepherd attacked."

"Does anyone *have* a mean German shepherd?"

She shrugged. "So it was a stray."

"Right." Jasha considered the dead Varinski stretched across her floor. "Where in hell did he come from? How did he get in?"

"He said he was from the moving company. And I let him in." She flushed in chagrin. "I thought you'd sent him to collect for the bill."

As wounded as he was, he managed to look more hurt. "Because that's the kind of thing I'd do."

"No, because I was mad." She allowed her head to lightly drop on his shoulder. "I'm sorry, Jasha. Sorry for the things I said, and thought, and . . . I'm just sorry."

"It's all right. We're both fools for love." Heedless of the pain, he pressed her against him. "What do you want to bet the police find a mover's body on the grounds without his uniform?"

"Oh, God, Jasha." She gave a dry sob and again reached out to hug him, then pulled back and lightly touched his bruises with her fingertips. "You keep saving me, and you're so hurt, and I thought you were going to die, and I just keep loving you, no matter how hard I try not to —"

"That's all I needed to hear." He wrapped his arms around her and pulled her close.

She tried to hold herself away. "I'm going to hurt you."

"It's a good hurt."

She gently relaxed against him.

He kissed the side of her face.

She kissed his shoulder.

If he hadn't almost been killed, he couldn't say this. But the Varinski could easily have won this battle. And there would be battles yet to come. If Jasha didn't speak now, he didn't deserve to have Ann. "Ever since we got back from Washington, all I could think was I wanted to go back into the forest where you had to depend on me to keep you safe. Here, every time you left my sight, I was afraid."

"I can't stay in lockdown all the time. That's not living." She tried to laugh. "I must buy shoes!"

"I know. Shoes are important." He squeezed her, trying to convey comfort, love, every good emotion. "But it's not just because I fear for you. I fear for me, too. Without you, I'm not whole. Maybe that's not the kind of love you want. Maybe you want a stronger man who doesn't need you. But this is the only kind of love I have, and it's yours if you want it." He felt the trickle of her tears on his shoulder. The salty water ran down his chest and into his wounds, and burned, but in a good way.

"It's exactly the kind of love I want, because it's exactly the kind of love I've been looking for all my life. But the birthmark . . . you don't need more villains in your life, and I swear to you, it does bring them."

Lifting her chin, he looked into her face. "What have I done that you should think I am so much less than you?" He was pleased to see her brimming blue eyes widen.

"What do you mean?"

"You're willing to accept me, and I've signed a pact with the devil. Someday, I'm going to have to pay him for my ability to change into a wolf. It would be so much safer for you if you ran as far and as fast as you could in the opposite direction."

"Well . . . you . . . that would be . . ."

"Cowardly? Why, yes, so it is. So why do you think I should run away from you because of a birthmark?"

"At least you can control your special . . ." She groped for a word.

"Freakiness?" he suggested. "Don't bet on it, Ann. I've spent the last week fighting every minute not to become a true Varinski and take you regardless of what you thought. I was doing so well, too, until I thought you were going to run into real danger, and then I . . ." The memory of those minutes in his office burned him with delight, and humiliation. Delight for the pleasure, and humiliation that when he was with her, he had no control. "My darling, I am so sorry. Please forgive me."

"There was nothing to forgive. It was rough, and it was fast, and it was . . . good." She touched his face as if she was memorizing each feature with her eyes and her fingertips. "Although I would believe your apologies more if your eyes weren't glowing red."

He groaned and closed them, trying to hide a desire too easily betrayed. "The birthmark makes you very special. But I already knew you were special."

"And I have worked so hard to be average."

He chuckled. "You are at least as average as I am."

It was a special moment, a once-in-a-lifetime package of emotions made clear, and only one thing could have interrupted them.

A huge yowl and a head butt from Ann's stupid cat.

Ann leaped back. "Kresley! My dear, darling boy, I thought you were dead." She tried to run her hands over his huge body.

Kresley shoved her aside, climbed into Jasha's lap, and plopped himself down.

Jasha groaned — and he would have sworn Kresley smiled.

Ann settled for stroking Kresley's head. "He saved me. When the Varinski was choking me, he saved me."

"Were those the scratches on the Varinski's chest and face?" Jasha scratched under Kresley's chin.

Kresley allowed the touch, and even deigned to rumble a purr.

"Some of them. The others I did."

"You did? With what?"

She explained, and showed him her hand.

He stared fixedly at it, but it looked normal. Normal. Yet through their time together, he'd learned one thing — the true miracle wasn't the icon. Ann was.

"I guess it was your blood mixing with mine, but why could I do it then?" She wore a puzzled frown, oblivious to the wonder of her. "Why not any other time?"

"I would guess that particular miracle took the perfect ingredients — your birthmark, my blood, and the rage you felt at someone killing an innocent animal." Yes, that made sense. She hated to see an animal, any animal, hurt. And when the Varinski hurt her beloved cat . . .

"Listen. I hear the sirens." He struggled to his feet and began to dress.

She watched with flattering interest, yet at the same time, her brow was puckered as her mind worked. "Jasha, I understand that your blood mixed with mine, and I had the ability to protect myself and my cat. But when I pulled out that arrow, my blood went into you, too. So what did you get from me?"

He finished buttoning his pants, then went down on one knee. "Salvation, my darling Ann — and love. So much love."

Jasha thought he and Ann would have to do some fancy talking to justify the blood and mayhem.

Instead, Sergeant Black easily accepted their explanations about the hostile stray dog, the guy in the mover's coveralls, the attack on Ann, and how Jasha saved her. He sent a patrolman searching the grounds, and they did indeed find one of the movers, dead and stripped of his uniform.

He didn't ask about the animallike scratches and bites on the Varinski's body. Instead he quickly zipped the body into a body bag and sent it to the morgue, assuring Jasha and Ann that the report would state that the killing had clearly been a case of self-defense.

Then, as the paramedics bundled Ann and Jasha into an ambulance, turned on the siren, and drove away, Doug Black watched — and his pupils glowed red.

ABOUT THE AUTHOR

Christina Dodd is a *New York Times* bestselling author whose novels have been translated into twelve languages, featured by Doubleday Book Club®, recorded on books on tape for the blind, given Romance Writers of America's prestigious Golden Heart and RITA Awards, called the year's best by *Library Journal,* and, at the pinnacle of her illustrious career, used as a clue in the *Los Angeles Times* crossword puzzle. Christina Dodd lives in Washington with her husband and two dogs. Sign up for her newsletter at www.christinadodd.com.

The employees of Thorndike Press hope you have enjoyed this Large Print book. All our Thorndike and Wheeler Large Print titles are designed for easy reading, and all our books are made to last. Other Thorndike Press Large Print books are available at your library, through selected bookstores, or directly from us.

For information about titles, please call:
(800) 223-1244

or visit our Web site at:
www.gale.com/thorndike
www.gale.com/wheeler

To share your comments, please write:
Publisher
Thorndike Press
295 Kennedy Memorial Drive
Waterville, ME 04901